Dream Lover

Dream Weavers, Book 4

Kimberly Dean

Published by Tiger Eye Productions, LLC

Dream Lover
Copyright © 2023 Kimberly Dean
All rights reserved.

Cover design by oliviaprodesign
Vector design by Marisha

ISBN-13: 979-8-9855505-6-6

PROLOGUE

October, Hunter's Moon

What a rush!

Hunter squealed as the dirt bike she was riding hit a bump and went airborne—for about all of six inches. The roar of the engine was loud in her ears. Grit coated her face, despite the helmet she was wearing, and the smell of exhaust plugged her sinuses. She and Emily had snuck into the adventure park under the cover of darkness, and they had the track all to themselves. Neither of them were very good, and it was a little hard to see, but the full moon was out.

She couldn't imagine being anywhere else.

They rode down a bumpy slope, and she jammed her foot down when they reached the turn at the bottom. A plume of dirt flew as the back tire dug in, and it slowed her down. Ahead in the race, Emily veered off toward the jump. A real one.

"Woohoo!" Hunter yelled. "Go for it!"

Emily's bike launched into the air, almost in slow motion. Time warped into fast forward when she came down again. Unfortunately, her back wheel didn't clear the mud puddle. It landed in the squishy mess and slipped, throwing her out of balance. Dirt and mud sprayed as she landed, bike outside the puddle, but her firmly in it.

Hunter skidded to a stop. "Emily? Are you all right?"

People suddenly swarmed the track from every direction, startling her. She quickly identified Emily's boyfriend, Zane Oneiros, and a bunch of men who must be his brothers. They raced to Emily and pulled the bike off her.

"Em, are you hurt?" Zane dropped to his knees.

Emily's voice was muffled inside the helmet. Hands shaking, he lifted her goggles. She grinned at him with a mud splatter on her cheek. "Ew, *mud*."

Hunter revved her engine. It was time to go.

"Uh uh," one of the brothers called.

Before she could scoot out of his reach, he plucked her right off her bike. It fell over, the engine cut out, and the Solstice Adventure Park was doused in silence once again.

"You're not going anywhere, Lunatic," the man said, handling her as if she weighed no more than a toy doll.

Fear exploded inside Hunter's chest. "I didn't do anything. Let me go, Oneiros."

"I don't think so."

She squeaked and tried to wiggle away, but he wrapped his arms around her. "Stop it."

She kicked at his shin. "You stop it."

"Ow," he yelped when she connected.

"You big oaf." She pulled her helmeted head back and was ready to head-butt him when she caught a look at him. "Oh!"

Hunter froze. Dear gods, he was gorgeous.

"On second thought..." she purred.

He scowled down at her, not trusting her sudden change in attitude. With her arms trapped at her sides, she wobbled her head at him. Seeing what she wanted, he cautiously helped her remove her helmet. Her hair spilled out, tumbling around her shoulders, as she looked up at him. He looked even better without the visor in the way. Talk about *yummy*.

"Hi, I'm Hunter."

He stared at her with his mouth agape, and the angry tension in his face turned slack.

"What's your name, handsome?"

He seemed to have forgotten it.

"Tony," Zane yelled.

"Tony." She smiled. Oh, what had the moon goddess delivered to her tonight?

Mud sloshed behind her as Zane pulled Emily out of the puddle. Hunter glanced over her shoulder to make sure her friend was okay.

"This stops now," Zane barked, jabbing a finger at her. "Do you understand? She's not one of your playmates anymore."

"Stop it." Emily caught his sleeve and yanked him back. Her eyes weren't sparkling with fun anymore. "This isn't her fault."

"The hell it isn't." The handsome guy holding Hunter snapped back to attention.

His hold on her tightened again, and she became agitated. She did a quick sweep of the Solstice Adventure Park. They had her cornered. There were three of them here.

Emily could only help so much, and she was ignorant about what was really going on anyway. Hunter's human friend was standing smack dab in the middle of an argument between Greek gods. Her boyfriend and his brothers were the Oneiroi, Greek gods of dreams, while she was the daughter of Selene, the moon goddess.

The Dream Weavers seemed upset that sweet, rule-following Emily was doing something wild and spontaneous under the full moon, rather than sleeping at home, tucked safe into her bed.

Hunter grumbled. They were spoiling her fun. Tonight was her night, the Hunter's Moon.

It was time to wield her power.

Her focus landed on the youngest Oneiros.

"Wow," she said, making her voice sultry. "That half-pipe looks like an awesome ride, doesn't it?"

The snow facility was closed, awaiting winter, but it was on the far side of the complex. It would get him out of her hair.

"Wes, don't listen to her," Zane snapped.

Wes was already turning around to cast his gaze across the park to the half-pipe. His face lit up. "Yeah."

He snatched up Emily's helmet from where it had fallen on the ground, swung a leg over her dirt bike, and hopped on the kick start. The roar of the engine was loud in the night.

One down. Hunter turned her attention back to the sexy one who intrigued her most.

"Wes, snap out of it," he yelled. His voice jumped when she wiggled in his arms, rubbing up against him. "Hey, stop that."

"Want to dance with me in the moonlight, big boy?" It had been her biggest wish for the longest time. She wanted to dance naked under the full moon with someone.

He tilted his head, and his hold on her gentled. Hunter looped her arms around his neck, and she followed when he hesitantly swayed from side to side.

"Tony!"

Footsteps pounded toward them.

"Over here," Zane called.

Dang it. Things were just getting interesting in a way she liked. Muttering under her breath, Hunter lifted her face to the full moon.

"No," Zane roared when she lowered her chin and looked over her shoulder. He leapt between her and the next brother who was trying to come to the rescue.

"Go get Wes," Zane told the latest arrival. "I've got this."

"Do you, Dream Weaver?" Hunter ran her hands along Tony's broad shoulders, and he grunted.

"Go home, Oneiros. Take Emily with you, and I'll let your brothers go." Hunter tried to use her influence on him. It had worked on all his other brothers so far, but Zane just glared at her.

"You've had your fun, but this is it. You stay away from her from now on."

"She's my friend," Emily said, even as she watched what was happening around her with growing awareness.

"She's not your friend, she's a Lunatic."

"Stop calling her that. It's rude and… and insensitive."

"Em, she's the one making you do these things. It's gone too far."

Mud flew as Emily whirled around. "So I always have to be the sensible one? The fuddy-duddy?"

Ah, there they went. Hunter looked up at Tony through her lashes as Zane and Emily got into it. It was about time they were honest with each other.

"Now, back to you, big guy, and our dance."

They swayed back and forth to the sound of bickering, and his hands slid down to her hips. The embrace turned purely sensual, and Hunter's brain went foggy. He felt as good as he looked. When he dipped his head, they were on the same wavelength.

She just wasn't ready for the jolt that went through her when their lips locked. Zeus's thunderbolt had nothing on this guy. His power swept through her senses, and she felt the moment it meshed with hers. Her nipples pinched, and her core throbbed.

She groaned deep in her throat.

It was good. Really good.

She wanted more.

She tugged his T-shirt out of his jeans and saw the corrugated muscles of his abs. The guy was ripped. She spread her hands wide on his chest as his fingers tightened on her butt. His tongue swept into her mouth when she touched him.

"Holy hell," he muttered.

Heaven. Hell. It was the best of both.

He yanked the riding jersey she'd borrowed upward, broke the kiss long enough to pull it over her head, and tossed it aside. His big hand covered her breast as they began dirty dancing rather than just swaying.

Hunter arched into his touch. She'd never made out with a god before, and he was ruining her for all others.

With one arm still around his neck as their dance

continued, she reached for the zipper of his jeans with her free hand. She laughed against his lips when he ground against her knuckles. Somehow, she managed to get his jeans undone, and she pulled the zipper down carefully.

"*Tony!*" Zane suddenly yelled.

Emily gasped. "They're dancing together under the moon. *Naked.*"

She might have shared her secret wish a time or two.

"*Anthony*, wake the fuck up!"

Hunter sighed. Why did all good things have to come to an end?

She stepped back from Tony and rubbed her lips together. "Too bad we're enemies, *stud.*"

She trailed her fingers over his impressive chest and, impulsively, leaned in to kiss him one more time. Deciding it was time to stop pushing her luck, she darted off to her loaner bike.

Zane made a move toward her, but she held up her hand.

"You wouldn't have your dream girl if it wasn't for me, Oneiros. You owe me." She grinned at Emily. "Thanks for sticking up for me. I *am* your friend."

Shifting the bike into gear, Hunter escaped into the night, laughing in exhilaration. The excitement and adrenaline made everything even more intense.

She'd kissed an Oneiros and gotten away with it.

"Best full moon ever!" she whooped.

CHAPTER ONE

He'd kissed the enemy.

Tony stared at the plate on the table in front of him. It was dotted with muffin crumbles, and the harder he stared, the more he realized how much it looked like a full moon.

He began fiddling with the salt shaker.

He'd kissed a *Lunatic*, a daughter of the moon goddess. He still wasn't quite sure how it had happened, but his brothers were sure to get to that soon. They were in full postmortem review around him, and half of them hadn't even been there to witness the fiasco. The kiss. The nighttime dirt bike ride. The showdown that he and three of his Dream Weaver brothers had lost—or won, depending on how you looked at it.

A dumpster fire. That's how he saw it—and not because that kiss had been hotter than hell.

He braced himself as AJ gave a play-by-play recap. It all came down to one thing. A Lunatic, energized by a full moon, had used her power of suggestion to play them like a fiddle. Which, come to think of it, looked a lot like his fork. He tapped the salt shaker against the metal tines and heard a high-pitched ring.

She'd played some of them more adeptly than others. Primarily him.

Damn it.

"There's Wes." AJ had to speak up to be heard. Their table was revved up to the point where the other breakfast diners were choosing tables far away so they could eat their pancakes in peace. The Oneiroi had the back room of IHOP all to themselves.

AJ hurried to pull out a chair, and Tony frowned. The formality was a little extreme. When he looked up, though, he saw Wes with his arm bandaged from wrist to elbow. The knot in his gut tightened. If he'd been more aware, if he'd kept his head, his brother might not have gotten hurt.

"How are you doing, Wes?" he asked.

AJ pushed the chair under Wes's butt as he gingerly sank down.

"I'm all right. Just some bumps and bruises."

"It's more than that if you're bandaged like a mummy."

Wes looked at the arm he cradled against his stomach. "Road rash."

Tony cringed. That burned like an SOB, and Wes had put a dirt bike down on concrete. Not that Tony had seen it. No, he'd been otherwise engaged. Hell, he felt lower than a snake for not having Wes's back.

"It looks worse than it is," his little brother said as he shifted in his chair, trying to find a more comfortable position.

Derek whipped out his phone and began texting. "Let me see if Shea has anything that could help it heal."

His girlfriend was a biochemist who specialized in skincare. There was nobody better to ask.

"Do you need help with anything?" Cael asked from the head of the table. They had nearly a full contingent out today, for good reason. "Is there anything we could do for you?"

His girlfriend, Devon, quickly jumped in. "Like cook meals or do laundry?"

"Nah, I'm good," Wes answered.

"You're not good," the oldest Oneiros countered. He glanced at Devon, and they exchanged silent communication fast. "Why don't you come stay with us for a few days?"

Devon reached out to cover Cael's fisted hand. The under-riding tension at the table couldn't be ignored. They were Dream Weavers, sons of a primordial goddess themselves. They were tasked with keeping the balance in the nighttime world, and one beautiful Lunatic had completely upended things.

One Lunatic. Tony shook his head to get his brain back on track. Her beauty didn't matter, stunning as she was.

Damn it.

"I don't want to get under your skin." Wes glanced around the table when nobody laughed. "See what I did there?"

"Yeah, I see fine," Cael grumbled. "Decision made. We'll follow you home after this, you can grab your things, and then you're staying in our guest room." He turned his hand over and squeezed Devon's fingers. "I'll set you up with a gaming system, and she'll baby you even more than she already does."

Wes had that effect on women. It was something about his puppy-dog earnestness.

Tony put down the salt shaker when Derek's gaze slid over to it, and he realized the ringing from the tines of the fork was sounding more like a warning bell.

Shit, he didn't think he could feel any worse until he looked up and saw Zane and Emily coming through the front door of the restaurant. Zane's hair was sticking up at all angles, and Emily looked white as a sheet.

The rest of the table quieted down when they saw the new arrivals. Bobby shifted over a seat so they could sit next to each other, but Emily didn't make it there before she blurted, "I'm so sorry."

Zane swung his arm around her shoulders, and Tony suddenly found himself on his feet.

"Em, it's not your fault."

Her pale cheeks brightened with slashes of red when she looked at him.

Yeah, the fault lay solely on someone else's shoulders. Namely, the woman he'd kissed.

And honestly, it had gone beyond that, to some heavy breathing, suggestive rubbing, and the quick shucking of clothes.

Tony's face flared hot when Emily's gaze broke away. He sat down heavily, and when he saw the bright white plate again, he nearly sent it straight out the window.

The situation was complicated on so many levels. On the surface, Emily and her "friend" Hunter had gotten more than a little wild during the full moon a few nights ago. At the root level was the reason why. None of them had known Hunter had a secret... a secret very much like their own.

Lunatics and Dream Weavers both descended from the Greek gods and came to power in the night. While Dream Weavers helped people sleep, though, Lunatics kept them up and inspired them to do crazy things—especially when the moon was full. That put their goals at opposite ends of the spectrum.

Suffice it to say, it made them enemies.

He rubbed his temple when his eye twitched. His lips shouldn't have gotten anywhere close to Hunter Mahina. Nor his arms, nor his hands, nor his—

"I'm still sorry." Emily's fingers bit into the purse she'd settled into her lap. "I don't know what I was thinking taking Zane's dirt bike on a joy ride in the middle of the night. I didn't mean to scare all of you or make you come running to help me."

"You get one of us, you get us all," AJ said quietly.

Zane gave a quick nod of thanks as he rubbed Emily's shoulder. She blinked and looked away, but then she saw Wes and her eyes welled up more. "Oh no. Are you okay?"

"I'll be good as new before you know it."

Zane swallowed hard, swung his other arm around the back of Wes's chair, and gave a squeeze to the back of his brother's neck. Zane and Wes, the troublemaker and the tagalong.

"Hell," Tony muttered, and cleared his throat.

"I can't figure out why I did something so irresponsible,"

Emily said. "I've never even thought about riding a dirt bike. Well, I dreamt about it once, but to go out in the middle of the night? With no lessons or asking if I could use it?"

Tony held back a growl. She'd dreamt it? That sounded suspiciously like a Zane special.

"It's so unlike me," she continued, "but I have no excuse."

"Yeah, you do," Zane said. "The full moon was out."

Her expression turned rueful. "I believe there might actually be something to that, but I also have to take responsibility."

"You are. You made me bring you here today to apologize."

"And I truly do," she said, her attention flitting over everyone around the table. "I just... I don't understand. Why did you join in? Why did you go riding after I wiped out on the mud jump, Wes?"

Wes gave a surprised cough. He hadn't had much of a choice once Hunter the Lunatic had put the suggestion in his ear. He adjusted his arm as he tried to come up with an excuse. "To get the bike away from you, and because it looked like... fun?"

Yeah. Taking a dirt bike down a snowboarding half-pipe with no snow sound like a blast. It wasn't fun. It was exactly how it sounded—*lunacy.*

Emily looked his way, and Tony was suddenly pinned. "Hunter always said she wanted to dance naked under the moonlight, but the... kiss? Have you two been seeing one another, and I didn't know it?"

Suddenly, he was under a spotlight with everyone at the table—hell, everyone in the room—waiting expectantly for his answer.

"I've never met that devil woman before. I did it to... distract her?" The statement sounded like a question to his own ears.

As if that was the answer for his enthusiastic engagement. And what about the desperate, clawing need? And the loss of half their clothes?

He crossed his arms, sat back in his chair, and let the words sit. He didn't have any more to say about that.

"Have you talked to her?" he asked, turning the tables around.

Emily bit her lip. "She's not answering my calls, but she texted."

Zane sat a little taller in his chair. "She did? What did she say?"

"She's sorry if we caused problems with your family."

"Like hell she is," Bobby muttered.

"Excuse me?"

"She shouldn't have pushed you to do that," AJ said, hopping in to cover.

"She didn't push me. It was my idea." Emily ran her fingers along the strap of her purse, pulling it tight. "I've been trying to break out of a rut and be more spontaneous. Like Wes said, it sounded like fun, and it got stuck in my head."

"A real friend would have stopped you from doing something so dangerous," Cael insisted.

Tony nodded. Yes, that right there. Emily needed to break off that friendship fast if there was one left. They couldn't have a sleep raider so close to someone in their family.

"You don't understand," she said. "Hunter has been suggesting I try new things because that's her job."

"What do you mean it's her job?" he asked, pouncing on the new tidbit of information.

"She's a life coach."

He let out a bark of laughter. "The Lunatic is a *life coach*?"

"Don't call her that." The snapback was a return to the new Emily, but she quickly quieted. "And she's *my* life coach... or she was... We went too far, and I think she's as embarrassed about it as I am."

Doubtful. Especially with the way Hunter had ridden away, whooping it up. He remembered that part very distinctly.

"Do you think we scared her off?" Wes asked.

Tony stiffened at the direct question, and he heard Cael

sigh. Again, the complexity made it hard to have an honest, open discussion. One moon-powered Lunatic had easily handled four Dream Weavers in the waking world, but four men standing off against one woman in the human world was not an admirable thing.

Emily hadn't known what was really going on, and it showed in her body language. "Well, there was a whole gang of you."

"That's because I put out the call for help," Zane said. "I didn't know where you'd gone, and I knew you weren't experienced on a bike. Next time, take my car."

More than one set of eyebrows rose. Zane's beloved Camaro? Okay, the guy truly was head over heels.

Emily's face softened. "I'll never do anything like that again. I promise."

Good. She sounded like the old Emily, the responsible, clear-thinking counterweight to Zane's wildness. She'd be on guard against any more of Hunter's rabble-rousing suggestions, if the demigoddess ever did reach out again.

Although knowing the Lunatic was out there, hiding in the daylight, doing gods knew what? It made Tony itchy. He was happy the little seductress was making herself scarce, but they couldn't let her ride off into the moonset. She'd just set her sights on another sleeper, maybe one of *his* charges.

Devon pushed back her chair. "Why don't you and I go find a girls' table, Emily? I think this calls for Belgian waffles with extra strawberries and cream."

Tony stiffened. What? No, they couldn't just end this here. They needed more information. This was a huge problem they needed to solve.

"Oh, I don't know…" Emily hemmed.

That was right. Stay. They'd only just learned what Hunter did for a living. Where did she hang out? Were any of her sisters in town? What else did Emily know?

Zane gave his girlfriend a nudge. "You don't have to sit here and beat yourself up."

"It's fine, Em," Wes said.

"I was there," AJ said, "and I don't blame you."

"Nobody does," Cael said. "Go with Devon if you want, or stay here with us. You're always welcome at the table."

"The Oneiroi table?" she said, the corners of her lips moving almost imperceptibly upward.

She knew what they were, and she liked the story of it all. The mythology, as she called it. She thought they were just keeping the story alive for their heritage. She didn't believe any of it was true.

But it was.

In this case, dangerously true.

"Waffles do sound good," she said, "and I don't want to intrude on your family time."

Tony's knee began bouncing underneath the table. She wasn't intruding. She was the star witness, and they needed to keep this discussion going. They needed her insight. She knew this Hunter woman better than anyone. How could they find her? How could they protect their sleepers from her? How could they protect themselves?

He leaned into the table, planting his elbows on either side of the bright white plate. They needed to do *something*. There was a freakin' Lunatic loose in Solstice. They couldn't just let this drop.

Zane kissed his girlfriend's cheek. "We're a package deal now. You're never intruding."

The color came firmly back into her face.

Yeah, yeah. Happy endings and all.

She gave Zane a quick peck on the lips, but then she started to rise. "I'll go catch up with Dev—"

"Can I get Hunter's number?" The question came out of Tony's mouth before it went through his brain.

Emily hitched halfway up from her chair. She wasn't the only one. Beside him, Cael flinched, and Bobby started hacking up a lung when his orange juice went down the wrong pipe.

Tony ignored them as his brain raced to catch up. It made sense for him to ask. *It did.* Emily had seen them in a lip lock.

She could jump to whatever conclusion she wanted about why he needed her life coach's number. It didn't matter what she thought. What was important was that he had a way to track the Lunatic down.

"Her number?" Emily squeaked. She slowly straightened. "Um, let me text her and ask first. I don't feel comfortable giving out her number without permission. Even to... well, *you*."

"Yeah," he said, his voice in a rumble. There went his element of surprise, although what had he been planning to do? He didn't have a plan. He was grasping at straws, but he couldn't just let it go. "You tell her I'm looking for her."

Let that ruffle the Lunatic's hair. Her long, dark, silky hair. *Shit.*

Devon's stare bored into him like he'd lost his freaking mind, but she kept her lips pressed together tightly. She caught Emily's hand and pulled her out of the back room to a table up front.

Zane followed Emily until she was out of sight, but then he twisted back around in his chair like a top set free. "*You want Hunter's number?*"

"He wants more than that," AJ muttered.

The crack was so out of character, it broke the tension. Everyone busted up, but Tony didn't get what was so funny.

"You know where she is, brainiac?"

AJ shook his head, still smiling. "No, but there can't be many life coaches in Solstice with that name."

Well, *duh.* The smart answer made Tony even more pissy. "She's loose in the city of Solstice. We need to do something about it."

Zane frowned. "Like what?"

"Isn't that why we have these Sunday breakfasts? To figure out that type of thing?"

"Whoa, whoa, whoa," Cael said. "Take it down a notch."

They were starting to get side-eye looks from the waitstaff, because they were all leaning in, with muscles bunched and voices raised. They were regulars, but this was getting out of hand for even them. As it should. Maybe they should have met somewhere more private, but they were here now. They needed to deal with this.

Cael lowered his voice, his words clipped. "This isn't a 'sleep raider attacking one of our charges in the dream realm' situation."

Tony jabbed a finger at Zane. "No, she was messing with one of our girlfriends in the waking world."

"Where we have no purview."

Tony's head whipped around to Derek. "What do you mean, no purview?"

"I mean that we hold court in the dream realm. The Lunatics rule night activity under the moon. It's a well-drawn line."

"Oh, come on," Wes said. "Even when they come after us?"

Exactly. Look at the guy. That Lunatic had initiated the whole sequence of events from working with Emily— although Tony wasn't sure how they had met up—to dropping suggestions in Dream Weavers' ears under the full moon. Hunter had to have known what Zane was the closer she'd worked with Em, right? Tony knew he'd felt *her* power the moment he'd shown up at the adventure park.

"She made the first move," Bobby said. "We need to push back."

Cael ran a hand through his hair. "Four of us already did, and, from the sound of it, she handed your asses to you."

"That wasn't pushing back; we were protecting Emily," Wes said.

"And still… your asses?"

"We can't let her get away with this," Bobby insisted.

"What happened the other night was bad," Cael said. "I agree it was in a gray area. I don't know of any other time when the Oneiroi caught a Lunatic actively influencing one of their charges, but it was in the waking world. We were on her turf, and she defended herself against us. If she came into the dream realm, it would be a different story, but it's not. So, I'll say it one more time. We are *not* going to escalate tensions by actively hunting her down."

"Why not?" Tony asked. "We haven't engaged before, but maybe it's time. We could solve a lot of problems—problems that come up once a month."

"Do you want to start a primordial war?" Derek asked, his eyes sharp. "The moon warring against the night? Because that's what will happen if we go off half-cocked and word of this gets back to our mothers."

If it hadn't already...

The Oneiroi eased back in their chairs. Selene versus Nyx? Now there was a scary thought. No doubt their mother would win, but she wouldn't be happy to be put in that situation. The night and the moon had a peaceful relationship. Nyx had let Selene drive her chariot across the night sky for eons.

Tony just wasn't ready to let it go. "None of that means we can't talk to this woman, this *Hunter*. She needs to be warned to keep her pretty little butt away from us and our charges."

"Pretty little butt?" Bobby repeated.

"He should know. His hands were all over it," AJ said. The guy was on a roll.

"I'm serious," Tony grumbled. "Look at Wes. She messed him up bad."

"What about you?" Zane said.

Tony's eyes narrowed. "What about me?"

"I had to tell you to pull up your pants, musclehead."

Tony's vision went blurry as irritation surged inside him. "It was the Hunter's Moon, *her* moon. She had extra power."

"Does she still?"

"How would I know?"

"You still thinking about kissing her?"

Of course he was. It had been a hot kiss. You didn't hold a woman like that once and forget—

Tony jerked as the real meaning of the question sank in. "She does *not* still have her claws in me."

"Are you sure?" Zane asked. He braced his elbows on the table. "I'm with Cael and Derek on this. We need to call this one a draw and move on."

Tony stared at him in disbelief.

"Why aren't you chomping at the bit to go find this woman?" he asked. Zane was weirdly subdued, which wasn't like him at all. His brother had been in love with Emily for years, and Hunter had put her in danger. "You have more reason than anybody."

"What do you think I was doing while you were all going loopy?" Zane shot back. "I already had this talk with her; I got in her face. She knows better than to come near Emily again. Why do you think she's not answering her calls?"

"But…"

Zane held up his hands. "Emily considers her a friend, and Hunter said something I can't forget."

Wes frowned. "What could she have possibly said to make you back down?"

He'd been halfway across the adventure park, so most of this was news to him, too.

"Emily and I wouldn't be together without her help." Zane shook his head. "It's the truth. I can't be in this fight. I'm out of it."

There was a long pause at the table. They'd had disagreements before, but never one where each side was so far apart from the other. After all the talk about protecting sleepers and maintaining a balance between good and evil in the dream realm, how could they think about walking away?

"Well, I'm not," Tony finally said. He pulled out his phone and did a search for life coaches in Solstice. When Hunter's picture popped up, his heart began pumping faster. Yup, that was her. Dark eyes, shiny black hair tamed to look professional, and lips that were anything but.

"Yes. You. Are."

The muscles in Tony's shoulders pulled tight. Cael didn't pull rank very often, but he heard it in those three words, and he didn't like it. With effort, he pulled his gaze away from his phone and locked it on his brother.

Cael was unmoved. Tony might be bigger and badder, but Cael was still the older brother. "Because we don't know how far her power of suggestion goes."

"What does that mean?"

"It means, what is up with you? Are you sure your head is cleared from the other night?"

"Yes, I'm sure."

"You're not feeling any aftereffects?"

"I'm fine."

"Then why the all-out push to see her again?"

"Maybe it's not the head on the top of his shoulders that's doing the thinking," Zane said.

Tony's shoulders bunched, and he damn near growled.

"That kiss did hit you hard." AJ's voice was quiet and calm, but sitting next to him, Tony could feel his brother poised to react, if needed.

"You were dancing naked with her under the moonlight," Wes agreed. "Dirty dancing."

"How would you know, Evil Knievel?"

Wes's jaw jutted out. "I have eyes."

"Which should have been on the half-pipe you shouldn't have been riding down in the first place."

"Enough," Cael said.

"Agreed," Derek joined in, backing him up. Reaching out, he swiped his finger across the screen of Tony's phone, moving the picture of Hunter out of view.

"Hey!" Tony snapped, jerking the phone out of reach.

Derek tilted his head, and his eyes went steely.

And Tony realized he'd just fallen for the trick hook, line, and sinker. *Shit.*

She wasn't still in his head.

She *wasn't.*

At least, not in the way she'd been the other night.

He dropped his head, fighting for his composure, and that damn plate was directly in his line of vision.

She'd made a fool of him on that dirt track, and he had no

interest in seeing her ever again. His concern was for his brothers. He didn't want any of them tangling with her. Her powers were strong, and if anything happened to one of them, he'd feel just like Emily, responsible for everything. Hell, watching Wes all sore and scuffed up was hurting his heart. He was the protector in this family, the biggest and strongest.

He needed to find a way to make Hunter stop going after vulnerable prey: their charges *and* his brothers. He knew what she was now; he knew what she did. He'd be ready for her the next time.

"We drop it," Cael said. "All of us. We're not going to do anything that will draw the attention of the gods. A Lunatic had a little fun, and Zane got the girl. Some of us are worse for wear, but we're calling it a draw."

"And we're keeping an eye on you," Derek said, his gaze unflinching.

The black clouds of tension gathered solely in Tony's head. They had no right to bench him on this. He should be their go-to guy. Cael and Derek might be the senior Dream Weavers here in Solstice, but they hadn't been there the other night. They had no idea what they were up against in this woman.

She was something.

Bobby flagged down a waitress for a refill on his water, and Tony drummed his fingers against the table as his brain kept churning.

The decision might have been made, but they couldn't stop him from living his life. He could work the Google thing, and he knew Hunter's haunts better than anyone other than maybe Zane. There was the adventure park, the city rec center, and Night and Day juice bar. Maybe he'd drop by a few places. He worked out, and he'd been known to drink juice.

He had no idea what he'd do if he saw her again, though.

He needed to work on a plan for that, because much as he hated it, Derek was dangerously close to the truth. She wasn't still in his head, but she was on his mind.

Because he'd kissed the enemy, and gods help him, he'd liked it.

CHAPTER TWO

Hunter rolled onto her back with a groan when her phone dinged the announcement of a new text message. She was awake, but she wasn't ready to get going. She was a night owl by trade. Anything related to mornings was a struggle for her, and it was the *weekend*.

Sunlight brightened her bedroom to the point where the curtains were glowing. Grabbing the empty pillow beside her, she flung it over her face—and then had to adjust it so she could breathe. She really needed to look into sun-blocking shades.

"Ugh."

Who was texting her at this hour, anyway?

She wriggled on the bed, trying to find a more comfortable position, but her toes were out from under the covers. She needed her toes covered in order to sleep. Flouncing again, she tried to find the missing sheet, but that just succeeded in waking her up more.

Her growl was muffled by the extra pillow.

Her clients didn't usually reach out on the weekend, although she did have a brunch meeting today. But that was brunch, and this was definitely breakfast time. Was he canceling?

If he was canceling, then she could sleep in. She should check.

More likely, though, it was one of her sisters. They weren't early birds any more than she was, but with everyone based all over the world, it was easy to get confused on time zones.

Giving up, she blindly reached for her phone on the nightstand.

One quick peek, and she was awake. "Emily!"

She missed her friend and former client. She rubbed her eyes and read the message, hoping that Emily wanted to get together or talk or something. They had fun together, but their escapade the other night had put a damper on their relationship.

The "or something" in the text made Hunter sit straight up in bed.

Tony wants your number. Should I give it to him?

Tony. Tony Oneiros. The big, muscled, hunky, bad-tempered Dream Weaver—who also happened to be a great kisser.

"He what?" Hunter squeaked.

Her heartbeat leapt from its resting rate into the danger zone in one second flat. He wanted her number? After what she'd done?

Or after what *they'd* done?

That, she could understand. It had been a great kiss, a steamy, knee-weakening make-out session. He'd *better* want her number after that.

But his brothers hadn't fared as well when they'd challenged her, had they? Poor little Dream Weavers stuck with no powers outside the dream realm. That night had been a whirlwind, a glorious jumble of activity and messiness and emotion.

"Ohh," she said in a huff when she caught on, "he's trying to trick me!"

She kicked at the sheet that now seemed to be everywhere, and it tangled around her legs. She had to fight to extricate herself before she could launch herself out of bed and begin pacing around her bedroom. She read the text again.

Nope, she hadn't misread it. Tony Oneiros wanted to get

in touch.

Her stomach tightened. He'd been good at the touching part, too. His big hands spanning her waist... His palms sliding down to cover her butt... She shook her head.

"Oh, Hunter, you've gone and done it this time."

She scraped her hand through her hair and flipped it to the side.

Her full moon had been one for the record books. Her sisters couldn't believe that she'd taken on four Dream Weavers by herself and lived to tell the tale. Half of them thought she was a hero, while the other half thought she was nuts—which was saying something.

Maybe Emily could give her some background on what this was all about. Hunter lifted her phone to text... or call... but she couldn't.

"Dang it." She was trying to stay on the right side of Zane Oneiros, Emily's boyfriend. He'd been the one Dream Weaver who hadn't fallen under her influence.

And he was the brother of the sexy, yummy one who had.

She chewed on her lip.

That was the beauty of her moon powers. Her subject had to have some interest in order to respond to her suggestions. She knew that. It was why Zane had been all growly and incensed. He'd been immune to everything she'd said, but his brother, the delectable Tony, hadn't.

Which raised the question, could the text be real?

Her belly squeezed, and she stopped pacing right in front of the glowing curtains. Warmth filled her from the inside out, and her thoughts went all ooey and gooey until she got hold of herself.

"Get real." They'd had a moment—a scorching-hot moment—but that didn't mean she could forget what he was. An Oneiros wouldn't cross that line. An Oneiros and a Menae? Never.

She made herself march to the bathroom to throw some cold water on her face.

It was definitely a trap, but why?

A thought occurred to her, one that made her ooey-gooey center congeal into a rock-hard chunk of ice. She knew the Oneiroi vanquished sleep raiders in the dream realm. They didn't intend to do that to her here, in the waking world, did they?

Cold water dripped off her chin. They wouldn't. The Menae ruled under the moon; everyone knew that. They wouldn't risk upsetting the upper echelon. There were still Greek gods out there who were way more powerful than them, and everyone had gotten used to nighttime being the way it was. They liked having the moon there to guide their way.

No, if the Oneiroi hurt her, they'd risk the extinction of their own kind.

And Tony hadn't acted like he'd wanted to hurt her. Even when he'd plucked her off her bike, he hadn't been rough. Just strong.

So strong.

"Oh, hell." Hunter grabbed a towel and scrubbed the water droplets off her face.

This was all her fault. What good had she thought would come from making friends with the girlfriend of an Oneiros? She'd put this all into motion by giving Emily her business card in the first place. The laced-up project manager had just been so frustrated and unfulfilled when they first met. So ready to break out of her structured little world.

She'd been trying to help. Honestly.

Hunter braced her hands on either side of the sink. She'd tried to do a good deed, and she'd succeeded. Emily and Zane were together now, but in the process, she'd outed herself to the enemy. They knew she was here now, and they didn't like it—even though they knew the rules. They were supposed to stick to the dream realm, but they'd come at her in the waking world under a full moon. She'd had every right to "wipe the floor with them," as her sister Strawberry had put it.

But she'd hurt their pride.

She stared at herself in the mirror. Was that what the request for her number was about? Was the blasted Dream Weaver trying to show how tough and brave he was? To get her going? To yank on her chain?

Her eyes narrowed. Of course he was.

She glared at the phone where it sat on the vanity. And she'd fallen for it. She'd gotten up early on a Sunday morning—no, she'd leapt out of bed.

He'd made her *pace*.

A grumble passed her lips. Oh, he wanted to play with her head? She was a master at that game.

Snatching up her phone, she began typing. Just as quickly, she backspaced. She needed to word this correctly. She needed to send Tony Oneiros' cute butt pacing. Lifting her phone, she started again. *Yes,* she typed. *Give it to him.*

He wouldn't be expecting that. She'd called his bluff.

See how he'd deal with that.

And if the request was for other reasons? More intimate ones?

She gave an all-over shake and did a mental reset. She'd deal with it then, which would be never. Because it would never happen.

She blew out a breath. What a way to start the day. She glanced at the time. She might as well get ready for her brunch meeting. It was with a prospective new client. She needed those, especially since she'd just lost one.

Emily.

The thought brought her mood back down.

She needed to pay the bills, so a Sunday brunch meeting it was. It was the only time her prospective client could meet, which didn't bode well. He'd need to find time to work with her if he really wanted to make changes in his life. The first problem she could see was that he worked too much.

They'd need to change that.

* * *

The wake-up call worked in Hunter's favor. For once, she

was early for an appointment. The sandwich shop was busier than she'd thought it would be when she arrived. She'd thought it a strange place to meet for brunch, but when she saw the breakfast sandwiches the place was serving, she understood why it was popular.

She grabbed an open table and ordered an iced coffee as she waited. She didn't need the pick-me-up, but it sounded good. Her energy levels were still running high. It was only a few days since her moon, but in another week or so, she'd be feeling the drain.

There was something to be said about adrenaline, too. Hers had been pumping since that text message.

She looked at her phone for the hundredth time, but she still hadn't gotten a return message from either Emily or the not-so-sneaky Oneiros. She took a sip of her sweetened coffee and let the mocha flavor roll over her tongue. She wondered how *he* responded to mornings.

She hoped she'd given him a jolt in return.

The door to the sandwich shop opened, and she sat up straighter. There was her guy. She recognized his name and his face from all the magazine and news stories. She gave a wave as his gaze swept the restaurant, and he smiled.

Warmth settled in her chest, and it was a pleasant feeling. Nothing like the ball of fire she'd experienced when a certain grumpy Dream Weaver had glared at her.

She turned the phone over so it wouldn't distract her during her meeting and stood to greet the newcomer. "Hi," she said. "I'm Hunter."

"Hi, Hunter." The handsome, dark-haired man reached out to shake her hand. "I'm Pete. Pete Larimer."

* * *

She'd given him her number.

Well, she'd given Emily permission to pass her number along, which was the same thing. Tony was still staring at the text message the next day. The number glared at him, practically pulsing as his eyes went in and out of focus.

What did it mean?

Was she calling his bluff? Did she think he wouldn't use it? Or did she figure he could get it off her website anyway? The number was the same, so it *was* a wash. Offering it made her look good in Emily's eyes, and it made the kiss more understandable to her friend too.

He tapped his finger against the side of his laptop. Oh, she was cunning.

Or did she think she still had power over him?

Did she?

He went through a quick self-check. They knew Lunatics were crazy powerful under a full moon. He rolled his eyes at his unintended pun. They were powerfully crazy, too. Beyond that, though, he and his brothers were pretty much in the dark about what their capabilities were.

In the dark… He let out a snort. He was picking up right where AJ had left off.

"What's so funny?"

His head snapped up. *Shit.* He was supposed to be working. He swiped his finger across his phone's screen to hide the message. "Was that ten?"

His client was already poking her nose into his space, looking at the laptop display. "Two sets of them. Whose number was that?"

Shoot. She hadn't been looking at the next exercise—she'd been sneaking a peek at his phone.

"None of your business," he grumbled.

"So, it's a girl," Kimora said with a grin.

He rolled his standing desk out of the way and cleared a space on the gym room floor. "Let's move on to speed skaters."

Her grin twisted into a grimace. "Well, you don't have to get cranky about it."

"You want to get better at those quick cuts on the court, right?"

"Yes," she muttered as she took a drink from her water bottle.

"These will help with those."

"I know. That doesn't mean that I have to like them." Still, she walked over to the space and eyed the hash marks taped onto the floor. She was a pro who wanted to keep climbing the rankings in the tennis world, and she knew she had to put in the work to do that.

Tony looked at the workout he'd planned for the day. "Three sets of ten."

With her hands propped on her hips, she gave a sharp nod. Determination set her features as she moved into position. In a flurry of motion, she started lunging jumps from side to side. The goal was to strengthen her lateral movement on the court. She needed to be able to get to distant shots, plant herself for a good return, and then dash back to play defense.

Her breaths turned harsh as she pushed herself, launching from one leg to the other. He glanced at the heart monitor readout. She was in the anaerobic zone, but they were looking to improve performance, not cardiovascular capability.

"That's good form," he said as he made a note on the record he was keeping.

He glanced at the phone again, even though the screen remained dark. He remembered some heavy breathing during that kiss…

"What's her name?" Kimora asked, panting as she took her first break between sets.

"Huh?"

"The girl. The one attached to that number."

He narrowed his eyes on her.

"Come on. I need to think about something other than the fire burning in my lungs."

"That fire should be in your legs."

"Yeah, yeah. Don't try to avoid me. What's her name?"

"I don't want to tell you that."

"Why not?"

Because the woman was as much a pro about ferreting out gossip as she was at crushing overhand volleys. At the same time, she hated being a fixture in the gossip magazines. The irony didn't escape his notice.

"Because I don't know if I'm going to call her," he said.

"Why not?"

He pointed at the mat. "Stop stalling."

She gave him a glare but returned to the starting position. In a split second, she exploded back into motion.

Why was he not going to call Hunter Mahina? Because Cael's voice was in his head reminding him to stay out of it. Much as he disagreed, he typically wasn't one to rock the boat. That was Zane and Wes's specialty.

But she'd dared him by sending him her number. She didn't expect him to use it.

Which was precisely why he should.

It would rock her off her game, maybe make her vulnerable. Then they could talk about her leaving the city *or* the country. She couldn't stay, that much was clear, but he had no intention of using force. He was a big, strong guy, but vulnerability made him want to protect. They were talking mind games here.

Of which she was a pro.

"Hunter?" Kimora was suddenly at his side again. She looked at the computer screen as she used a towel to wipe the sweat from her brow.

Godsdammit. He'd spaced out again and typed the wrong name.

"A girl named Hunter?" His client flipped the towel over her shoulder. "With a cool name like that, you have to call her."

"Yeah." More and more, he was coming to the conclusion that he really did.

"Why the hesitancy?" Kimora was enjoying this way too much. "Are you afraid that she sees you as prey?"

"*No.*" Although his sweaty client wasn't that far off-base. The Lunatic had been a threat to his brothers. She was still a threat to their charges, all the sleepers out there in Solstice who needed sleep and dreams.

But she hadn't felt like a threat as she'd rubbed up against him with her arms wrapped around his neck.

Kimora's eyebrows lifted. "Or are you afraid you like her?"

His heart gave a thump, and he finally looked at the woman. "I'm afraid she's playing me."

The playfulness disappeared from Kimora's face. "Why would she do that?"

It was her nature.

"She's known for being a wild child."

"With men or just overall?"

"Overall." He pushed away from the table and moved to reconfigure the pulley system on the weight machine. He adjusted the pin in the weight stack and pointed at the ankle strap. "Side leg lifts."

Kimora complied without complaint this time, but he'd made a mistake with his choice in exercise. She could breathe while doing it, which meant she could still talk.

"I think you like her, Tony," she said as she swung her leg in a controlled motion.

He busied himself stacking up the orange cones they'd used for a previous floor exercise.

He didn't like Hunter. He only knew her enough to dislike her.

"I'm intrigued by her," he admitted.

And was attracted to her.

Hardcore attracted.

"Isn't that enough to at least call her to find out if it could lead to more?"

That was what was niggling at the edges of his brain... The thing he shouldn't consider but couldn't stop obsessing over. Did she *really* want to get in touch?

His heart rate jumped, and he looped one of the cooling towels around the nape of his neck.

"Being intrigued by someone is the best thing ever." Without being told, Kimora turned and moved on to the next exercise, reverse leg lifts. "I mean, the physical is one thing, but if a guy can get into my thoughts? Mmm."

Hunter had gotten into his thoughts, all right. The question was how much she'd controlled them—and how much had been him acting on his own. Because that was another problem, in and of itself.

"You have to call her, Tony."

Yeah, he did, because she could get into anyone's head, and he and his brothers were the only ones who knew that. She was a dangerous woman. Someone needed to figure out how to mitigate the risk, and he'd prefer it be him.

The vision of Wes and his bandaged arm returned, and it straightened Tony's head right out. He removed the cooling towel, folded it into a square, and placed it on an open spot on his table.

"You're right. I'll make the call."

* * *

Hunter was leaving a drawing class when her phone rang. She waved goodbye to her client, who hadn't actually taken the class, but volunteered as a model. It was a big step for him to get away from the numbers and equations of his engineering classroom and into the creative world. And hello, it wasn't like he'd had to take off his clothes.

Although maybe that could be a next step. She didn't think it was out of the realm of possibility.

She stepped out of the pathway to the art studio and into the garden area to answer the call. She didn't recognize the number. "Hello?"

"Hi. It's… uh, Tony."

Her breath caught, and she tripped on a crack in the sidewalk.

He cleared his throat. "Tony Oneiros."

"I know."

"I'm calling."

"I can hear that." Hunter slowly sank onto a plastic chair at one of the outdoor tables that filled the garden/outdoor eating area. With the way her knees were weakening, she better sit before she did a face plant. "Why?"

Oops. She hadn't meant to ask that out loud.

"We need to talk."

Hearing his rumbly voice made her want to do more than that. She fluffed her hair. "So talk."

"In person, I mean."

Was it hot today? Glancing up, she saw that the sun was bright, but it was October. If anything, the soft breeze was actually a bit cool. Yeah, she shouldn't trust herself right now. "Why?" she asked again.

"You know why."

She slumped back into her chair. Oh, she recognized that grumble, and it was just as sexy now as it had been the other night.

She shouldn't do it. She knew better than to accept. The Menae did their best to stay off the Oneiroi's radar, but she'd taken a different approach, hadn't she? She'd marched right up and kissed this one.

She gave in. "When?"

Automatically, she pulled up a calendar on her phone. They weren't that far out from the full moon. Another week, though, and she'd be at low ebb. She couldn't meet with him then. She needed to be sharp and ready around this one.

"Tomorrow over the noon hour?"

They were going to have a meal together? Excitement lit her, but darn, that didn't work. "I have a lunch meeting with a client."

He paused, and the silence was heavy. "A life-coaching client like Emily?"

This time, the chill didn't come from the weather. "It's my job." Sensing that was a point of contention, she quickly proposed another time. "What about around five?"

"I'm working then. How about midafternoon?"

Now she was curious about what he did for a living. "That should work. Where?"

"Night and Day?"

She stiffened. Her juice bar? She didn't like him invading

her territory. Zane knew that she and Emily had done karaoke there. As she thought about it, though, that might be a plus. It was territory she knew. "As long as there are people around."

That was a deal-breaker. She might like to take chances, but she wasn't taking one like that. If they came together, there were going to be witnesses around. They wouldn't have a clue what was going on, but if things got heated, humans would provide protection.

"I'm not going to hurt you." He sounded offended. "We just need to set some ground rules."

Her energy level came down from where it had been buzzing around her head, landing somewhere closer to heart level. "You're coming alone?"

"It will just be you and me."

The energy dropped again to swirl around her core.

"But don't think about using your powers on me again."

It dropped once more, falling flat at her feet.

She got it. He wasn't calling because he was interested. He was calling because she'd bested him and his brothers the other night when they'd try to spoil her full moon.

He was looking to protect himself, too.

She frowned at the withering pots of flowers that had seen the better days of summer. He didn't know she was on a downward slope, powers-wise. That much was clear. She scrunched up her nose. She'd learned that he didn't have powers outside the dream realm—at least none on the scale of hers—but he didn't need anything extra, did he? Those Greek god genetics had given him plenty of physical strength and beauty, which were powerful enough.

At least, she was plenty susceptible to them.

Night and Day it was.

"Agreed," she said. "Two o'clock?"

"I'll be there."

She let out a nervous puff of air. This was so rigid and tactical, like a meeting between spies of opposing nations. It was exciting and dangerous, but he'd made the first move and he'd kept her off balance the entire time. She hated having to be on guard and watch every word.

She wasn't good at it.

"What's the dress code?" she asked impulsively.

"What do you mean?"

"You've set rules for everything else. Clothes were optional the first time we met."

She smiled when he didn't answer. Point scored. He was the one off balance now.

She knew to quit when she was ahead.

"See you tomorrow, Tony. I can't wait."

CHAPTER THREE

Tony made sure to arrive at Night and Day early. In fact, he'd had a late lunch at the juice bar and was doing paperwork as he waited. He'd wanted to be the first one here. It was all about establishing territory and setting up boundaries.

This meeting was important, and he had a message to deliver for his kind. He took the responsibility seriously.

Seriously enough that it made trying to do paperwork impossible. He rolled the paper umbrella that had come with his drink back and forth between his thumb and fingertips as he stared at the laptop screen. Kimora's performance was improving on her side-to-side movement, but now they needed to work on the transition to charging the net. He needed to devise a strategy on how to improve her muscle memory there.

Because his muscle memory was shot right now.

He knew the answer to this, but he couldn't keep his attention on his work. The umbrella made a *fwipping* sound as it caught the air and spun. He hadn't been able to keep his attention on his work last night, either. He'd had a hell of a time transitioning into the dream realm, because his thoughts were on Hunter and this meeting.

Maybe some balance board work would help Kimora.

A zing of energy made his head snap up and his gaze lock on the door. The Lunatic was here. He felt her the moment she walked in the place.

Gods, she was beautiful.

Attraction grabbed him in the chest when she looked straight at him. No need to scan the place to find him. She felt him, too.

Like knowing like.

She hesitated two steps inside the door, and his thighs bunched when he thought she might run. But then she gestured at the counter, and he gave a nod. He kept an eye on her as she went to place an order.

She was a tiny thing, at least compared to him. She wore jeans and a stretchy top to accommodate for the cooler weather, and he liked how the outfit clung to her curves.

He blew out a hard breath. "She's the enemy, you idiot."

It didn't matter how cute she was. He needed to remember the calamity such a small package could bring.

His brow furrowed. Speaking of which, her energy felt different today. The tone was the same, sexy and alluring, but the volume was turned down. That answered one question. Her power wasn't as strong during the day—or maybe this far removed from a full moon. Or both. When was it in the lunar calendar, anyway?

Okay, so he hadn't answered any questions, but he'd come up with more.

Her drink order was delivered, and she turned to face him. He saw her chest rise and fall as she summoned her nerve to start walking to his table.

Tony closed his laptop with a bang, shoved it aside, and gave the paper umbrella a toss. She'd bested him the last time with soft words in his ear. He wasn't going to let her manipulate him again.

"Hi," she said softly.

Damn. His good intentions wavered. He liked her voice.

"Hello." Best to be formal. He couldn't let things decline into the personal like they had last time.

Although, come to think of it, she'd jumped into that kiss, too, and she hadn't had anyone pushing her to do that.

He shifted in his seat. "I wasn't sure you'd come."

"I can't resist a dare."

Of course she couldn't. Good to know.

He nodded at the other side of the booth. He'd chosen it over one of the high tables. More room for him to spread out, and he liked the privacy of it. They needed to have it out, and he didn't want to be sitting out in the open where anyone might overhear.

She looked over the space as if determining exit paths, and then checked the counter, where plenty of people were working. She slid into the booth seat, leading with a massive bag that was half her size.

And then they were face to face.

The air tingled as their Dream Weaver and Lunatic energies collided and then joined. A rush went through Tony, and his thighs clenched again.

Hunter wiggled in her seat and took a quick sip of her drink through the straw. "So, what do you want to talk about?"

He stared at her a full five seconds before his brain kicked in. This wasn't about attraction or flirting or getting to know one another. It was about drawing lines between them. He folded his arms across his chest. "Things got out of hand the other night."

She pushed her hair over her shoulder. It was caught together at the back of her head in a bright purple clip, but it was long enough to still cascade forward. "In some ways."

"In all ways," he said firmly. "You and Emily breaking into the adventure park after hours, dirt biking in the dark…"

"She was good, wasn't she?"

"She… That doesn't… You sent my brother Wes on the half-pipe."

"I needed some space. You were all surrounding me."

Him in particular.

"Because you entranced me." Tony steeled himself. He wasn't going to let her turn this around on him. "I went there to find Emily. You were the one who had me engaging in…

ahem... other things."

Like making out as if their lives depended on it.

He swore he saw a tinge of color highlight her cheekbones.

"Is your brother all right?" she asked.

Huh. She was deflecting, which meant she wasn't so casual about their make-out session after all.

Or was she playing him again?

"Like you care," he muttered. He needed to remember why he was here. He needed to deliver a message. A strong one.

Her big brown eyes widened. "I do. You were all swarming around me. I needed to protect myself."

"So you sent him off to break his neck?"

"I mentioned the half-pipe because it was on the other side of the park. I didn't know he was going to try to ride a dirt bike down it."

"Yeah, right."

Her spine snapped straight. "I give people nudges, but they make their own decisions from there."

In an instant, she went from indignation to horror. Her mouth dropped open, and she clamped a hand over it.

Tony looked at her, stunned. Okay, there was a piece of information that nobody had known about Lunatics. "Kind of like when I lead sleepers into dreams."

Her eyebrows rose, but then she slowly lowered her hand. "I probably wasn't supposed to tell you that."

He picked up the paper umbrella, and the *fwipping* noise resumed. "Me either."

Although it was something that Dream Weavers really wanted others to know. They didn't intentionally deliver nightmares. Sleepers sometimes needed bad dreams to deal with the complexities of their waking life. It was how humans processed things.

So, if she just gave people nudges, what had the kiss been about?

Tony stared at her lips as she took another sip of her

drink. Shaking his head, he snapped himself out of it. "Yeah, so, the point is, after what happened, I think it's time for you to move along."

She went still. "Excuse me?"

"You heard me."

The top napkin in the dispenser on the table had a corner sticking out. He jabbed at it with his finger, trying to tuck it back in, but that left it with a pucker in the middle. He plucked out the entire thing and smoothed the napkin on the table before him.

Hunter's gaze went to the napkin and then returned to his face. "So that's what this meeting is about? You're trying to run me out of town? It's a 'this town isn't big enough for the both of us' situation?"

"So, you understand."

This time, she was the one who sat back and folded her arms. "Where would you suggest I go?"

"Careful."

"No, seriously. Tell me. There's an army of your brothers out there. Where am I supposed to go where people don't sleep?"

That stumped him. He hadn't accounted for that. He folded the corner of the napkin in and gave it a crease.

Her eyes narrowed. "I've been here all along, and it hasn't been a problem."

"It's a problem now." He folded in the other corner so the napkin had a nice point. "What made you target Emily, anyway?"

"Target?" Hunter let out a huff. "I gave her my business card because she was so obviously lovelorn over your cocky brother. She hired me."

Zane *was* cocky.

"Did you know that he was an Oneiros when you agreed to work with her?"

"Of course I did. I could feel him like I can feel you."

Just like that, the air between them zinged again. They both felt it, but neither of them was willing to look away first.

"Why take that risk?" Tony asked.

He won the stare-down when her gaze flicked around the restaurant. "It sounded like fun."

Fun? She'd done it on a lark?

More likely, she'd done it as a test. Just like he was poking her with questions and trying to get answers, she'd been trying to get the inside scoop on Dream Weavers through her new client.

Although the stories about her escapades with Emily had been what first intrigued him. Emily's new friend had sounded self-assured and engaging. Sexy, before he'd even met her... long before that kiss...

"Well, it needs to stop." He tapped the handle of the paper umbrella against the point of the paper arrow he'd just made. "We can't have a Lunatic running around town, messing with people's minds."

She choked on her drink mid-sip, and he passed her the next napkin.

Which messed up the one behind it... He jabbed that one with his finger, too.

"Lunatic?" she sputtered. "You call us Lunatics? With a capital 'L'?"

He frowned. "That's what you are."

Her eyes danced even as she rolled them. "Oh, I need to tell my sisters that one."

She pulled her phone from her bag and began to text, which made Tony nervous. They'd just tracked down one Lunatic. They had no idea where the rest of them were hiding, and he certainly didn't want to draw any more of them to Solstice. One was plenty.

Especially this one.

She let out a snort. "It is catchy. I'll give you that. Luna for the moon."

"And Lunatic for the crazy effect you have on people." The second napkin ended up in a ball in the middle of his palm. "Like the way you kissed me."

And there it was, the grenade landing in the middle of the

table.

"Well, isn't that the pot calling the kettle black?" She set her phone down so hard on the table, it *thunked*. "Isn't playing with people's minds right up your alley, Dream Weaver?"

He sucked in air so sharply, his chest ached. "That's not how dreams work. They restore people's sleep."

"And the full moon opens a release valve the same way," she snapped.

Tony was taken aback. Was that how they saw themselves?

Hunter checked that she hadn't cracked her phone's screen before tucking it into her bag. "We're the Menae, not Lunatics. We're the daughters of Selene, who's just as high-ranking a goddess as your mother. There are fifty of us, compared to the legions of yours. I have just as much right to live here as you do."

Tony tapped the umbrella stick against the table so hard, it accidentally tore a hole in the napkin. A waitress who was on approach to check on them stopped, pivoted, and went to talk to an elderly couple instead.

Hunter ran a lock of hair around her forefinger as she held her ground. "In fact, you seem like you could use more of my 'Lunatic' ways."

His brow furrowed. What the hell was she getting at?

"It was a good kiss, Tony."

He snapped.

"No." He pushed aside his assortment of napkins and paper umbrellas. "Stop it. You're not going to bewitch me again."

She flinched, and the color washed out of her face. "You think that's what it was?"

"I know that's what it was."

"So all this…" She looked around the table and then back to him. "The phone call and this meeting was seriously just to tell me to leave Solstice?"

Of course it was. Had she not been listening? "What did you think it was?"

She shook her head and gave a jerky cutoff motion with her hand. "Got it, message received."

She pushed her half-finished drink aside and reached for her bag.

Tony felt a twinge of uneasiness. He'd come here for a fight; he hadn't expected her to act hurt. "Hey."

She pawed through her bag, searching for something. "No, I've got it, although you should know that my response is for you to go straight back to Erebus where you came from."

She finally yanked her keys out of the dungeon of her bag. Something else tumbled onto the table. She reached to retrieve it, but then pushed it across the table at him.

"Here, if you don't want to kiss any more, try this. It should help with all that nervous energy bottled inside you."

Tony held up his hands, not wanting whatever she was giving, but he was confounded when he saw a plastic toy of some sort. "What the—"

What did she mean, "if he didn't want to kiss any more"?

She was spry, though. She'd slid out of the bench seat and was halfway to the door before he could react.

"Hunter." He swiped up the gadget, shoved it in his pocket, and hurried after her. "Hunter, wait."

* * *

Hunter was disappointed. She'd known it was a trap. She'd even prepared herself for it, but the more time that had gone by, the more hopeful she'd become. How could she have convinced herself that this meeting could have gone any differently? This was what she got for being optimistic, for always trying to believe the best in people.

She pushed open Night and Day's door and felt the chilled breeze smack her in the face. The day was overcast and nasty; she should have taken a hint.

Hefting her bag higher on her shoulder, she put down her head and marched toward her car.

She hated drama and fighting. It wasn't her way. Well,

unless it was a K-drama on Netflix or fighting while wearing one of those big bubble suits.

She didn't hurt people intentionally, whatever that big oaf thought. Why had she worked herself up into coming here? What she'd felt was a spark between them was obviously the flare of anger on his part.

"Hunter."

She wrapped her arms around herself as her hair whipped in the wind. She didn't want to talk to him anymore. She wanted to go somewhere to clear her head, but where? The pool was closed for the season, and the axe-throwing place was no fun alone.

"Hunter."

She hitched to a stop when Tony passed her and planted himself in her way. He moved fast for a big man, and he was hard to get around, too.

When she sidestepped, so did he.

"What did you mean, 'no more kissing'?"

Gah. She'd thought that had been pretty clear.

"This is my car," she said, pointing to his left.

"Yeah, well, this is my truck," he said, pointing to his right. He dipped his head. "Did you think that was why I called you here?"

"No." Although anyone with a pulse would have thought it would come up. "It doesn't matter what I thought. I got the hint."

His eyes narrowed. "No, I think I finally did." He stepped forward. "You wanted to see if there was something there, didn't you?"

She wasn't going to answer that. She put her head down and bulldozed right toward him, expecting him to get out of her way, but he didn't budge. She bounced off him when she collided into him, but he caught her by the waist.

And then eased her closer again.

"That might have been the deciding factor for me, too," he said.

She looked up at him sharply, and she heard her pulse in

her ears. His gaze swept over her face and then stuck on her lips. Next thing she knew, he covered them with his own, and they were kissing again like they'd never stopped.

Oh, this was what she remembered most from her full-moon night.

She spread her fingers wide on his hard, muscled chest. He blocked the harsh wind from her, and all she felt was warmth and excitement. The buzzing energy returned, the one they'd formed together the last time, swirling back and forth around them.

He let out a low groan just as she felt it center in her core, and his arms tightened around her. He cupped a hand over the back of her head as he deepened the kiss. Their mouths became more intimate, and he licked over her lower lip.

Mm, that was nice.

She went up on tiptoes and wrapped her arms around his neck. Her bag swung forward, though, and got in the way. Dang it, she needed to learn how to travel more lightly.

She adjusted it out of the way, and he grunted when their bodies made contact. His hips swung forward, making her want to rub against him even harder, but then something bumped against her hip.

"Shit," he said, breaking the kiss.

With one arm, he swung her to the side until she was pressed against a very big truck. Watching her closely, he removed her bag from her shoulder and set it on the hood. A computer bag landed there next.

Planting his hands on the truck on either side of her, he leaned in again. He brushed his mouth over hers once… and then twice… and then she launched herself at him.

The kiss turned hot and indecent within a heartbeat, all grabby hands and rubbing body parts. It was only the sound of a horn honking that made them pull apart.

Tony stood between her and the offended driver as he sent them a glare. The elderly couple from the juice bar was standing just outside the door, though, smiling and giving them two thumbs up.

Embarrassed, Hunter moved until Tony's big body hid her from them, too.

His eyes were glazed when he looked down at her, and his lips were puffy. Something else had puffed up against her stomach, too.

"It's good, isn't it?" she whispered. "This thing between us."

A muscle in his jaw clenched. "Are you doing this?"

She pulled back sharply, hurt to the quick. She reached for her bag, but his hand closed over hers.

"We're supposed to be enemies."

"Who says?"

"History."

"What does that have to do with us?" She jutted out her chin. "Or the future?"

His shoulders bunched as he leaned in. "Do you swear you're not using your powers on me?"

What powers? There was no moon out. What did he think she could do, snap her fingers and he'd come running?

Which could be a lot of fun...

She poked him in the chest. "You kissed me, buddy. I didn't have to tell you to do anything."

He caught her finger and slowly lifted her hand until it was back around his neck, where he apparently wanted it. "Yeah, well, I'm about to do it again."

The kiss he gave her this time was hard, deep, and a little naughty. Hunter felt herself melt against his truck as he crowded her. She felt surrounded by him. Deliciously surrounded. Erotically captured.

This was escalating fast, but she had no problem with that. She'd been thinking about him for days, lusting for more than just a taste this time. He thought she was inside his head? He'd taken up residence in hers.

Hidden from view, she slid a hand down his stomach to the front of his gym pants. His groan cut through the howl of the wind.

Yeah, that wasn't puffy. It was hard.

They both struggled to catch their air. "We need to find someplace more private," he said.

She nodded fast.

"Your place or—" He stopped.

The trust wasn't there yet, which made absolutely no sense. They were talking about being intimate, but he didn't feel comfortable having her in his home? Honestly, though, she didn't feel comfortable inviting him to hers, either.

"The motel across the street." The answer came to her in a flash of brilliance.

He swiveled his head around and spotted the place.

"If you're up for one of my suggestions," she said softly.

He was moving before she finished talking, swooping her up again and planting her in the passenger seat of his truck. He plopped their bags on her lap and gave her another fast kiss. "Hell yeah. Sounds good to me."

CHAPTER FOUR

The key to the motel room slowed them down. It was the old-fashioned metal kind with notches and grooves. They got the door opened fine, but getting the key out of the lock was another story. Tony finally gave it a yank, risking breaking it off in the slot, and it screeched free.

They looked around the room as they entered. The furniture was worn, with a visible chip in the corner of the dresser where an old television sat.

"At least it looks clean," he said.

"Do you think the guy who checked us in knew what we were here for?"

"No, I'm sure he thought we look tired and needed a nap."

Hunter laughed, and the sound turned giggly. She wandered around the room, feeling light. Her heart was racing fast, and even her fingers were tingling.

"That's the energy I remember," he said, his voice rumbly.

She dropped her bag on the lone chair in the room and squeezed her hands together. "This is new to me."

He froze mid-step. "You've never done this before?"

The heat raging in her abdomen flared, but for an entirely different reason. "I've never had a nooner... done a nooner... However you say it."

He shifted at the word, and so did she.

It was a good word.

"Technically, it's midafternoon."

"But it's the middle of a workday, and we're at a cheap motel."

"Second thoughts?"

"No." She was in. She was always excited to try new things… but that wasn't what was important right now. She was about to jump into bed with a Dream Weaver. A sexy, grumpy Dream Weaver who touched her like he couldn't get enough of her.

Even if he didn't trust her.

"What about you?" she asked.

He looped an arm around her, picking her right up off her feet. "I'll probably regret it tomorrow, but this place would have to be on fire to get me to leave."

They tumbled onto the bed and began tugging at clothes. Their own, each other's, whatever was closest.

Hunter arched her neck when his lips found the sensitive spot under her ear, and she dug her fingers into the back of his T-shirt. She pulled it up until he had to stop so she could pull it over his head.

It exposed his delicious, muscled chest again, and she spread her hands wide over it. She could feel his heart pounding as fast as hers. He began tugging up her top. He worked it over her trembling stomach, but stopped when he exposed her bra.

She'd chosen her outfit carefully this morning, including her bra and panties. She hadn't planned this. She hadn't thought it would happen, but she'd liked the thought of sitting across the table from him wearing something tempting, even if he didn't know it. The pink bra with the front closure was turning out to be a good choice.

A tight sound left his throat, and he forgot about her top entirely. He dealt with the front clasp of the pretty bra, and then his big hands were sliding up under the cups to take their place.

"Ohhh," Hunter groaned. She arched hard into his touch,

and her heels dug into the mattress.

They were racing even faster than she and Emily had at the adventure park. He kissed that spot on her neck again, and her hold on him became a little desperate.

He molded and shaped her curves, and her nipples poked into his palms. Feeling her reaction, he played the stiffening peaks with his thumbs.

"Tony," she gasped.

"You've been in my head for days."

"Mine too." The word went high when he gave her left nipple a soft pinch.

The throbbing spurred her into action, and she pushed at his gym pants. He'd dressed casually—no flipping through outfits for him—but she loved it. It made him easier to get naked. She hooked her thumbs into his briefs, and he lifted his hips to help her.

He got the tab of her jeans undone and gave a yank on her zipper. Hunter's thighs clenched when his knuckles bumped against her. She ground against the back of his hand as it caught between them.

"I'm hurrying as fast as I can," he said, his voice strained.

She pushed his gym pants down as far as she could reach and grazed her hands up the backs of his thighs. The sound he made was guttural, and he jerked his hand out from between them so he could get his cock to the place where she was doing all the rubbing.

Hunter trembled. He was big and hard. She twisted to get into a better spot. So, so big.

"Damn jeans," he muttered as he pulled hers down.

The waistband dug into her hips because he'd only gotten the zipper halfway down. She stuffed her hand between them to right the problem, and he reared upright. His stare locked on to what she was doing, and he reached for his pants again.

She froze. "No?"

"Hell *yes.*" He grabbed her wrist and put her hand right back where it had been. "I'm looking for a condom."

Oh, yes. *That.* She found the tab of her zipper and pulled it all the way down. His weight still bore down on her, but she wiggled her butt as best as she could to get her jeans off.

"Oh, gods," he groaned when he saw her pink panties.

They were damp. She'd gotten wet when he first plucked at her nipples.

She rushed to twist, shove, pull, and beg them to disappear from her body when he tossed a handful of condoms from his pocket onto the bed.

Her eyes went wide. "A handful?"

"I told you I wasn't sure what the situation was." He ripped open the first package and rolled the protection onto his straining cock.

Apparently, they'd prepared for the meeting in different ways.

Things were getting urgent.

Hunter kicked her legs, trying to work her jeans down further. She caught at his shoulders, and he rolled back onto her, shifting his legs to work himself into place.

They shared a shocked look when they both found themselves stuck.

Hunter jerked her head off the mattress to see what the problem was, and Tony looked over his shoulder.

"Shoes."

"Aaah," she cried, trying to toe them off.

"Fuck it," Tony cursed.

"I'm *trying.*"

He let out a snort of laughter. He managed to kick off one shoe and free a leg, but it didn't help matters. "This isn't working."

Hunter clutched at him. She didn't want to stop. She was close—close to something amazing. She could feel it.

Tony's jaw clenched, and he eyed their situation. Showing those fast movements again, he planted his hands on the bed on either side of her and pushed himself up onto his knees.

His erection flared straight up at her.

"Don't go. Don't stop," she said, trying to tug him back down.

"We're not," he said as he caught her by the hips.

Before she could figure out what that meant, he flipped her over and pulled her up onto her knees.

Hunter's heart nearly cracked her ribcage, it began beating so hard. Scrambling to find purchase, she pushed herself up on shaky arms, so she was on all fours before him. Her jeans were bunched around her knees, and she was sharply aware of the bareness of her most private parts before him. She craned her neck to look over her shoulder at him as he positioned himself on his knees behind her.

It was a tight fit.

"This?" He slid a finger down her wet crease, circled her opening, and penetrated her before pulling it back out. "Or take time for the shoes?"

Her air choked in her throat. Oh, gods. Her belly spasmed, and her pussy clenched tight.

"*This,*" she croaked, swinging her entire body back, seeking that deliriously arousing touch.

What she found was even better. He pushed the head of his rock-hard cock into her, and she let out a cry of pleasure. His fingers dug into her hips as he held himself a few inches inside her.

Their bodies did the talking from that point on. He stroked his hands up her stomach and then back down to the spot where they were joined. His fingers tripped against her clit, and she melted around him. When he thrust again, he reached the hilt.

Their moans were loud enough to carry through the thin motel wall.

They savored the connection for only a short moment before they began to move. Digging his knees into the mattress, Tony began to pump into her, drawing out the strokes, going faster and then slower, only to go hard again.

Hunter's toes curled, and her fingers snagged in the bedding. She could feel all of him from this position, the doggie style she'd never tried. She dropped her head, and her hair spilled in a cascade around her. It swung forward and back, forward and back, as he took her deeply. Her shirt was crammed under her armpits. Her breasts bounced, her nipples tight and pointy as the open bra dangled beneath her.

So damn sexy. So damn good.

If they'd had no time to deal with the shoes, they had little time to stretch out the act itself. Tony's thrusts became more regular, and that meant hard and fast.

Her head snapped up when his toying with her clit got more serious. And unrelenting. Her eyes popped open when he plucked and thrust at the same time, and she caught the reflection of the two of them in the framed picture hanging over the bed.

Against the backdrop of a vase of purple violets, she saw the two of them together. Him fucking her from behind... her rocking back to take him... Desperately. Hungrily.

"Ton-eeeeee," she cried as she came.

The orgasm ripped right through her, making her body arch. He thrust into her one more time, and then he was coming, too. It was fast, dirty, and fantastic.

She slumped onto her elbows when the climax finally let her go, and she felt his breaths against her back when he came down onto all fours atop her. That caused a secondary orgasm to ripple through her, and then they were both out of breath *and* energy.

Hunter rested her head against her forearms as she felt Tony moving sluggishly. He pulled out of her carefully, and the drag of flesh made her moan in pleasure one more time. He mumbled something she didn't hear, but she felt his weight leave the bed and then him tugging at her shoes.

Her jeans and panties went next, and she heard noises of what she assumed were his clothes. The mattress dipped as he crawled up it, all the way to the pillows.

"Gods help me," he said with a whoosh of expelled air.

She turned her head on the pillow to look at him. "I guess clothes were optional after all."

His lips twitched, and then he reached for her. She lifted her arms obediently so he could get rid of the pullover that was trying to strangle her. He collapsed back against the pillow with her splayed out atop him and flipped the bedspread over them backward. They hadn't even had time to fold back the covers.

"I don't think I'm going to regret that," he finally said.

"I like nooners, Dream Weaver."

He chuckled. "Good to know. I'll mark it down under things I've learned about the Menae."

* * *

Because he was definitely making a list. This was one thing that that wouldn't go on it, though, for his brothers to see.

Holy shit.

The more his heart slowed, the more Tony's mind raced. If he'd had any idea that it would be like this with her, he would have gone running in the opposite direction.

Oh, who was he kidding? He would have broken the land speed record to follow her on the night of the full moon.

He stroked his hand down her side and cupped her bottom as she rested limply atop him. That had been intense and the best sex of his life.

And it had been with his enemy.

She didn't feel like his enemy, though, as she snuggled atop him. Light shone through the thin curtain of the motel room window. It made it impossible to deny what had just happened.

"You'll fry your brain if you keep thinking so hard."

"Too late. Already toast."

His synapses were having serious trouble firing correctly.

What was he doing? What was he thinking taking her to bed like this? Even meeting with her was out of bounds. Cael had warned him. What was he supposed to do now?

She propped her chin up on her hand. It put her close, and her dark eyes were observant. He reached to undo the hair clip that was now cockeyed on the back of her head and sticking straight up in the air. After tossing it on the bed beside the condoms, he indulged himself in sliding his fingers through the long tresses.

"I'm not regretting it," he said. Seriously, he'd come so long and hard, he'd seen stars. "I'm just re-indexing things in my head."

"You do that a lot, don't you?"

He froze. Was she more than he expected? Did Lunatics—scratch that, *the Menae*—have abilities to look inside thoughts in addition to affecting them?

"Stop it. I can't read minds, but I can sense energy… Yours in particular, for some reason. You get all spun up in here." She tapped his forehead. "And you get it out, apparently, by doing this." She cupped his bicep as if to measure it.

Red flags still waved in his head. "You promised not to use your powers on me."

She lifted an eyebrow. "I'm not. I'm providing life-coaching advice, free of charge."

"Oh, yeah?"

"You don't need to be a Greek goddess to get a psychology degree." She sighed when he continued to glare at her, and rested her head again on his chest. "Enjoy the moment, Tony. I sure am."

His hand tangled in her hair. That had been what attracted him to her in the first place, way back when he'd started hearing about her escapades with Emily. She'd sounded like a free spirit, someone who was able to take life as it came and roll with it. That was something he tried to do, but could never achieve, no matter how much he projected an easygoing, laidback image.

Nobody expected the big, tough guy to get wrapped up in his head the way he did.

But she'd seen it.

One conversation with her, and she'd seen it.

He backed away from that thought. It was dangerous ground, especially with her. He might want to fuck her, but he couldn't let her see any weakness. She might not be superpowered during the day, but he'd seen what she could do.

This one played the long game.

"What did you do for your lunch meeting?" he asked.

"Do?"

He might as well make the best of this—outside of the sex part, which already couldn't be topped. He was here; he should try to learn more about her kind. "Yeah, you took Emily hula hooping and karaoke singing."

Back then, he'd been dying to meet a girl who could live that way.

She stretched under his touch like a cat when he massaged the back of her head where the clip had been. "Oh, this new client isn't ready for anything like that. I can barely get him out of his office and away from his computers. We had lunch at a sandwich shop in the same building as his company."

"What does he want to change about his life?"

She shook her head and sat up without an ounce of self-consciousness. The bedspread slid down to pool around her hips as she straddled him, and Tony's erection started to perk back up.

Damn, but she made his mouth water.

"I can't tell you that. I need to keep some things confidential, or people won't trust me."

"Interesting standards." He settled his hands on her thighs. They were sleek and taut from all that dancing, bike riding, and whatever else she did. He tried to concentrate. Was that how she lured her victims in? By gaining their trust and then using the knowledge to escalate them for her nighttime gig?

She spread her hands over his chest... and then his abs. The touch was more serious than a tickle, and she rocked aboard him when he reacted. "When's your appointment start?" she asked.

"What appointment?"

"The one around five."

Oh, damn. That was right. He had other obligations today. He looked at the clock on the nightstand. "An hour or so."

She cocked her head, and her hair fell forward so one breast played hide-and-seek with him. "What do you do for a living that allows you to take nooners? *Have* nooners? Shoot, I need to learn how to say that now that I'm doing it."

Doing it. Like currently in the act of—and maybe continuing to do so in the near future.

Tony's hold on her thighs tightened, but he relaxed his hands to stroke her up and down. He saw no need to keep that secret. She couldn't use it against him. "I'm a trainer, a sports performance trainer."

Her nose scrunched in the cutest way, and he felt his resistance to her slip a notch. He hitched it right back up in place. He was *not* going to end up as one of her patsies.

"Do you run basketball camps or something?"

"No. Well, sometimes…" Pulling back from temptation, he folded his arms under his head. "I work with elite athletes to give them advantages over their competitors."

Her eyes lit up. "Like who?"

That info she could use, and he didn't share it anyway. "People ranging from high school stars to college athletes and pros."

"Now that's interesting," she said softly. His stomach clenched when she leaned forward and planted her hands on either side of him. Her hair swung forward, curtaining them both as she looked down into his eyes. "We both help people to improve their lives."

The comparison made him uncomfortable, for their day jobs *and* their night ones.

"So why is it so hard to fix our own?" she murmured.

He frowned. "What's wrong with yours?"

She sat back on her haunches and swept back her hair. "I have this group of handsome, angry Greek daemons who want to hunt me down and exterminate me."

"Hold on." He pushed himself up on his elbows. "Nobody is exterminating you."

"Really?"

The crack in her voice couldn't be faked, and it made him

angry—but with himself and his hotheaded brothers, not her. Cael was right. They weren't in the dream realm here, and things had to be handled differently.

"No. We're not happy with your antics—and you definitely need to stay away from Emily—but we're not going to harm you."

She folded her arms over her breasts. "You just want me to move to another town where other brothers of yours might not have the same policy."

His lips flattened. She had him there.

"Fine. You can stay." He'd forgotten he'd asked her to leave anyway. He dropped back down against the pillow. "There, your life is fixed."

Her mouth dropped open in shock. She blinked once and then started to climb off him. "I hope you're a better sports trainer than you are a life coach."

"Why? What else is wrong?"

"Nothing."

He sat right up and caught her. "Hold on. Tell me."

She let out a huff. "It's just not easy being a spirit goddess, you know?"

For as bright and bold as she usually was, the admission got him *right there*. Oh, he knew. The responsibilities and pressure of his night job were weighty. Did she regret the things she did for hers? What was required of her as a Menae?

"I know," he said. "Trust me, I know."

He rubbed his hands up and down her back.

He'd worried things had gotten too down and dirty. The shoe thing had tripped him up. He'd just been so intent on screwing her, he hadn't worked out the logistics, but apparently, she'd been as turned on as him.

Call it the male ego, but he wanted to prove he could do better. Not the end result, but the ramp-up to it.

"We have the room for the rest of the hour."

She went quiet for a long moment before shrugging one shoulder. "You did bring a whole handful of condoms…"

She still seemed dejected, and he didn't like it. He'd met

with her to have it out. He'd been ready for a fight because he'd seen her hold her ground.

He didn't like seeing her sad.

Rolling them both, he planted her underneath him on the bed. Her eyes flared, but then she was tugging the bedspread out from underneath them as he dealt with the condom situation.

The fit was easier this time when he mounted her, settling into the cradle of her thighs. She wrapped her sleek legs around him, and he thrust into her slowly. Her back arched and her breasts lifted as he settled deep. Tony dropped his head.

So good. So hot. So forbidden and dangerous and out of control.

He began thrusting, and her fingernails bit into his back.

He didn't know what he was going to do about her. Maybe she *was* using her powers on him; maybe she wasn't. If he got close to her, though, he could learn more about the Menae. Then he and his brothers could figure out how to rein them in. It was as good of a reason as any, because he wasn't giving this up.

Not yet.

CHAPTER FIVE

Pete Larimer wanted a girlfriend, one who liked him for him and not his money. It turned out that was harder to find than it sounded.

Hunter looked around the venue. At least twenty circular tables were donned with white tablecloths. Centerpieces were done in seafoam green, which was the color of the charity. Tables along the edges of the room held items up for bidding, and excitement loomed in the air. Maybe tonight they'd have better luck.

She'd tried several approaches to help him meet women, the first being to send him to the grocery store. Everyone had to eat, and a grocery store didn't have the pressure or the hookup undercurrents of a bar. Nobody was drunk, and his tech-celebrity status might go unnoticed. She still thought it could have worked, but he'd been held up at the office for something or another and hadn't made it to the store until after eight o'clock.

The late hour had reduced his chances of meeting anyone compatible to essentially zero. She knew *she* hadn't been happy driving her own cart around the empty aisles as she ran recognizance for him.

She let out a puff of air and flipped through the pamphlet for the event to find the agenda.

They'd tried wall climbing next, but it turned out that

talking was challenging when you were holding on to a manmade façade by your fingertips. It hadn't turned out to be her thing, either, which was a bummer. She was short. She couldn't reach some of the handholds that others could. She'd been banished to the kiddie wall, which had been fine for her assignment to watch Pete's interactions, but bad for her ego.

Tonight, though, they were onto something. She could feel it. She smoothed the linen napkin on her lap. Pete was a bachelor being auctioned off for a date. Her job was to scout the audience and make sure the bidding war was robust.

The idea was perfect. Bidders would, in theory, be wealthy enough that the money thing shouldn't be a problem. They'd also be philanthropically minded, which she'd learned was important to her client. At the very least, he'd end up with a dinner date.

If they ever got the show started.

She looked at her phone for the time. She'd been working long hours for this one, and her days had been packed, too. Goal setting seemed to coincide with the start of the school year. It slowed down for the holidays before ramping up again for New Year's resolutions.

A text message popped up on her screen. *Want to meet up tonight?*

A zing went through her. It was from Tony. They'd been scandalously meeting for nooners in secret, but their schedules hadn't jibed for three days now.

She missed him.

They still walked on eggshells around each other. Sensitive topics were definitely avoided when they talked, but once they touched, they couldn't stop. So they didn't talk much, and they didn't delve into their differences. They stuck to the physical. For a Dream Weaver and a Menae, it seemed to work.

At least for now.

She did the math fast. Pete was the first bachelor up. The organizers wanted to start the show with a bang, and they had the Solstice Sentinels' star receiver for the finale. She could sneak out once Pete had strutted his stuff down the runway and they learned who bid on him.

I'm at a thing, but it shouldn't take all evening, she typed. There was the auction, but dessert was also supposed to be served.

Are you up for something different? he asked.

Her eyebrows rose. There were way too many ways to interpret that. Were they not having sex? Or were they having a different type of sex? Her earlobes got hot. It didn't matter. Both options got her blood pumping. They might not fully trust each other, but she trusted him in this. When he touched her, he brought her nothing but pleasure.

Delirious, muscle-melting pleasure.

She sent a dancing banana emoji with a question mark.

No dancing, he returned, *unless I'm supposed to read that in code.*

She let out a laugh so sharp, a woman at the next table looked at her. Hunter pressed her lips together and sent him a karate man.

I have no idea what that's supposed to mean, so I'm just going to go with no.

She picked a musical note.

I could add some music.

She smiled. *I'm in.*

When can you meet?

Let me get back to you.

She went off in search of Pete and found him backstage. He looked nervous, but more tired than anything. "How are you doing?" she asked.

He pulled at his collar. He looked amazing in black tie, but she could see it wasn't natural for him. "Are you sure this is going to work?" he asked.

No, but they needed to keep trying. "Yes, because you're going to end up with a date."

Of that, she was sure.

He sat down on an abandoned chair that had seen better days and rubbed his face. "All this for one date—and the woman will be paying for it."

Hunter hugged her clutch to her chest. Fatigue was coming off him in waves, and she was on the downward path herself. "Listen, why don't I talk to the organizers? We'll have you go on dates with the top three bidders. How about that?"

He shrugged and rested his forearms on his thighs. "I guess."

"Come on, Pete. Liven up. This is supposed to be fun."

"I know. It was just a late night."

"Working again?"

He nodded. "I was checking out a new feature that goes live next week."

She rolled her eyes. She didn't want to get into a boring tech discussion. "What did I tell you about that?"

He sighed. "That I'm paying smart people to do those things, and I need to get off the computer and into the real world."

"And that's precisely where we are." Fortunately, activity backstage began to pick up. It must be time to start. She waved her hands, encouraging him to his feet. He tugged at his jacket sleeves, straightening them out, and ran a hand through his dark hair. "How do I look?"

Tired. "Flash me those pearly whites."

That got a response out of him. He really was dashing when he wasn't working himself into the ground.

"There," she said. "Those bidders out there are going to use all their money on you, and there will be nothing left for all the other bachelors."

"I just hope I don't end up with a big, fat goose egg."

"You won't. That's why I'm here." The organizers spotted him and waved him over to start the lineup. Hunter walked with him. "I'll start off the bidding and see if there are any interesting women out there for you." She'd been schmoozing, chatting up the attendees, and generally being the perfect wing woman. "Once your winner is announced, though, I need to head out."

He looked at her sharply. "You're leaving? Before we can debrief?"

"We can talk about it tomorrow. You need to go home to sleep anyway."

His eyes narrowed. "You have a date, don't you?"

Ooh, sore subject there. But she wasn't really going on a date, was she? It was a booty call.

Or was it?

An excited shiver went through her. Tony had said he wanted to try something different.

"I'm meeting a friend."

That was debatable, too, but she didn't have time to think through the minefield of her relationship with an Oneiros.

Pete sighed. "Just get me through this first, all right?"

"Of course." What was personal time, anyway? At times like this, she wished she worked the standard nine to five.

Oh, who was she kidding? That would drive her nuts.

She patted Pete's arm. "You'll do great. Just remember to smile and make eye contact."

She hurried away from the backstage area when the organizers started giving her the evil eye. The queue of handsome men were supposed to be bachelors. "I'm not a girlfriend," she said when a gray-haired woman with a clipboard glared at her.

I'm not anybody's girlfriend, she thought as she pulled her phone out of her tiny bag. She wasn't sure what she and Tony were doing. It was sexy and exciting and a little risky, considering what might happen if either of their families found out.

See you in an hour or so, she texted.

That turned out to be cutting it close. The entertainment portion of the night didn't start until after dessert was served, and then the emcee was chatty. Pete had barely left the stage before she was running for the door. She sent him a text with an excited peacock, but once she hit send, she was off the clock.

Her foot was heavy on the accelerator as she drove across town, and she was relieved to only be five minutes late when she pulled into the parking lot at Night and Day. It was their meeting spot. For reasons.

She got the first word in when she stepped out of her car. "I said 'or so.'"

"I'm not complai— Whoa." Tony's gaze swept over her. She hadn't had time to swing home to change, so she was still in her little black dress. "You look good."

The way he dragged the word out into two syllables made it sound better than any fancier compliments he could have chosen. Warmth spread inside her chest.

"That must have been some event tonight."

"A bachelor auction."

His head snapped up, and the warmth cranked hotter. Interesting. He didn't like that.

"I got the bidding going for my client."

The proprietary light in his eyes faded a bit, and then his fingers began tapping against his thigh. "Huh. Well, you're overdressed for what I planned."

"Which was…?"

He tilted his head toward his truck. Her heels helped her out when she walked closer, because the additional height allowed her to see the truck bed. Literally. He had a blow-up camping mattress back there.

Her jaw dropped. "You've got to be kidding."

He blushed. Red slashes lit up his cheekbones as he stood under the street lamp in the parking lot.

"Not for that. I thought…" The tapping against his thigh became faster. "Maybe we could go stargazing out at Comet Tail Lake."

She went still. They were actually going to do something date-ish?

"It's a middle ground for the two of us, and if it leads to other things…" He waggled his eyebrows and gave a lopsided grin.

She reached for the truck to steady herself. He was irresistible when he slipped and did that—forgot they were enemies and just enjoyed the moment of being together.

"I'd like that."

"Yeah?"

The cheap motel was getting expensive, she knew. She wasn't sure how much personal trainers made, much less ones specializing in sports performance. She'd beaten him there earlier this week and paid. That had led to the biggest argument they'd had since he tried to run her out of town.

"Absolutely. It's a beautiful night for it." Not giving him time to think about it, she circled his truck and climbed into the passenger seat. She liked doing the nooner thing, but they never got out of the motel. Making love to him under the stars? Even if it was in the back end of a pickup, that would be magical.

She just couldn't read too much into it.

"Do you have a jacket?" he asked as he climbed in beside her.

With him looking at her like that, she didn't need one. "It's so nice, I didn't wear one."

He glanced into the back seat. "I think I've got an old one somewhere if you get chilled."

Things went quiet in the cab as they headed out. They didn't talk much when they met up. They were usually on a schedule, and talking wasn't the priority.

Here, though, the silence was uncomfortable.

"Was your day busy?" Hunter asked.

He made a sound in the affirmative. "High school basketball is right around the corner, and I had a late session with my tennis pro…" He cursed under his breath when he shared more than normal, but then he kept going. "She had an interview at our normal time, so we had to move it to later than usual."

Hunter craved the information, anything more she could learn about him, but she couldn't let it show. "Oh, good. So, you weren't waiting long?"

"Only about five minutes." He kept a straight face when she gave him the stink-eye, and he turned onto the highway. "So… a bachelor auction?"

He'd shared. She could do the same, if she kept it vague.

There had been a lot of men at the auction. "I'm trying to shake up his routine and move him toward his goals."

"That would get *me* out of my comfort zone."

She tried to imagine him in a tux. It wasn't difficult. She was a pro at fantasizing, and what she saw in her mind's eye was enough to make her toes curl inside her pointy shoes. "I had to fight to get him to go, but you'd do well."

His eyebrows went in different directions. "How do you figure that?"

"Because you're confident." He wasn't bold like his brother, Zane, but he knew how to hold his ground. And put him in a tux? Forget about it. "And you're hot."

A muscle in his temple spasmed.

She shrugged. "I'd have to pony up my paycheck to hold off the other bidders."

The lighting from the dashboard was faint, but she could see his surprise. "You'd bid on me?"

A date with him? One where he wasn't all defensive and snarly?

Butterflies swirled in her chest, so close to her throat that she just nodded. She focused on the white center line of the road, but her hand bumped against his on the shared armrest between them. The butterflies took off in every direction when he hooked his pinky finger around hers.

She curled her finger, holding him back.

The silence wasn't as uncomfortable for the rest of the drive. It was intimate and cocooning. She was almost sad when they pulled into the park entrance, but then she saw the view when they arrived at the lake.

It was beautiful, with the night sky sitting like a dome atop it. They were outside the artificial light of the city, and she could see so many more stars. The park was quiet. Nobody else was around. There was barely even a breeze.

"The park is closed."

He let out a grunt and detached their pinky hold. "You're already getting me to break rules."

The pang of disappointment was sharper than it should

be. "It's not me," she said, looking up at the half-moon.

He swung the truck around, shifted into reverse, and parked so the bed was facing the lake. "Trust me, it's you."

The butterflies returned.

Hunter got out of the cab, and she was careful as she slid down onto her high heels. She had to climb to get into the monstrous thing, and she didn't want to twist an ankle. Once steady, she looked out again over the lake. She had good night vision, and she was sure he did, too.

He propped a hand atop the tailgate as he watched the quiet lake. There was so much going on beneath the surface there—both in him and the water. "Summer's last gasp," he said.

The temperature had swung upward again, which was unusual for late October. He lowered the tailgate, and Hunter braced her hands on it, preparing to jump. She let out a squeak when he caught her by the waist and lifted her.

"Thanks," she said as she scooted back on her rump.

He caught her behind the knees to stop her. "Those shoes are something else, but they need to come off."

"Oh, right." She didn't want to pop the air mattress.

His hands slid down her legs to her ankles. The straps were delicate, and he showed care as he dealt with them. He stored her shoes safely on the corner of the tailgate, but he caught her off guard when he returned his attention to her feet and rubbed them.

"*Mmm.*" She sighed and let her head fall back.

He worked out the tightness in her arches before climbing into the bed of the truck beside her. Together, they scooted toward the cab until they could stretch out full-length, side by side.

The view before them was spectacular, with the lake surface reflecting the moon and stars. Hunter lay back to take in the beauty of the night sky. The shades of darkness varied, with a smudge of light here and the glow of a planet there.

The half-moon bathed her with its light. Not too much, not too little. She was at her most *normal* now, her energy on an even keel. In a week or so, though, that moon would shrink from a crescent to no light at all, and things would suck.

"The moon and the night," she said softly. "They're intrinsic to one another."

Tony tucked his hands behind his head. She could feel his warmth. How could she not? He took up more than half the mattress.

"Our mothers are good friends," he noted.

It left the obvious question hanging in the air. How had their children gotten to be at such odds?

Hunter didn't want to think about that. She brushed away a moth that fluttered too close.

"There's the Big Dipper." She followed the line created by the two stars at the front of the dipper's cup up until she found the brightest star in the sky. "And that's the North Star."

"Sure, take the easy ones."

"I'm shockingly bad with constellations." She felt a nip at her arm, and she swatted at it. Not a moth this time, but a mosquito. She tried not to scratch at the bite, but she couldn't help it.

Tony pointed to her left. "Draco, the Dragon's Head."

"Where?"

"See the star halfway between the Big Dipper and the North Star? That's the tip of his tail."

"Oh, I see it."

"His body is coiled around the Little Dipper and then his head turns back the other way." Tony traced the outline but jerked suddenly and smacked at his pointer finger with his other hand. "Ah, I didn't count on mosquitoes still being out."

"We haven't had a freeze yet." Hunter didn't like winter when the skies were often overcast, and she couldn't spend time like this under the moonlight.

Did he know how good this felt to her? To be soaking up the moon's rays while listening to the sounds of the water lapping against the shore and an owl hooting in the trees?

"Nobody knows how I fit in with all this," she whispered as she looked at the expanse of the night sky above them. Their ancestors still lived amongst the stars. "Except you."

She rolled her head on the air mattress. In the confines of the truck bed, he was close. "My sisters are spread out all over the world." Shoot, that was another secret she probably shouldn't have spilled. "At least your brothers are close."

"Some of them. I don't know all my brothers, but it must be lonely for you."

"I'm busy, and they call, but when I slow down…" This time, she remembered to stop. "Yeah."

He stared at her. With the moonlight bathing him, he'd never looked more handsome to her. "Having so much family around causes different expectations for me."

Her fingers tightened where she'd laced them together against her stomach. He was loosening up around her, sharing more bits and pieces. Was he beginning to trust her?

She spoiled the moment by slapping at her leg just below where her dress covered her skin. "Ouch."

"Damn things." He sat up and waved his arms to chase them away.

"They like me, for some reason," she said as she tried not to scratch.

He let out a snort. "I know how they feel."

She went still when he looked over his shoulder at her.

"For some reason," he repeated.

Then he was leaning down, and her heart rate jumped. His mouth covered hers softly, and his fingers tangled in her hair. She caught at his shoulders. She loved when the energy in the air changed like that. She'd only experienced it with him. Tonight, under the night sky, it felt even more powerful.

He pivoted atop her, and the kiss became hungrier. More urgent.

He planted a knee beside her hip. "Ow," he said as he rocked his weight back.

"What's wrong?"

"The mattress doesn't have enough air, and the truck bed is hard against the knees."

She cupped his face and leveraged herself up for another kiss. "So spread out atop me."

The growl he let out was low and sexy. He lowered his weight onto her carefully, and she opened her thighs to get more comfortable. When his weight and his hardness settled against her in all the right places, she was the one who let out a moan.

And it wasn't because anything was *too* hard.

He planted a hand beside her head. It breached the bottom, too, but he didn't complain because she was dragging his T-shirt up his back and exploring the smooth skin she found there.

"*Ah.*" He smacked at the back of his neck.

Hunter nearly hit herself in the eye when she felt a stinging bite on her temple. "Make them stop."

"Gods damn it," Tony said sharply.

She jackknifed to the side to reach for that bite on her bare leg that was driving her crazy.

"That's it," he said as he sat back on his haunches. "They're eating us alive."

He held out a hand to help her up, and they scurried to get out of the back end of the truck. He hopped down, but when she started to launch herself, he got in her way. He tossed her shoes into her arms, and then picked her up. "Get the door," he said as he carried her to the passenger side.

He wasn't letting her bare feet touch the darkened ground. She did as told, and he deposited her on the seat before closing the door. He trotted around the back end, flipped up the tailgate, and made a dive to the driver's-side door. He nearly landed on her as he jumped inside.

He slammed the door behind him, and the interior light was doused again.

"Did any get in?" he asked.

"I don't know," she said as she itched and scratched and ran her fingers through her hair. "I don't hear any."

That high-pitched whine was unmistakable.

He scratched at his knuckles like he was trying to draw blood. "A perfect night and a perfect plan," he grumbled.

Hunter couldn't help it. She started to laugh. "Two Greek gods foiled by insects."

"You really want to laugh at this?" he asked as he planted his feet on the floorboard so he could rub his back against the padded seatback harder.

"Yes," she said as her giggles grew into belly laughs.

He slipped and let out a bark of laughter. And then another.

Hunter fell against him as she tried to catch her breath. He caught her hand to stop her from scratching her arm.

He thought it was that easy?

Spinning around, she climbed over him and straddled his lap. His eyes went wide at the slick move, but he dropped his head forward when she ran her fingernails up and down the back of his neck, scratching the spot for him.

His hands clamped down on her hips, and she jutted one side out to try to get it closer to the bite she had on her thigh.

Next thing she knew, they were kissing and rubbing each other anywhere they could reach.

Until she bumped against the horn, and it let out a blare, scaring the owl. Its shadow swept across the cab of the truck as it flew to another perch.

"Fucking thing won't sound when I need it to," Tony snarled. He caught her by the waist and twisted them both away from the steering wheel. The console got in the way when he tried to lay her down.

"Go back. Back." Reaching down, Hunter found the controls on the side of his seat. She pushed it, and the driver's seat reclined. Tony fell back with her splayed atop him.

It was better.

She kissed him again, and he pushed one hand into the low-cut neckline of her dress to cup her breast. Her nipple tightened, and she wiggled against his erection. His legs shifted, and his knee banged into the steering wheel.

"Shit," he said, collapsing back against the nearly flattened seat.

"Can we not catch a break?" Hunter braced one hand against the door rest and the other against the console. As humungous as his pickup was, there wasn't enough room to do this. She clawed at her thigh as the itch flared.

The sound of their heavy breaths was loud in the confines of the cab. The moon shone through the back window, highlighting the twisting of their clothes and their mussed hair.

Had their mothers spotted them together? Was that why nature had turned against them? Did they not approve? Why not? Wouldn't the two of them getting together improve relations between their family lines?

Tony flicked the button at the side of his seat, and it began to rise.

Hunter sighed and climbed off him.

"Buckle up," he said as she settled into her own seat.

She guessed that was it.

"Are we going back to the motel?" She knew she was putting herself out there, but she didn't want to go home. She'd missed him this week.

"We'll go to my place."

Her head snapped around. "What?"

His hand paused over the ignition. "Unless you don't want to?"

Want to? She snapped her seatbelt into place and began strapping on her shoes. "Drive!"

CHAPTER SIX

Hunter was excited and nervous. He was taking her to his home. It had been an unspoken agreement before now that going to either of their places was not an option. All those midday rendezvous had been at the motel, because while they were attracted to each other, the trust didn't extend beyond the bed.

They'd just moved past that. Leapfrogged right over it—because of mosquitos.

She pressed her lips together to stop a giggle. They'd even jumped over the "your place or mine" discussion.

He was taking her home.

He turned out of the park onto the main road, and the moon was right in front of them. Her excitement sharpened. Maybe the moon goddess had seen them and approved? Earth was a big planet. The moon couldn't keep her eye on everything, but maybe?

She heard a tapping sound over the roar of the tires. Tony was drumming his thumb against the steering wheel like he was sending out a frantic message in Morse code.

Was he second-guessing his decision? She wasn't going to ask.

"It was a fun idea."

He scratched the back of his neck. "They drank gods' blood. Do you think that will get them through the winter?"

"Why?" She grinned. "Are we going to try again in the spring?"

His lips twitched. "Maybe."

She reached out to his hand on the console and hooked their pinky fingers together. "It's got to be stronger than tiger's blood."

He let out a bark of laughter.

The lights of Solstice became brighter as they drove toward it, and the pinpricks of distant stars disappeared. He headed for a quiet, older part of town that had smaller houses, but big yards. The houses were tidy and well kept. No music blared, and the streets were empty. The neighborhood was getting ready for sleep, although lights still shone in windows here and there. A man walking his dog was the only movement she saw.

He turned into a long driveway, and she looked at his house with interest. It was a one-level ranch that was nothing fancy, but wonderfully homey. Dark shutters lined the windows, and two big planters bordered the front door. The outdoor light showed they were overflowing with well-kept mums and other autumn foliage.

He pulled up to the detached garage, shut down the engine, and silence loomed once again. It was charged with anticipation.

Hunter scratched the bite on her arm, and he caught her hand. "Stop that."

"They're driving me crazy."

"Me too. Let's get inside and find something to put on them."

The promise of relief had them both bursting out of the truck. He came around the front to make sure she landed safely on her heels before leading her to the back door of his home.

Inside, he bustled her through the kitchen and down the hallway. When he finally hit a light switch in the bathroom, it was nearly blinding. Hunter tried not to scratch, but she rubbed her knuckles against the rising lump on the side of her leg.

He opened a drawer and then the cupboard beneath the sink before finding a bottle of calamine lotion. "Here. Let's try this."

He gave the bottle a shake and squeezed out a dollop on his fingertip. He aimed at her leg, and she pulled up the hem of her little black dress so he could coat it liberally.

She did a little dance. "It's not working."

"Give it a chance. Let it dry."

He squatted down to get a better look, and she felt him apply more lotion to another bite she hadn't realized she had. And then a third. They all immediately started crying out for her fingernails, and her feet did a pitter-patter dance.

"Ah," Tony said. "You made me get it all over."

"Douse me with it."

"Hey, there are two of us in this condition." As if saying it out loud made it worse, he began scratching at the small of his back.

She'd probably given the monsters access to that smooth, bitable flesh when she tried to strip his T-shirt off him. Hunter clamped her hands onto the vanity as she tried to hold still. He'd shifted over to look at her other leg, and he was so close she could feel his breaths on the back of her thigh.

Her eyes popped open. "Hydrocortisone."

She grabbed the tube out of the drawer he'd left open. Wasn't that stuff supposed to help with itching? She skimmed the label to confirm before popping the top. She squeezed out a glob onto her finger and turned around fast. Squatted as he was, the position nearly put his face in her lap, yet it was her application of the cream to the bites on the back of his neck that made his eyes go round.

"Oh yeah, baby."

They took a look at each other and realized that relief might be at hand. They started tearing off clothes and treating each other's bites as fast as they could. When Tony grabbed the hydrocortisone to get the mosquito bites on her arm,

Hunter poured calamine lotion on her fingers and reached around his waist to find the bumps on the small of his back. She pushed his T-shirt up and off him so the pink liquid wouldn't smear.

"Not the face," she said when he took the bottle from her and put a dab on the itchy bite on her temple. With the darker tone of her skin, the pink patch would jump right out.

"You're damn cute, you know that?" he said, giving her a fast, hard kiss.

Her mind blanked. They were going for relief here, of all kinds. He could paint himself up like a clown for all she cared, and she'd still take him to bed.

A very muscled, sexy clown.

"Ah, my feet," she said as she kicked off her shoes. She rubbed her heel against the top of her other foot.

"Switch," he said as he passed her the hydrocortisone.

She caught his hand so she could get that irritating bite on his index finger and then looked over his arm as he squatted down to treat her feet. While he was there, he pulled down her panties, and she let out a squeak. It surprised her even more when he laughed.

"Playing doctor never had quite this meaning before."

He spun her around, and she went up on her tiptoes when he found a bite on the curve of her butt. No wonder she'd been squirming against the seat of his truck.

"To-ny?" All this touching and rubbing was having side effects.

He stiffened when he heard the tone of her voice, and then stood up fast. "Right."

He plunked the itch medicine onto the vanity and caught her by the waist. She climbed right onboard, wrapping her legs around his middle as he started moving to the bedroom. With no panties, the denim of his jeans was rough against her flesh. She wiggled harder.

His blunt fingertips scraped up her back, looking for a zipper.

"It's a pullover."

"So pull it over already."

She worked her dress out from where it was caught between them, and he caught the tab of her bra. It snapped against her, but he finally got it unhooked. They tumbled onto the bed together, and she went for his jeans.

* * *

Tony shoved down his jeans and boxer briefs. He couldn't believe he'd brought a Lunatic here, to his home. He'd let her inside willingly. Intentionally. But it was Hunter, and now that she was in his bed, his need for her was at a level that was insane.

He shifted as she grabbed his jeans from where they bunched at his thighs and yanked them down. Her bra dangled from her shoulders, but it was all she wore as she twisted to get his shoes off his feet. They'd learned their lesson.

Light spilled into the room from the hallway bathroom.

Gods, she was beautiful. So spunky and full of life, especially when she forgot they were supposed to be on opposite sides.

She started to toss his jeans to the floor, but then she remembered another lesson. She lunged to snag them back, and she gave him a grin as she dug into the pocket where he kept the condoms.

That grin...

Her mischievous side should be a warning. He shouldn't like her. Not a Lunatic... Menae... Whatever they called it.

Or, at least, he wasn't supposed to.

As she climbed aboard him, straddling his thighs, he lost the distinction between love and hate. She looked sensual as she perched above him. She was delicate in form, but her body was tight. He reached out to pluck her unhooked bra away from her breasts, and she offered her arms as he stripped her bare.

He caught her breasts as she reached to drop her handful of treasures on the nightstand. All except one.

He had a boxful of them in the drawer of that very nightstand, but he wasn't about to tell her that. Not when she looked so pleased with herself, and not when he had his hands on two of the firmest, softest breasts he'd ever discovered.

He pinched her nipples, and she let out a thrilled gasp. She returned the favor by scratching her nails up his thighs right to his balls.

"Careful," he said when he nearly bucked her off.

She caught her balance and ripped open the condom wrapper. "No way this would have worked on that air mattress. Next time we'll have to add more air."

Next time.

He had a fleeting worry about fingernails as she unrolled the condom over him, but then there was nothing but pleasure. She rose onto her haunches, and he slipped a hand between her legs. Her thighs clenched, trapping his hand as she let out a cry.

"Oh, that's... *Ohhh!*"

He rubbed the tip of his finger against her, and her entire body quaked. Catching her ass with his other hand, he pulled her into position. Eager to take him, she slid her knees wider on the sheets. The sounds they both let out were carnal as she sank down onto him, taking him inside her.

Tony's fingers dug into her hips. "Hunter."

"I know," she said with a pant. His vision glazed when she began to move, pumping slowly. Lifting her arms, she piled her long hair atop her head. She looked like a goddess—because she was.

And, for the moment, she was his.

Slamming his heels into the mattress, Tony thrust up into her, throwing her off her rhythm. She let out a cry. He did it again, and the time for slow and sexy passed.

Leaning forward, she caught his shoulders and began riding him. He captured one of her breasts, and then reached back to grab the headboard. They were rocking and rolling, their bodies coming together in sharp slaps. The agony and the ecstasy. The merging of two perfect counterparts.

He didn't analyze that thought as the need and the drive to take her overwhelmed him. When she arched and came, he caught her. She was breathtaking in that moment, a picture of pure bliss.

Flipping them both over, he thrust deeply, keeping the connection going. He could feel the flutters of her orgasm, and he lifted her legs higher, propping them on his shoulders as he kept fucking her right through it. The cushion of her body and the sounds of her moans drove him toward the finish line, but the temptress pushed him through the winner's tape when she dug her claws into the bite at the base of his neck. Satisfaction had him spilling his load.

The house was quiet when Tony rolled his weight off her.

"Wow," she said.

"Yeah." It was always good between them, but that had been something else.

She snuggled up beside him and rubbed her toes against his shins. He trailed his fingers up and down her spine, trying not to agitate any of her bug bites now that they'd both sufficiently distracted themselves.

There was something about having her here in his home. There were no thin walls with paying customers next door. There were no time limits or excuses to be made. They were still sneaking around, but they'd just taken it to another level.

One he wasn't sure he wanted to examine too closely. Not when it felt this good.

She stirred beside him.

"Uh, give me a few moments," he said when she reached for the nightstand. And by a few minutes, he meant that he'd need a few hours. Maybe less if he got a protein drink from the refrigerator.

Instead of another condom, though, she picked up the blue plastic toy thing she'd practically thrown at him when they first met at Night and Day.

"You kept it," she said.

He'd been carrying it around in his pocket every day,

although he wasn't quite sure why. "What is it, by the way?"

"You don't know?" She held it up into the ray of light that slanted across the bed from the hallway. "It's a fidget spinner."

"A what?" He didn't particularly like the word *fidget*.

"It helps some people calm their thinking, or at least rein it in so the thoughts are moving in the same general direction." She gave it a whirl.

It wasn't loud, and he liked the smooth action. He was an engine guy. He liked figuring out how machines worked, whether it was in his truck, at the gym, or the human body itself. But this thing looked like something you got out of one of those machines with a claw arm. "Why would you give me a toy?"

"It's not a toy, it's a tool." She put it back down as if a little disappointed.

He picked it up again. Yeah, the action was nice. A little hypnotic, actually. "I like it. I just didn't know what it was for."

He let the fact that she'd thrust it at him in the middle of a fight pass.

Why had she done that? He knew that Lunatics were supposed to be manipulative, but it didn't seem like a trick. He'd have to do a web search to learn more, but it seemed like she was trying to help.

Maybe her life coaching took precedence during daylight hours?

Or maybe being a Menae was different than what he and his brothers had been taught?

It was too much to consider right now, especially with sleep pulling at him. It was late, and he needed to get to work.

Shiiiit. He flinched so hard on the bed that Hunter reached for him.

"What?" she asked. "What's wrong?"

Work. "Who's your Dream Weaver?"

"Excuse me?"

"Right, you wouldn't know that." He kept slipping up

around her. More importantly, though, he couldn't have one of his brothers finding her here. They had a rule not to invade each other's privacy. Sleepover partners were taken care of by whosever bed they were in, but the primary Oneiros always knew. After spending so much time with their charges, a Dream Weaver could identify them by their brain wave signature alone. It was like a fingerprint.

He let out a long breath. Damn it. This was why it couldn't work between them. Even if he did trust her, or was beginning to trust her, his brothers would—

"I don't dream."

The confession cut right through the darkness. Tony looked over at her. She'd shared that freely and openly, and it was huge.

"*You* don't dream?" Because they'd messed up on assignments? "Or Menae don't dream?"

She hesitated for half a moment. "We don't dream."

Confused, he rolled onto his side. "But you're half human." He'd checked. He'd done a lot of homework on his Greek ancestry in the past few days. "Your father was Endymion, a mortal man."

She shrugged self-consciously. "I don't know what to tell you."

"Why tell me at all?"

"Because you would have figured it out once all you Dream Weavers started talking."

That was a good point, because they did talk... like gossipy girls at the high school lunch table sometimes.

But it was a key disclosure, especially for the two of them and whatever this relationship between them was. "So none of my brothers are going to visit you tonight."

This time, she was the one who looked poleaxed.

"Oh, right." She looked at the clock. "Do you need to go?" She pulled the covers to her chin. "Do I need to?"

"No." The answer came out before he even thought about it. He didn't second-guess himself, even though there were all kinds of implications threatened by that decision. "Unless you want to?"

He was bone tired, and the calls of his charges were loud in his ears. He didn't want to get up and traipse across town when he was so relaxed, and she was right where he wanted her. But if that was what she needed...

"I could drive you back to your car."

The awkwardness was killing them both. Their words were stilted, and even their movements had gotten unsure.

"Can we do that in the morning?"

Yesss.

"Definitely." A sleepover felt right, although he did need to address a few things. He flipped back the covers. "Stay put. I'll be right back."

He checked to make sure they'd locked the door then pointed his key fob at the truck to ensure that was secure, too. They'd scrambled inside the house so fast. He lived in a quiet neighborhood, but it was always best to take precautions.

Like putting his briefs back on when he found them beside the bed.

He'd gotten the bathroom light, but Hunter had turned on the bedside lamp. Her gaze stuck on his clothed state.

"So no more..." She tilted her head at the rumpled comforter.

He shrugged and got back into bed. "Maybe, if I get through everyone fast." Hell, she'd shared something private with him. "Being naked in the dream realm was never a problem until Devon started showing up there. Suddenly, it's indecent."

"Who's Devon?"

Crap on a cracker. "I can't tell you that."

"Okay." She lifted the covers so he could slide underneath them. When he doused the light, she relaxed at his side. "What happens now?"

"I'll wait until you go to sleep."

He could feel the vibration in the air. She wanted to ask more but was holding back. She was curious by nature.

"Do you help with that, too?" she whispered.

"No, the Sandmen do that."

"You're not the same?"

Damn, they'd lost a lot of their history over the years. "No."

Although, if she didn't dream, did Sandmen visit the Menae? How did they fall asleep without them? Maybe it was a different process entirely?

No dreams. He couldn't wrap his head around the concept. He didn't dream, but he experienced them through humans up front and firsthand. Other sleep raiders like Somnambulists, Night Terrors, and Spasmodics lived in the dream realm, but Lunatics were in the human world like him and his brothers, the Oneiroi.

They were turning out to be more alike than he'd ever thought.

"Can you access humans' thoughts during the day?" he whispered.

She didn't answer.

Yeah, that question was probably over the line. When he looked at her, though, he realized she wasn't being secretive. She was sleeping. She'd slipped off quickly and easily.

And since he was still in the waking realm, he had no idea if a Sandman had been involved.

His hands fisted in the sheets. If they were, they'd better keep their mouths shut about what they'd seen. Although in their world, Dream Weavers were so far beneath them, they'd probably see no value in the gossip.

"Whatever," he mumbled. The politics were exhausting.

Closing his eyes, he savored the feel of his comfortable bed and his intriguing new lover beside him. He hadn't expected the night to end up here, but he couldn't say he was unhappy about it.

He'd deal with the fallout later.

Once he'd resigned himself to that major decision, making the transition was easy. With Hunter in his bed in the physical world, his spirit form jumped into the dream realm.

It was time to bestow some dreams.

CHAPTER SEVEN

The brain waves of Tony's charges were loud when he entered the dream realm. He was late, and many of his sleepers were ready for him. He was usually regular with his services, so the disruption in schedule was not appreciated. He quickly got to work.

Routine was important when sleeping. It was just like muscles in the human body. If they were worked regularly, they responded well. If workouts were infrequent or too aggressive, the body responded with aches and pains. Fatigue and headaches were the same result on the mental side.

Concentrating on his senses, he traversed the night to get to the sleeper who was calling the loudest. Make that sleepers. He found brothers, aged eight and six, sleeping in one bed. He remembered that, when one of his younger brothers would crawl into his bed to sleep, usually because someone had told them a scary story about sleep raiders. And if it was a story about Night Terrors, that nearly always happened. At least he knew neither of these two had had a bad dream, because neither had made it that far into the sleep cycle yet. That was on him, though, because they were ready. Both were in deep sleep. It provided the muscle repair they needed after time on the playground and karate class, but their brains needed a different kind of sleep to restore them.

That was where dreams came in.

He did a sweep of the house for any sleep raiders. When he found it safe, he reached out a hand to each of them. He might as well multitask to make things quicker. It took concentration to do this, especially when his intent wasn't to have them share the same dream, but he was up for the challenge.

He felt good tonight. Really good.

He detected delta waves, first in the six-year-old and then the older child. He latched on to the passing waves and led them up. Their heart rates increased, even as their muscles locked down, and then they were both there, on the precipice of dreaming. The older brother chose his story first, and Tony let him go on his way. The younger one was slower to formulate his path. Instead of a story, all he wanted to dream about was his toy truck.

That was fine. The kid might play with it all day, but if he didn't have any other things to work out—like having to eat broccoli at dinner or worrying about his upcoming test for his yellow belt—toy trucks were fine.

Sleepers knew best what they needed, not him.

He drew his touch away from the children's foreheads. The dreams seemed to be taking. It was time to move on.

He made it through five or six of the most urgent cases before he turned to efficiency. He could bestow dreams to sleepers faster when they all lived together, and he had a bunch of charges living in the same frat house at the university.

He headed their way, and for the first time in ages, he paid attention to how he felt as his spirit traveled through the dream realm. A fizzle of energy circled him, feeling tingly and soothing at the same time. It was how *he* recharged after an eventful day.

So, so eventful.

He manifested in one of the larger sleeping rooms in the house where twin beds were lined up, one after another. It looked more like army barracks than a place conducive to studying, but what did he know? He'd never been a frat boy.

Zane looked up when he felt a new arrival and cocked his head when he made the identification. He was bestowing a dream on a fraternity member who'd passed out on the rug. "Nice of you to join us. Isn't this one of yours?"

Tony peered closer. Great, the fraternity had held another party. Dreaming wouldn't stave off the hangovers these college kids would be feeling come morning. "Uh, yeah. Thanks for picking him up for me. I'm getting off to a late start tonight."

"No kidding. This is the third charge I've picked up for you."

Tony shrugged and moved to the closest bed. The situation had been reversed plenty of times.

He placed his palm over a mouth breather's forehead to start the process and let out a wheeze. *Gah.* Not even being in the dream realm protected him from the stench of alcohol on this one. He steeled himself, did his job, and then considered which sleeper to approach next. Were there any teetotalers here?

Zane's forehead rumpled. "You're mellow tonight."

"I'm always mellow."

Zane snorted. "Yeah, right." His brother paid little attention to the guy in front of him, who was snoring like a motorboat, as he led him into a dream. "There's something different about you."

Tony rolled his eyes and went to the next bed.

"Let's see. It's Thursday night."

"Party night." Obviously. As a trainer, it disturbed him to see young people in this state. Did they not know what they were doing to their brains and bodies?

"Not for adults like us."

Tony coughed. Suddenly, Zane considered himself an adult? It took more than a steady girlfriend to reach that status, but if anyone could tame him from his wild ways, it was Emily.

Although there was something to say for wild ways.

Tony scowled. Hunter was a wild child, too, but she had

other sides. He'd seen them.

Zane folded his arms over his bare chest. "It's too late for a sporting event, even accounting for overtime, and you're chilled out, even though you're hours late to the dream realm."

Tony didn't like where this was heading.

Zane rocked back on his heels. "Zeus's lightning bolt. *You got laid.*"

Tony gave him the side-eye. Could he say it a little louder? There had to be other Oneiroi around who hadn't heard.

Speaking of dream weaving, he sensed one of his charges in the room across the hall. Turning around, he went that way.

Zane was right on his heels, and Tony swore when they both nearly ran into AJ. The ghost. He was as quiet in the dream realm as he was in the waking world.

"'Scuse me," he said, rounding his other brother to get to the kid who was slumped over a desk. He checked his charge's breathing. Everything seemed fine. He doubted the guy had been studying, but his arms were curled around his laptop like a pillow.

"Tony got laid tonight," Zane announced.

AJ's head whipped around. "Yeah?"

"Why is this news?" Tony asked. He adjusted his hand on his charge's forehead. The guy's brain waves were all over the place, even though he was sleeping. "I've been known to date."

"Yeah, yeah. Women love you, but you're picky."

"You're relaxed," AJ said.

Zane bobbed his head. "That's what I noticed, too, but I called him mellow."

"I don't even know what that means."

Tony frowned. He was having trouble leading this sleeper up to the dream realm. The guy wasn't in light sleep, but at the same time, he wasn't in deep. His sleep waves were scattered somehow, like they didn't know what to do.

Dumb kids and their partying.

Zane swung his arm around Tony's shoulders. "It means that whoever this woman is, she rocked your boat so hard, you're still lying in bliss on the beach."

As freakishly close as that description was, Tony sent a questioning look at AJ.

"In a good way," his quieter brother agreed. "Your head is always filled with about a dozen thoughts at one time."

Tony finally got his charge into the dream realm. "I think you have me confused with Derek."

"Nah, Derek's ten steps ahead, while your thoughts are always in different directions," Zane said.

Whatever.

Tony turned to the next bed, the one where the guy sleeping on his computer should be.

"That one's mine," AJ said, stepping in.

"Who is she?" Zane asked.

Tony looked around. He didn't see any female coeds in here. For once.

"The woman in your bed, numb nuts."

Tony jerked his head up, and his so-called mellow left him. He couldn't have them going down that trail.

Zane let out a hoot. "Someone will tell me. You know they will."

Tony pulled his thoughts together. It was all right. He'd covered for this. Hunter didn't dream, so none of his brothers would be summoned to his house.

Unless Zane went there just to be nosy.

A chill went through him, and his hands fisted. If Zane crossed that line, so help him, there would be a war of the gods coming. Oneiros versus Oneiros.

"Unless one of you went home afterward." Zane rubbed his chin. He was like a dog with a bone when he sniffed out something like this.

Tony kept quiet. They wouldn't know. They could never know that he was sleeping with a Lunatic... *Menae*, whatever. "I don't know what you're talking about."

Zane snapped his fingers. "It's the tennis player, isn't it?"

Tony was so stunned that he didn't know what to say.

"That's it. Your client, Kimora. That's great, man."

"Son of a…"

"No, seriously. It's time you met someone."

"I'm not talking about that." Tony jabbed his finger toward the kid on the computer. "My charge just bounced out of his dream."

Zane frowned and started paying attention. "Did someone else give him one before we got here?"

"I don't know. His brain waves feel weird."

Tony moved aside so Zane could cup his hand over the sleeper's forehead.

AJ moved closer. "Curved monitor. A sound bar. Gaming chair. He's a gamer. I bet it's the blue light wrecking his sleep patterns."

Tony picked up on the clues that he'd missed. That made sense. "Bobby was talking about that at IHOP the other week."

The blue light from electronic screens was becoming as big a disruption to sleep as the sleep raiders they fought.

"I looked into it," AJ said. "It screws with people's circadian rhythms, because most blue light comes from the sun. When humans stay on their devices or watch TV after dark, they don't get the signal that it's time to sleep."

Zane removed his touch from the college kid's forehead. "I got him back into a dream, but I don't know if it's going to hold."

"Technology," AJ said with a shake of his head.

"It's messing up so many things." Tony looked around. Someone would have to come back for the hardcore partiers who were still going strong, but otherwise, they seemed to have gotten to everyone. "Time to move on."

"Whoa, big guy." Zane stepped in front of him. It was brave for a pipsqueak, or stupid. Zane could be either. "Speaking of screwing, we're not done with our conversation."

And yet, somehow, he always managed to be both.

"Yeah, we are," Tony growled. There was something about the word alone that he didn't like. *Screwing.* "I'm out of here."

"Do you prefer Kimony or Tomora?" Zane asked, even as Tony began to disperse.

He was still solid enough to give his brother the middle finger. "Screw yourself, asshole."

He vanished with the sound of AJ's laughter filling his ears.

* * *

Hunter watched Tony as he woke. He'd been so quiet and still for so long, it was like watching life be breathed back into him. His chest rose and fell under her hand, and she stroked him in relief. She'd been checking to make sure he was breathing for the past half-hour.

"You're back," she said when he opened his eyes.

"Mmmph." He yawned and took a stretch that made something crack.

It was good to know that neither of them was an early bird.

His eyes slowly came into focus. "Morning."

His voice was husky and sexy, but his eyes were cautious.

"You go to the dream realm in your mind," she whispered, as if it was a secret that shouldn't be shared outside this room.

He didn't exactly stiffen, but she felt the tension poised and ready to spring.

"Something like that."

And he'd let her stay. He had to be vulnerable when he did that. He hadn't stirred at all when she made noise, and she'd been up for a while now.

Something sweet and rough filled her chest. He probably figured that she couldn't lead him into trouble if he was sleeping, but he'd trusted her not to hurt him while he was otherwise engaged—and that made her want to protect him. He should have steel doors on this room. Bars on the windows. Filtered air.

"I will never let that be used against you," she promised.

"Thank you," he said softly.

It opened the subject to her, though, one she'd been dying to know about forever. "What's it like there? In the dream realm?"

He thought about it for a moment. "Unpredictable."

"With sleep raiders lurking around every corner?"

"Not quite, but you do have to watch your back."

"What's out there? Or do I even want to know?"

He shrugged. "You probably already do, but in the way that humans perceive them, as sleep disorders. There are Somnambulists that make people sleepwalk and Apneacs that that their breath away."

"Like with sleep apnea?"

"Exactly, and then there are the Night Terrors. They may be the worst of the bunch."

She frowned. "What if something happens to you there?"

His eyes narrowed as he considered her. "The Oneiroi are the most powerful beings in the dream realm."

That was good to know, but it didn't answer her question. People with night terrors woke up screaming. They had to be formidable opponents. What was he not telling her? If something happened to him there, would he not wake up here?

That terrified her.

He was strong, but surprises could happen. Accidents or setups. Even the best fighters and the strongest soldiers could be defeated by one wrong move, a miscalculation, or even the tiniest distraction.

She had to think of something else. "Is it dark or is it in Technicolor? Are there alien creatures running around?"

"It's quiet, and they do their best to hide from us." He plumped the pillow under his head. "It's nighttime—or, at least, it is on my duty."

"Even there?"

"It's this world, just once removed."

Curiosity got the best of her. "But I've heard that dreams don't always make sense, and why is there so much discussion on the color thing?"

"That's inside sleepers' dreams. I don't always go into them. I just lead them there and let them set whatever path they choose."

"But can you? See what they dream?"

"I can."

"Tell me one?"

"One of my charge's dreams?"

"You have assigned sleepers?" Her thoughts raced. So he must get to know people deeply, from the inside out. No wonder the Oneiroi were known for being ferocious. They were protectors.

"Can you tell me a dream from last night? Or isn't that allowed?"

He propped himself up on an elbow. "Let's see… I had one woman dream about working at a zoo."

"Aw, does she like animals?"

"She's a first-grade teacher."

Hunter laughed. So the answer to that question was yes.

"Another guy dreamt about his teeth."

Her laugh bubbled over. "His teeth? What does that mean?"

"Who knows?" He looked at the clock beside the bed. "You hungry?"

"I've got bowls on the table and cereal ready to pour."

"Good woman."

Hunter had worried about the morning after, but there was no awkwardness or drama. They shared a quick breakfast, but it was a weekday. They needed to get going, even if they didn't have strictly structured work schedules.

Tony drove her back to her car, and she hopped out into the Night and Day parking lot, wearing her little black dress and a jacket he loaned her. She unlocked her car but turned back to him before getting inside. "I had a good time last night. And not just the… *you know*. I liked spending time with you."

"Me too."

And there it was, the awkwardness.

Like a gentleman, he'd gotten out of his truck and followed her the few steps to her car. They stared at each other. It wasn't supposed to be like this between them: the attraction, the interest, the sharing of secrets... He pulled the fidget spinner out of his pocket and gave it a spin. "Are you doing anything tomorrow night?"

Excitement jumped inside her chest, but she made herself stop and do the math. Saturday should be okay, but any time after that, things would be dicey. Her energy would be draining. But Saturday? She could power through if he wanted to get together. "I don't have plans."

"Want to do something?"

"Like what?"

"I don't know. I picked stargazing. Your turn, life coach."

She thought about it for a second. "Have you ever thrown axes?"

As soon as the idea left her lips, she knew it was a mistake. She'd gone axe throwing with Emily, and it had turned into a thing with his brothers. She didn't know if Tony had heard about it. The activity had just been on her mind. Like always, she'd gone with the impulse.

His weight shifted. "You want me, a Dream Weaver, to give a Lunatic an axe?"

She knew it was a joke, but it landed as flat as her suggestion had.

"Sorry, no." She burrowed deeper into his oversized jacket. It was colder outside today. "Bad idea."

"I'm sorry, that came out wrong. All of it." He shoved the spinner and his hands into the pockets of his jeans. "I don't know how to do this, Hunter. I've been taught my whole life to be cautious of you."

"Me too, but I think we're doing okay."

"As long as we keep our families out of it."

She nodded. That was where things got messy.

He rocked back onto his heels and then forward again. "Why axe throwing? I thought you liked trying new things, and I know you did that with Emily."

That answered that question. What other discussions had the Oneiroi had about her?

She waved her hand. It was a silly thing. "My goal was to hit the target last time I went, but I never did because…"

Oh, smooth, Hunter. She kept stepping in it again and again.

"Because my brothers chased you out of there before you could."

She gave him a forlorn look. They'd just agreed to try to keep their families out of whatever was going on here.

"It's probably a bad idea to go." She scuffed her shoes on the asphalt. "They might go back. I can only imagine how they'd freak out if they saw us together."

"Where'd you go?" He pulled his phone out of his back pocket.

"Axe Me Anything."

His thumbs moved fast, typing out a search. "Looks like there's another place across town called Kick Axe."

"Really?"

He nodded and tucked the phone back in his pocket. "Let's do it."

"You don't mind? You don't think it's stupid?"

His expression softened. "Helping people meet their athletic goals is what I do. I'm kind of bound by oath to help you."

She let out a squeal and threw her arms around him. "Thank you. It's been driving me nuts."

It was the life coach inside her.

He patted her on the back. "Then it's a date."

"Yes." She didn't leave those words hanging. It was *a date.*

CHAPTER EIGHT

Hunter was still tripping over the concept later as she went through her messages at the coffee shop. She had a date with a Dream Weaver. Her, a Menae. It was difficult to get her mind on work or anything else, but she focused when she saw a message from Pete.

He wanted to talk about the bachelor auction.

The auction. Had that been just last night?

She looked at the time. He'd sent her a meeting invitation for later this morning. She had just enough time to drink her coffee and get ready for her day. Was that how he ran his business? Scheduling meetings at—she squinted at the email—one sixteen in the morning?

She made a note to discuss that and returned to her text messages.

There were a boatload from her sister, Strawberry, who still worried about her full-moon encounter with the Oneiroi.

Are you safe in Solstice? You embarrassed them.

Maybe it wasn't a good idea for you to expose yourself like that. They know you're there now.

The Neanderthals.

Let me know if you need me to come be your backup or help you pack.

Where are you? I'm getting worried. Call me!

Hunter sighed. There had been no way to avoid telling her

sisters. It was tradition, Menae telling the story of their full moons. Her dirt-biking escapade would have been enough, but to add Dream Weavers to the mix? At this point, the story had reached epic status.

And she hadn't even told them about the kiss.

I'm fine, she typed. She didn't have time for a call right now. She had to prepare for her meeting with Pete. *My relationship with Emily, my client, is protecting me.*

The fact that she was sleeping with—*and now dating*—an Oneiros didn't hurt, either.

Her sister did bring up an intriguing question, though. Why did the Menae need to live in the shadows when the Oneiroi were no more powerful in the real world than human men? The description of them as Neanderthals did rub her the wrong way, though. She didn't like being called a Lunatic.

She wanted badly to reply to that, but she scratched a bug bite instead.

"Ugh," Hunter mumbled. Where did her loyalties lie? Sneaking around with Tony was changing her impression of the Oneiroi, but she was learning some important things that her sisters should know. Was she betraying them by keeping secrets? Or was she putting herself first?

She blinked fast when Berry returned a message almost instantaneously.

Love you.

Hunter returned an emoji of a heart and put her phone down. She rubbed her hands over her face. If she was going to meet with Pete, she needed to get her head on straight.

Where were her notes about the auction? She took a bracing drink of coffee and flipped through her notebook.

"Hunter?"

She glanced up. "Emily!"

Speak of the devil. She sprang from her seat and went in for a hug before catching herself. They hadn't really talked since that infamous full-moon night.

Emily closed the distance and wrapped an arm around her shoulders while holding her coffee out of the way. "It's so good to see you."

"What are you doing here?"

"You introduced me to this place, and I like their coffee." Her friend peered at the cup on the table. "Double shot of espresso?"

Hunter laughed. "Not yet."

But soon.

They looked at each other as words suddenly left them.

"Are we okay?"

"I'm so embarrassed about what happened."

When they did speak, it was right on top of one another.

Hunter gestured to the open seat at her table. "Do you have time to join me?"

"A little." Emily slid into the booth. She was dressed up today. She was still in jeans, but instead of a T-shirt, she wore a silky tank top and blazer. "I've got to get to work, but I'm ahead of schedule."

"How are... *things*?" Hunter asked, trying to find a way to phrase it. There was so much wrapped up in that word.

"They're good." Emily reached out and squeezed her hand. "You really helped me sort through everything, like why I was limiting myself and what I truly wanted."

"Like Zane."

"Zane and other things. I'm sorry I got drunk on the freedom and pushed it too far."

"You were having fun."

"It was dangerous, riding at night." Emily's lips twisted. "I'm especially sorry if Zane's brothers scared you."

Hunter fought not to roll her eyes. They'd tried.

"Or if they crossed any lines."

And that would be in reference to Tony. She scratched at a bug bite on her arm. "That kiss was mutual. You weren't the only one acting drunk."

"I wasn't sure what to do when he asked for your phone number."

"I appreciate your running it by me before you gave it out."

"Has he called you?"

Emily was leaning in, and her eyes were wide. She was dying of curiosity, but Hunter didn't know how to respond. If Zane learned what was going on, he'd flip his blond wig. "We met at Night and Day to talk. The discussion… didn't go well."

Technically, it was the truth. Tony had been intent on making her leave town that day. Things had only gotten better outside the juice bar when they *stopped* talking.

Emily looked crestfallen, and Hunter felt horrible for telling a half-truth.

"That's too bad. He's always been nice to me, and he's a cutie."

Hunter rubbed harder at the bug bite, trying not to use her nails. Oh, her girl didn't know the half of it.

Emily took a drink of coffee. "He's the one who wanted the video of you hula hooping, by the way."

Hunter stopped, mid-itch. "What? But that was before."

Before the full moon. Before they'd even met.

"Right? He was disappointed when you didn't show up at the barbecue at Zane's house, too." Emily shrugged. "I think he's been crushing on you for a while. That night, I just assumed that he'd looked you up and you'd already met?"

"Uh, no." The information was blowing Hunter's mind. She rubbed at her temple, trying to put everything together. "That night was a first."

On so many levels.

"Maybe he was just nervous when you met afterward?"

That was one word for it. Nervous, angry, bullheaded, and fidgety—kind of like she was right now.

"Stop that." Emily pulled her hand away from the bug bite she was trying to scratch off her temple.

"They're driving me crazy," Hunter whined.

"I know how it feels. I was bit the other day when I was doing fall cleanup work in the yard. Where'd you run into them?"

"Out stargazing."

"Here." Emily handed her a tube from her bag. "My friend Shea gave me this. It works better than anything else I've tried."

Hunter began using the ointment liberally. "So, I know we're not working together anymore. You don't need me now that you've figured out your life, but… are *we* still friends?"

Emily looked taken aback. "I've got nothing figured out, and yes, we're *good* friends."

Hunter smiled as a weight lifted from her shoulders. It felt good to have someone to talk to, even if Emily didn't understand what was truly happening in the nighttime world of sleep and dreams. That was only one part of her life.

"It won't cause problems between you and Zane?"

"He has concerns about us spending time together, but I decide who my friends are." Emily flipped her short hair. "And he needs to understand that *I* was the bad influence on *you.*"

Hunter smiled. It was clear Em wanted to be a bad influence. Who was she to dash that dream?

She passed back the tube of ointment and folded her fingers together tightly. If it was working, she didn't feel it yet. "I promise to try to be boring."

"No, don't do that. You don't need to change… Oh!" Emily said, noting the time again. "I'm sorry, but I really need to go. I'm interviewing for a product owner job today at High Score."

Hunter perked up. "That's great."

"You think so?"

"You'll kill it." Hunter began gathering up her things. "I've got to get moving, too. I have a meeting with a bachelor."

Emily frowned. "So, no to Tony?"

Yes to Tony, but not today.

"It's a new client."

"Oh," Emily said, brightening. "That's great, too."

"Let me know how the interview goes?"

Emily crossed her fingers for good luck and headed to the door. "I'll text you."

Hunter grabbed her keys out of her bag and swiped up her phone to follow, but an idea occurred to her. It was so good, she stopped in her tracks. With a smirk, she opened up her phone's video gallery. She found the one she wanted and sent it to a certain Dream Weaver.

He'd wanted it? Now he had it.

She couldn't wait to hear what he had to say about it at their date.

CHAPTER NINE

Hunter met Tony at the axe-throwing place on Saturday night. Picking an outfit was a challenge. What, exactly, did one wear that would catch his eye and still allow her to throw an axe with confidence?

She hadn't been joking. She wanted to hit that target so badly, she could taste it.

She looked around the place when she entered, but she didn't see him. He was an easy guy to spot: big, tall, and so good-looking it made her eyeballs sweat.

Then again, he was even easier to feel.

When someone entered behind her, she felt a wave of power and her belly clenched.

His hand touched her waist. "Hey there, been waiting long?"

"Just got here," she said breathlessly.

Oh yeah, he packed a punch. The surge of energy came from his Dream Weaver powers, subdued as they were outside the dream realm. The tingle in the pit of her stomach, though, was all about the magic they made together.

He looked around. "Not bad."

"It's nicer than the one Emily and I went to."

"Good. Fresh start for both of us."

Oh, how she wished.

"Let's check in at the counter."

Whether consciously or not, he didn't remove his hand from her waist as they figured out how everything worked. She was impressed that he'd called ahead to reserve a lane and timed it so they could have dinner first. It showed forethought. Caring. She knew he was always in his head, but this time his thoughts had been about her, and they hadn't been about ways to get her to leave town or rein in her Menae tendencies.

They were led to a booth next to the windows and handed laminated menus. The place was eclectic. The theme was somewhere between Knights Templar and Paul Bunyan.

Tony shook his head as he looked around. "Who came up with this and thought, *Hey, there's a nifty business concept?*"

"I don't know, but they're brilliant."

"As long as nobody loses a toe."

"Hey, I'm not that bad."

He looked at her sharply. "I hope not."

"I hit the wall, usually." Hunter looked through the menu but had a hard time paying attention. They were out in public together. Intentionally spending time together.

Her inner life coach was *so* rooting her on.

Their waitress arrived not long after they sat down, and she looked at Tony with the eyes of a hungry wolf. "What can I get for you?"

Such a come-on line.

"Why don't you take her order first?" he said, barely noticing the obvious ogling. "I'm still deciding."

He scored points for that. Hunter knew what it was like having Greek god genetics, but he barely looked at the waitress in the tight red T-shirt.

She sat a little straighter, trying to fill out her stretchy green top. Hunter green for luck. It was cute with a knot at her hip. It had been her fourth or fifth wardrobe change.

"I'll have the ribs," she said as she put her menu down at the head of the table. "With lemonade."

This place had the same policy as the last one of no alcohol on the premises. Whoever had come up with the business concept had also thought about liability.

Tony's eyebrows jumped, and his lips twitched. He put his menu down atop of hers. "Make that two."

The waitress leaned closer, trying to draw his attention to her double Ds. "Any sides with that?"

"Coleslaw," Hunter said.

"Vegetables. Sounds good to me."

Hunter felt the waitress's gaze finally swing her way. Once she did, the woman's head dipped, and the unspoken challenge evaporated. She swept up the menus. "I'll get that in fast, so you'll be ready for your lane."

Tony waited until she was out of earshot. "It's hard for humans to compete."

"Aw," Hunter said. "That's sweet."

"You're beautiful."

Her breath caught.

"And ballsy." He chuckled. "What kind of a girl orders ribs on a first date?"

"Why wouldn't I order ribs?" Her real question was if this actually qualified as their first date or if last night had.

He shrugged, and she appreciated once again the muscled landscape of his shoulders.

"They're messy, and you eat them with your fingers... unless you're planning to use a fork."

"A fork? But that's why they put wet wipes on the table." She pointed at the canister. No little individual square wrappers for this place.

His smile came out of nowhere. "Some people get self-conscious."

"Like your impression of me could get worse," she said. And immediately regretted it. Why? Why would she remind him of that?

"My impression of you is... improving."

A warm ball of sunlight settled in her chest. "Ditto. Stargazing was a nice idea," she said softly.

On cue, the bites on her arm began to itch. She gritted her teeth to try to avoid scratching them, but finally gave in with a quick rub with her knuckles. Tony cursed and reached for the back of his neck. It was like yawning; the action was contagious.

"Next time I'll have to remember the mosquito repellant."

Ew. She hated that stuff.

"Or netting." Her eyes popped open wide as the idea took shape. "Netting, now there you go."

"Are you kidding? Like we wouldn't have gotten tangled up in it once we... you know... got busy."

The look he gave her was heavy-lidded, and that ball of happiness in her chest dropped even lower.

"Hey, none of that," she said. "Not yet. I want to hit that target first."

His eyes danced. "I do like a woman with goals."

Did that mean that he liked her? More and more, Hunter was hoping so.

Their ribs arrived before she could ask, which was probably a good thing. Just the smell alone had her salivating. She ripped off a section of paper towels from the roll that sat next to the wet wipes and spread it across her lap.

Tony chuckled at her enthusiasm, but followed her direction. Soon they were both elbow-deep in eating and enjoying every bite.

Who had time for self-consciousness? He'd already seen her naked. What was barbecue sauce compared to that?

* * *

Tony was enjoying himself. Even more, he was enjoying her. This was the outgoing girl he'd heard so much about before he even met her, Emily's friend who was up for anything and lived like a free spirit.

She'd intrigued him back then.

He was close to obsessed with her now.

She'd pulled her hair back into a ponytail and was eating with gusto. Where could a little thing like that put so much food? He knew the meal wasn't exactly health-conscious, but she buzzed about with so much energy every day, he knew she'd work it off.

Although her energy levels had been coming down every time he'd seen her. Was that because they were becoming more comfortable together?

Finally, she reached her limit and pushed the plate away. She drained her lemonade, wiped her hands, and sat back in the booth patting her trim stomach.

He looked at his watch. "Right on time. Our lane should be ready."

She let out a groan. "I'll waddle right on over."

"You did it to yourself." He slid out of the booth and held out a hand to her.

It felt right when she tucked her smaller hand in his, but he wasn't going to analyze that right now. That fidget spinner she'd given him sat in his pocket, doing its job even though he wasn't playing with it. She'd taught him that he needed to not get so wound up in things. Sometimes, he just needed to let things happen.

That was easier said than done, but he'd been thinking about it a lot.

They followed the signs to the action. The tables were up front, while the throwing lanes were in the back. He'd checked online for the safety protocols that were in place, and they looked like they put their words into action.

"Lane eight," he said. She tucked behind him, still holding his hand as they passed a group that was definitely more on the Paul Bunyan side of the spectrum.

"Welcome, folks," the safety monitor said when he spotted them. "Let me walk you through things."

Tony listened intently. Keeping athletes safe and performing well was his job. He picked up on the concepts quickly, and Hunter was soaking everything up. She wasn't slapdash about things like he'd initially thought. She put a lot of consideration into her decisions, even when they got on the wilder end of the spectrum.

She and Emily had worn all the protective biking gear when they went out on their joyride.

Which was rationalization if he'd ever heard it.

He let go of her hand. "Ladies first."

She looked at him, as if sensing something was off. "Okay."

He watched her choose her weapon and line up. Damn, she was cute. His gaze slid down to her jeans that hugged her ass in just the right way.

"*Hi-yah!*"

His chin snapped up just in time to see her let loose of the axe. It dropped quickly as it traversed the length of the lane, but it stuck when it hit the wall a foot above the floor.

She shrugged and turned to look at him. "At least it stuck."

"What was the call of the attack for?"

"To channel my energy into the throw."

"Excuse me?"

"It helps." She turned with a flounce and patted his ass as he was choosing his axe. The intimate touch made his spine snap straight. "Show me how it's done, big guy."

The glint in her eyes made his jeans tight. Oh, he saw how it was. She didn't play fair.

Two could play at that game. He gave a stretch and squeezed his back muscles as he pulled his arms down in a classic bodybuilder pose.

When he sent a peek over his shoulder, he saw her gaping at him.

Oh yeah, he was onto her, and he had some sway over her, too.

He toed the line on the floor of the lane and eyed the target. He remembered the instructions they'd been given and gave the axe a light toss. The moment it left his hand, he could tell he hadn't put enough into it, but he still placed the throw halfway between Hunter's and the bull's-eye.

She came up to stand next to him. "How did you do that?"

"Doesn't matter. We need to figure out what works best for you." He walked to the wall to retrieve their axes. "Try again, and I'll watch your form."

"Uh huh. I've heard that before."

He chucked her under the chin. "Throw the axe, dynamo."

Determination set her jaw, and her eyes narrowed as she eyed the target. Tony stepped back into the safe zone and paid more attention to her throwing this time, rather than her form.

There was nothing wrong with that.

"*Hi-yah!*" she screeched as she gave it another whirl.

Heads turned from the crew-cut Army types three lanes down, and Tony bit back a growl. "Keep your eyes on the target in front of you, boys."

Hunter was consternated. "It didn't stick."

Her second throw was, in fact, on the rubber-padded floor. The axe had hit the wall with the top of its head and bounced off.

"Do it again," he said, passing her his axe.

And again, the *hi-yah* rang throughout the bay. Like she wasn't noticeable enough already with that face and that body.

He shook his head. "I see the problem." He picked up another axe and headed her way. "You're not strong enough to throw one-handed. You should use the two-handed overhead toss he showed us."

"But that's not as cool."

"What's more important? Looking cool or hitting the target?"

She took longer to answer than he thought she would. "Can't I do both?"

"After you bulk up that arm. I could give you some exercises if you're serious."

She flexed her biceps and then looked at his. "Okay, I'll try the two-handed way."

She took the axe, but he stopped her when he saw the way her feet were staggered. "You want to hit your target, not the one in the next lane."

He caught her by the hips and turned her so she was squared up to the wall. She tucked in right under his chin. He aligned her arms so her elbows were close to her ears rather than splayed out to the side. "Now focus on the bull's-eye," he said into her ear, "and give the axe a flick."

He could feel the concentration rolling off her as he backed off. She inhaled deeply and then did exactly as she was told. The blade of the axe hit with a solid *thunk* in the outer ring of the target.

"*Woohoo!*" Hunter hooted, the heels of her boots leaving the floor when she jumped. "I hit it. Did you see that?"

He gave her a fist bump when she practically skipped his way. "I did. Good job."

"But I forgot my yell."

"Next time."

The smile she gave him was blinding. Reaching out, she rubbed his arm. "Go show me how it's done."

"Oh," he groaned. "Oh, yeah. Right there."

She'd found the cluster of bug bites on the back of his arm.

"Sorry," she said, pulling her touch away fast.

He wasn't, although once those bites got attention, they wanted more.

He ignored them as he chose an axe and took his stance again. He eyed the distance and took a practice swing. When he let loose on the second, he added more *oomph* to it than he had the first time. The axe sailed through the air, impaling the wooden board, but way too high above the target. If they doubled the length of the lane, he might have hit it.

"Good one," she cheered anyway. She walked with him as they retrieved their weapons. "You know what I think you need?"

"What?"

"A yell." She looked around as if it was a secret that she didn't want anyone else to know.

"I'm not going to yell."

"Why?"

"Because people look at you when you yell."

"People always look at me."

"Yeah, I've noticed." He patted her backside. "Get your spunky ass back on the line. I want to hear that *hi-yah* ringing from the rafters."

Her laugh was like a bell in this place of weapons and testosterone. "Don't dare me."

Yeah, daring a Lunatic probably wasn't the best idea.

"Menae," he whispered under his breath.

He watched her take her stance at the throwing line, taking into consideration all the guidance she'd been given. Her hips were square to the board, her elbows pointed at the target, and her eyes narrowed. Tony knew the moment she let out a short but sharp "*hi-yah*" that this was the one.

The axe flew in a line tilted forward under the weight of its head, and the blade let out a solid *whomp* as it buried itself in the bull's-eye.

Hunter jerked in surprise, then pointed at her accomplishment. The crew-cuts and the Paul Bunyans all let out cheers.

"Tony!" she squealed, pointing to show him.

"Way to go, babe."

She exploded into action, running at him full bore. He had only a moment to brace himself before she leapt at him.

"*Oof,*" he said when she collided with his chest. She was tiny, but she was bullet fast.

It was the last coherent thought he had when her arms and legs wrapped around him, and she gave him a big smack on the lips. His hands clamped over her butt as she kissed him silly.

"*Ahem*, folks," the security monitor said.

Tony kept her close when she dropped her legs, but the slide of her body against his caused other problems. "She hit the bull's-eye," he said rhetorically.

"Congrats," the man said. "Maybe we could stick to a high five next time?"

Tony nodded and cleared his throat. His cock was already

trying to give her a high five. "Yes, sir."

Hunter's eyes danced. When she pulled back, she kept him shielded. "I did it."

"You did." She'd reached a goal she'd set for herself, and damn if that didn't touch him. Some people didn't work toward anything at all. At the other end of the spectrum were athletes who busted their butts for small marks of improvement, but it was work to them. They didn't celebrate their wins like she did. Maybe he needed to change that.

"You're up," she said.

Indeed he was.

He blew out a breath and tried to focus. He concentrated on his own technique, but just as he let loose, he took her advice. "*Hwuh.*"

The axe stuck, dead center of the target.

"Tony!" Hunter let out a yelp of excitement and rushed over to him. A peek at the lane monitor made her keep her feet on the floor this time, but she bounded up to him and gave him a squeeze. "*Hwuh?*" she said with a laugh.

He wrapped his arms around her. "It sounds more manly than *hi-yah.*"

"I told you it would work."

The way she beamed up at him with her hair tumbling down her back just about did him in. "Yeah, you did."

He shot the lane monitor a glance. The guy's back was turned. What the hell? He gave her another swift kiss.

By the time the guy turned around, they were both whistling innocently and retrieving their axes—after Hunter had taken a picture of them for proof, of course. They couldn't tell anyone. If she showed the photo to anyone, there was nothing to say one was his, but they'd both know.

Tony nudged her with his elbow. "Want to start keeping score?"

"You're on. What's the prize?"

He thought about it for all of a second. "You hula-hoop for me."

"You watched it! I've been waiting for you to say

something."

He knew she had, and of course he'd watched it. She'd sent it to him. What was he going to do? Not watch it?

Okay, maybe he could have not watched it ten times in a row.

"What did you think?"

He thought that he now understood why Zane wouldn't show him the video of Emily hula-hooping. "It looks like good exercise."

She swatted at him.

He smiled. "I like the flicky thing you do with your hands."

"But that has nothing to do with the hoop."

He shrugged.

Her eyes flared. "What do I get?"

"What do you want?"

Oh, that was the wrong question to ask this woman.

Too late.

"You to dance with me naked under the moonlight again."

CHAPTER TEN

Tony arrived late to IHOP for the regular Sunday morning Oneiroi breakfast meeting, although he couldn't say that he was sorry about it. He was usually on time or even a little early, but he'd gone out with Hunter last night.

Which showed that whatever he thought, she *was* influencing him. The question was whether or not there was a magical component to that influence...

Screw it. It had been just about the best date ever, and she'd stayed over again. The punctuality cops would have to cut him some slack.

"There he is," AJ said. His gaze ran over him, and his brow crinkled when he saw Tony's easy strides.

He had no urge to rush. He felt languid, man. For the first time in his life, *languid*.

Wes cranked his head around to look over his shoulder. "We were starting to get worried. You're usually the first one here."

"Late again?" Zane said. "That's twice this week."

"Shush," Emily said to her boyfriend. "Like you have any room to talk." She smiled at him. "Hi, Tony."

Huh. Maybe having the girls here was a good move. He hadn't liked it when they started showing up, but they helped temper the testosterone that sometimes got out of control. He hadn't had to knock anyone's heads together for a while now.

"I'm just saying, Tomora must be going strong."

Zane might be off the market, but that hadn't done anything about the guy's mouth, unfortunately.

"Tomora?" Wes said.

"Tony's getting hot and heavy with the tennis pro."

Tony's thigh muscles seized up as he was halfway lowered to his seat. He forced them to relax and eased on down. There were times when it was best to just keep quiet. If his brothers wanted to run down the wrong trail about whom he was seeing, he sure wasn't going to stop them—especially when he was trying to throw them off the scent anyway.

"Kimora Ikeda?" Shea asked, perking up. "She's impressive, Tony."

"I like her too," Emily said. "What's she like off the court?"

Heads turned, and he was caught off guard. "Uh, Kimora. Yeah…" He drummed his fingers, which agitated the bug bite he'd gotten on his index finger. He began to scratch it. "She's focused, driven, nosy…" He realized he needed to say something nicer. "Powerful and pretty?"

Personally, he preferred his women tiny and spunky.

"Stop that," Shea said, leaning in to catch his hand. She analyzed his skin. "Is that a mosquito bite?" She went scrambling in her purse. "I might have something to help."

Now that he remembered it, the spot flared up and demanded attention. He curled his fingers into a fist to try to keep from giving in. "I didn't think I'd need bug spray this late in the season."

"Where did you go?" Derek asked.

"Comet Tail Lake." And why had he been there? Tony straightened his knife next to his spoon. "Went out stargazing."

Emily's head snapped up so quickly, her neck nearly cracked, and Tony flinched in his seat. Oh, shit. *Fuck.* There was a look in her eyes that made his intestines knot.

She knew the secret. He didn't know how, but she did.

"Getting in points with Mom?" Wes asked with a laugh.

Tony looked at his younger brother without really seeing him, because his peripheral gaze was locked on Emily. She was smiling, and it made a cold sweat break out between his shoulder blades. Was she happy about the pairing or excited because she had hot gossip?

If she gave them away, it would all come tumbling down... this thing he had going with Hunter... his inside track on learning more about the Lunatics... his brothers' trust in him...

Shea came up with a tube of cream and passed it to him. Thank the gods, something to do with his hands. He began to dab it all over.

"What were you doing under those stars?" she teased softly.

That sent blood straight to his earlobes. He swore they were on fire. He capped the tube and shoved it back at her. "Thanks."

He began straightening the packets of sweetener in their little holder and caught AJ's frown. He shoved his fingers into the front pockets of his jeans instead and found that fidget spinny thing Hunter had given him. It was as good of a time as any to give it a test run. He eased it out of his pocket and gave it a flick.

"When was the last time any of you spent time with her?" he asked. "*Mom*, I mean."

The spinner took off, whirling round and round. It was smooth in its motion, and silent, which was awesome. His shoulders relaxed from where they'd lodged up next to his ears. Okay. This was workable. He gave the device another push, and it responded like a perpetual motion machine.

Those ball bearings were slick.

Just like his response. It landed home with pretty much everyone at the table, and they backed off him fast. Nothing like bringing up Mom to get them back in line.

"I think that's our cue, Emily." Shea gathered up the tube of Biodermatics skin cream and her purse.

Emily did the same, although she winked at him before turning to find another table. A wink meant a secret. She wasn't going to give them away, right?

Right?

"Let's place our orders before we start," Derek said as he signaled for the server. Cael was out of town, and Derek was all business when he was in charge.

That was good. Maybe they'd get out of here early. Tony hoped so; he was hanging on by a thread.

He stared at the menu, not really seeing it. They came every week, though, so they all knew the offerings by heart. He considered the basket of ribs he'd eaten last night, so he balanced it out with an egg-white omelet with Canadian bacon and veggies. He might be a Greek spirit god who spent all day in the gym, but not even he could keep his physique without watching his diet.

Derek waited until the server was out of hearing distance before he launched right into the agenda. "Is there any follow-up on our last meeting about the Lunatics?"

"Menae."

Tony's fingers tightened so hard on the spinner, it stopped running. There was no way to get that word back. It had just flown right out of his mouth.

"The Menae," he repeated, doubling down when he felt all eyes on him. "I did some research this week. It's the olden term for Lunatics. Like Dream Weavers are the Oneiroi."

Zane rolled his eyes. "Potato, po-tah-to."

"No, that's good," Derek said. "We can't forget our history, or we're bound to have to learn it all over again."

Tony's fingers loosened their death grip, and the fidget spinner began whirling again.

"They're still crazy bitches." Wes bent and straightened his arm. He no longer looked like a mummy, but he still had a big old piece of gauze taped over his elbow.

Tony's eyes narrowed. He could see where the guy was coming from, but they weren't. Crazy *or* bitches. At least not from what he'd seen.

Hunter was just curious and up for anything.

He stopped. Maybe he did need evaluating. He was beginning to doubt everything he knew about the nighttime world. But did he really know? Did any of them?

He'd had fun with Hunter at the axe-throwing place. She was more settled than he'd ever seen her, with her energy at a nice, low hum. She'd been content just to be out and doing something she'd set her mind to. She hadn't been set on causing a stir, although her joy at hitting the target couldn't be contained.

"Nobody did anything stupid like try to track her down," Derek said. He didn't even form it in a question, because he knew what the order had been.

Tony fidgeted with the spinner. They all knew he'd asked for her phone number. He'd called her, which they had to all expect, and she'd met him at an impartial place, so technically, he hadn't tracked down anything. She'd come to him.

"The waking world is their turf," Derek said, his tone even sterner. "We're all clear on that?"

It certainly was her world. She'd had the Paul Bunyans and Knights Templar at her feet last night. He'd gotten a bit defensive at the attention they paid to her.

Fuck, he was in a bad spot.

"Good," Derek said. "Then let's talk about what happened this week. I want to make sure we're staying alert for all sleep raiders and not obsessing about Menae because we know there's one in town. Got it? Okay, AJ, you're up."

Tony listened with half an ear as AJ began talking about one of his sleepers with insomnia. He tried to focus, but he was in his head, and he was in deep.

What was happening to him? Was she manipulating him? They'd spent most of their time together during the day. She supposedly got her power from the moon. Or was this connection developing between them real? If it was, that caused even more problems. She was a Menae, for gods' sake, and he was an Oneiros.

"Tony?"

"Yup," he said, pulling his legs in and sitting up straight. "Insomnia."

Derek's eyes were sharp. "You're awfully distracted today. Do you have something concerning to report?"

Oh, he had concerns up the wazoo. He was just covering them somehow by playing with a kid's toy under the table. He heard laughter out front in the restaurant and saw Emily. Oh yeah, he had concerns.

"Actually, I do," he said. "I had to fight to get a college kid to take a dream."

"That's right," AJ said. "I forgot about that."

Yeah, it was right. He could be having secret rendezvous with the enemy and still do his job.

"He was sleeping on his laptop," Tony said. "We had a hunch it might be another case of too much screen time, like Bobby reported a few weeks ago."

Bobby held up his hands. "Told you so."

"This is getting to be a problem," Derek said.

"Has anyone figured out a way to stop it?" Wes asked. "Other than to get people away from their screens?"

Because that was a trick that nobody in the world had learned how to do.

The effects were spilling over into the nighttime world, though, so they needed to do something. They were the Oneiroi. They batted around ideas until their food arrived, and then talked some more. Figuring out the solution to brain wave malfunctions wasn't something to be done on an empty stomach.

And, apparently, it took more than an hour.

They were no closer to an answer when they packed up to leave, although they all agreed to keep an eye out for more cases.

Tony caught up with Wes on their way out to see how he was doing.

"You got any other tennis players on your client list?" his younger brother asked.

It was a good sign that he was on the mend.

"No," Tony said. He'd have to think twice before setting up one of his brothers with a client. That was tricky territory, although Hunter put her clients out on a runway for bidding, apparently.

He realized the fidget spinner was still in his hand, and he shoved it into his pocket.

"She doesn't have to be a tennis player." Wes swung his arm as if testing out his range of motion. "Pickle ball player would be fine. Or a gymnast." His eyes rounded. "A gymnast would be awesome."

"Yeah, because you're both known to take a tumble."

Wes rolled his eyes. "Haha. You're a funny guy."

He gave Tony a shove and went off in the direction of his car. It was parked next to Zane's Camaro, and Tony's steps hitched when he saw Emily looking his way.

Please let me have read her right. His stomach clenched when she smiled at him and gave him a thumbs-up. He waved weakly, almost dying when Zane nearly caught the signal.

He pulled out his phone before his ass even touched the driver's seat of his truck.

"Huh-llo?" Hunter answered, her voice groggy.

He should have let her sleep in his bed while he'd come here, but they weren't at that stage yet. She'd insisted on getting up and going home, even though it was clear she wasn't a morning person. None of them were, but she was bouncing back more slowly than he was today.

"Hey."

"Hi," she murmured. He could practically see her sinking back into her pillow.

"We've got a problem."

She let out a groan. "What is it now?"

"Emily knows."

"Emily knows what?"

"About us."

That brought her into the land of the waking. "How?" she squeaked.

Well, that blew that theory. "I thought that maybe you'd told her."

"Why would I do that? Zane and I have an uneasy enough truce as it is. If he found out I was seeing you, he'd go bonkers."

That was true, although Tony didn't like it. They were intentionally keeping their relationship a secret, but he should be able to see anyone he liked.

Hunter inhaled slowly. "I did see her the other morning at the coffee shop. I didn't say anything, though. I swear."

Tony began tapping his fingers against the steering wheel. Then how the hell had she made the connection? They'd been talking about Comet Tail Lake...

He stared at the spot on his index finger that he'd treated with Shea's ointment. "Ah hell. The mosquitos."

"What?"

"Are your bites still bothering you?"

"Yes, but I only told her I went out stargazing."

And bingo. "There it is."

"Oh, gods." Hunter let out a hiss. "That's diabolical."

The bloodthirsty demons were still biting them in the ass.

"Did she say anything? Do your brothers know?"

"Not yet, but I can't tell what she's thinking."

"As long as she doesn't let it slip to Zane, we should be okay." Hunter let out a gasp. "She's texting me!"

"Shit. She's in the car with him. I just saw them leave the restaurant."

"What do I do?"

"Don't answer."

"She'll just call next."

Because she was onto something juicy. "Distract her, then."

"I can't lie to her, not after everything that happened."

And she knew. He'd seen the gleam in her eyes. "I think she's happy about it."

Hunter paused. "Are you saying I should bring her to the dark side?"

Tony hung his head. He was already there. If Zane found out they'd involved Emily in this, there'd be hell to pay.

"Do what you've got to do. Loop me in after," he said in resignation.

"*Fuck,*" he cursed as he hung up. He looked out the windshield of his truck at the IHOP landscaping that was more than ready for fall cleanup. This sneaking around stuff was getting harder every day. Sooner or later, the truth was going to come out.

And yet he couldn't find the will to stop.

* * *

Hunter didn't know how Emily managed to get them into a nail salon for mani-pedis that afternoon, but she did. They met at a cute little shop that looked out on the park where they'd ridden scooters during their first life-coaching session, and it was nice. Hunter really had missed her friend.

Emily greeted her with a smile. "It's not hula hooping or karaoke, but it sounded like fun."

"It does, and I need it." Hunter looked at her nails. They'd taken a beating during that indoor climbing session with Pete. Besides, she didn't have the energy to do much more today.

They went to look at nail polish colors. "This may be the most normal thing we've done together," Emily said as she considered the selection of pale pinks.

Hunter arched an eyebrow. "And when was the last time you did it?"

She knew her former client's penchant for routine. Getting out of a rut didn't always mean doing something bold and out of character. Sometimes, it just meant taking the time to do something you enjoyed.

Emily wobbled her head in acknowledgment. "Point taken. It's been a while."

Impulsively, she chose a brighter, but not quite hot pink, nail polish. Hunter went for a deep teal color.

"That will look good on you," Emily said. "On me, it would look like a five-year-old's mistake."

They laughed and began discussing whether to stick with one color or choose another for their toenails. Soon, their manicurists were ready for them. They sat side by side at separate tables as they underwent all the buffing and shaping that had to be done before the painting began.

It was hard to talk with strangers listening in, but they tried. That was what people did at nail salons. They chatted. Hunter wasn't under any misconceptions. Emily had chosen this activity for a very specific reason.

"Tell me more about your interview," Hunter said, trying to head off the big stuff. "I got your text, but you didn't seem excited."

"It went okay, I think."

"But?"

"They had a lot of questions about why I want to switch roles. I told them I want to do something new, but I got the feeling that's an issue for them."

Hunter let out a huff as she turned. "That's because you're a high performer. They're focused more on what they think they'd be losing instead of realizing what they'd be gaining— someone who already knows the company and how things work."

Companies could be so short-sighted. People needed new challenges to stay stimulated and motivated.

"Eh eh. You mustn't move." With a scowl on her face, the manicurist switched to another tool to clean up the slash of teal polish that ran across the side of Hunter's finger.

Frustrated, Hunter planted her feet and turned only her head. "People like to think they have others all figured out. They don't know what to do when someone does something unexpected."

"I know." Emily was good at staying still. She was already getting her second coat of polish. "That's why I mentioned I was looking at product owner positions outside the company too."

"Atta girl."

"I remember the things you taught me."

Hunter felt all warm and sunny inside. This was exactly what she tried to do for her clients, instill them with the confidence to make their lives better for themselves.

Once their manicures dried, they moved over to the pedicure stations. Each was equipped with a big leather massage chair. She chose the full-body setting and went boneless when it began working. "Oh, my gods, this is heaven."

As much as she enjoyed spending time with Em—and despite the adrenaline that had flowed through her when Tony told her their secret was out—she'd had to drag herself here. Her energy levels were dropping quickly.

Emily took a sip of the ice-cold lemon water they'd each been given. "Ah, that's refreshing. Do you need a cappuccino?"

"I had two before I came." Hunter rolled her head on the padded headrest. "Are you still hula hooping?"

"Yes, I love it. Are you ever going to come back to class?"

"Maybe."

They shared a look. There was a lot behind that answer, and they both knew what it was.

"Zane knows I'm here with you right now. Come back. Class isn't nearly as much fun without you."

"How are you two doing?"

"Good." Emily's cheeks turned pink to match her nails. "Really, really good."

Hunter believed it. Zane had loved her for years before they'd gotten together.

"I'll try to get to class in a couple of weeks." She wanted to hear more about the other steps Emily had taken since they'd stopped having sessions. "Have you done anything else new?"

"Tony let me take over the planters in front of his house. I asked him if I could since the poor plants were struggling."

Hunter lifted her head from its comfortable resting place. "I thought that was your work."

Emily's eyes sparked. "Can we talk about that now? You

and Tony?"

Hunter sighed and snuggled deeper into the massage chair. She'd known the real intent behind this outing. She was about to get grilled, but was that really a bad thing? She needed to talk to someone. "Okay."

"So you are," Emily said in a burst. "The two of you. You're seeing one another."

"Yes."

"I knew it." Emily looked horrified when some water from her soaking tub splashed onto the floor. The pedicurist mopped it up with a towel as if it happened a hundred times a day. "You're such a good match."

Hunter took a sip of her water and made a face. *Ew*, lemon. "You think so?"

"Absolutely. You're both fun, and you care about other people."

"Fun? Tony?"

"He teases me all the time."

Hunter was seeing more of that side of him, and she liked it so much. She was attracted to him when he was a grump, but when he got out of his head he was irresistible to her.

"It's kind of hot and heavy right now," she confessed softly so the women pampering their feet couldn't hear, "but you can't tell anyone. His brothers don't know."

"They are so oblivious." Emily rolled her eyes. "Can I at least tease him back?"

"No, don't. Please. It will just make him worry. *More*." That man had so many things going on inside his head that nobody ever knew about. "He might pull away from me."

Emily tilted her head so her short hair swung. "You really like him."

"I do, especially when we get past the family thing."

"Family thing?"

Shoot. Oh, well. That might be easier to explain. "It goes way back. We're kind of like the Hatfields and McCoys."

"And you're crossing the line for love? How romantic! That explains so much."

"Love? Whoa. Hold on." They were crossing the line for earth-moving sex, but love? Hunter rubbed her temple. Just the idea made her lightheaded.

Emily's eyes widened, and she reached for her. "Are you okay?"

"Hm?"

"You just went so pale. Are you feeling all right?"

Hunter wasn't, but that was normal. It just felt like she was crashing faster this month, and harder. She could feel herself sliding down the slope, and there wasn't anything she could do to slow down. She'd thought she'd have enough energy to get through a relaxing mani-pedi, but maybe not. "I'm feeling a bit rundown."

Emily's forehead furrowed. "With the way you're constantly on the go, I can understand why. What have *you* done since we last met?"

"Oh, you know…. A wall climbing class, a painting class, a bachelor auction." *Oops*, she probably shouldn't have mentioned Pete. Even her thought processes were slowing down.

Emily took the hint. "Maybe we should cut it short today."

"I hate to be a spoilsport."

"You're not. We're done anyway." Emily nodded when the pedicurist held up two pairs of foam sandals with toe separators. "Will you be all right to drive yourself home?"

"I'm fine." Hunter roused herself and turned off the massage chair. Just to be safe, she gulped down the rest of her glass of lemon water. The tartness hit her, and that did the trick. She opened her eyes and sat up straight. "I just need to go home and take a nap. Good thing it's Sunday."

"I'm glad we could get together. I think that you and Tony make a cute couple. I won't say anything, but I'll be rooting for you."

"Thanks." Hunter willed herself to her feet, and they headed to their cars.

"Text me when you get home?" Emily asked.

"Sure." The bright sunshine and crisp air livened Hunter

up enough for the drive, not to mention her cold feet. "This was fun. Let's do it again soon."

Preferably, though, sometime long after the new moon.

CHAPTER ELEVEN

Hunter curled up under a blanket on her sofa and made sure her toes were covered. Her head was as heavy as her entire body, and her thoughts were sluggish. She groaned when her phone rang and she saw it was Tony. He wouldn't let his messages just roll over to voicemail.

"Hello?" she answered.

"Em called me. She said you're not feeling well."

The fink. At least she was keeping their bigger secret. Hunter sighed. "I'm not, but I'll be better in a few days."

"A *few days?*"

She was too tired to come up with an excuse.

"You were fine the other day."

"I know." She'd used the last of her reserves to do it. "It's not serious. I just need sleep."

Sleep. She dropped her head back against the armrest. Talk about the wrong word to use with him.

"Let me come over."

No.

The gut response was instinctive. She was at her weakest right now. Her most vulnerable. She didn't want him to see her this way.

"Rain check?" she asked.

Did he know the level of trust he was asking of her? Although he did let her sleep beside him when he was weaving dreams. She rubbed at the ache in her chest.

"Tell me your address."

She'd been to his place, even stayed over, but he'd never been to hers.

"I'll bring over some chicken soup."

She almost gagged. "That doesn't even sound good."

"What does?"

Oh, he was sly. That wasn't an acceptance on her part.

"Twelve hours in bed."

His voice dropped. "I can make that happen."

She groaned when the ache in her chest dipped to her core.

"Hunter, let me come over and take care of you."

And he thought he didn't have any powers outside the dream realm. Hunter realized how weak she really was when she found herself rattling off her address and telling him she was craving spicy food.

"I'm on my way."

She let the phone drop from her hand onto the cushions and stared up at the ceiling. She should probably clean up. Her house wasn't messy, but it looked lived in, with pillows strewn about and a heating pad plugged into the wall.

She just couldn't summon the will to do anything about it. Her energy levels were tapped.

She couldn't even find the will to go change or put on makeup. She was in comfy sweats and a Solstice Satellites T-shirt. She'd managed a shower today, but putting her hair in a ponytail was about as stylish as she'd gotten.

She hugged her pillow and, even knowing Tony was on his way, nodded off. She didn't sleep, but she fell into that hazy in-between for long enough that the knock on her apartment door made her jerk. She rubbed her hands over her face.

She had to physically push herself to her feet and grab the back of the sofa to get her momentum going toward the door. Uneasiness fluttered in her chest. Well, this was a test now, wasn't it?

She wasn't sure who was taking it, though, him or her.

His knocks started up again, louder this time. "Hunter."

She got that full volume when she opened the door. Her gaze dragged up his body. It was not fair how good he looked, especially when he was dressed as casually as she was in a T-shirt and jogging pants.

"Hi," she said.

"Hi. You look ready to drop."

She should have put on the makeup. "I feel like it, too."

Ushering her back inside, he put a paper sack on the table. Looking around, he spotted the nest she'd made for herself, and he guided her back to it.

She slumped sideways into her pillow and the arm of the sofa. "You didn't have to come."

"Yeah, I did."

She looked him over. "Were you at a training session?"

"Yes, but it's the last one for a while." He lifted her legs onto the cushions and noticed her bare feet. He covered them with the blanket.

"The tennis star?"

"She has one tournament left before it's the off-season."

Off-season. Was that what she went through once a month?

"How does stir-fry sound?" he asked.

"With spicy red pepper?"

"For improved energy. Chicken for protein, green peppers to fight inflammation, and onions for antioxidants."

She actually felt the pang of hunger. "Yummy."

"Give me fifteen minutes."

She lifted her head off the pillow. "You're cooking?"

"You need something healthy, not something that will weigh you down." His gaze ran over her. "Although you feel light as a feather right now."

She let out a snort. "I feel like a lead weight."

He squatted down to look in her face. "It's the moon, isn't it? Or more precisely, the lack of it."

She pressed her lips together, even as a chill ran through her.

He pulled the blanket up to her chin. "I can read a calendar. I just didn't know you were so attuned to it."

"The Oneiroi aren't supposed to know," she whispered.

"This is the drawback you were talking about, isn't it? The downside of being a Greek goddess?"

She blinked when she felt the prick in her eyes. He remembered that?

"Do you go through this every month?"

She nodded. "With the cycle of the moon, but you can't tell that to anyone." She caught his hand. "Please don't endanger my sisters."

"I won't."

She licked her lips. "I shouldn't have let you come over."

"Yes, you should have." He sighed. "We've got a lot of rules to follow, don't we?"

"I hate rules."

"I know." He ran a hand over her head, stood, and headed for the sack of groceries. "Have you been home all day?"

"Yes." She could normally make it through these lulls with caffeine and determination, but this was more than a lull. "I canceled my appointments today—even the one with my most important client."

Pots and pans clattered in her kitchen. "The bachelor?"

"Mm hm."

"Are you taking him to a nudist colony or something next?"

Something in his voice roused her. Was that jealousy? Or were her ears on the fritz, too?

"It's not the full moon again yet." Secret information spilled out of her again, but she didn't care. "Some things have to be worked up to—and that's probably not a good idea for him anyway."

"Sorry," Tony said. "I'm still trying to figure out how it all works."

She heard a drawer roll out, and she turned her head so she could watch him cook. It felt nice to have him here, puttering around her kitchen. Not scary or dangerous, like she'd been warned, but protective. Intimate.

Would it really hurt to tell him things? Or could it make the situation better? His brothers called them Lunatics, but they'd never been exposed to the reasons why she and her sisters did the things they did.

"A new moon is the time to plant the seeds or start a new project. I'm trying to get him to focus on the reason why he hired me—his personal goal—but he just can't get his nose out of his computers."

Whoops. Divulging client personal information *was* going too far.

Tony made quick work of the vegetables with a knife from her knife block that she'd never used and plopped them in the pan with the noodles. "We've been noticing that, too. Computers and gaming and streaming TV are messing up people's sleep patterns."

"Screen time affects dream time?"

The sizzle continued, even when he stopped stirring. "That's it, exactly."

Interesting. "They can't get to sleep, or the quality of their sleep is poor?"

"Both, but I'd say the quality suffers more."

"It's the same during the day. Quality of life is degrading for all those people with their noses in a phone."

"Or those forty-inch monitors."

They looked at each other. It was one of the longest discussions they'd had about their abilities, and it felt like they were onto something. Maybe…

But Tony didn't let his stir-fry get limp like she did. He plucked the spicy chicken combo out of the pan with a pair of tongs and dropped it into two bowls. "Stay where you are," he barked when she started to get up to move to the table.

He brought her the bowl, a fork, and a napkin right where she was. All she had to do was sit up to accept them. She tried a bite as he returned to the kitchen. "Mm, that's good."

Healthy with a zing that tried to perk her up, but didn't

quite do the trick.

She appreciated the effort, though, and she was on her third bite when he returned with a glass of water and his own bowl. He sat down on the recliner beside her, and they ate together.

"What are you watching?" he asked.

"An old horror movie." Old enough to be in black and white. "Vampires, I think. It's a Halloween marathon."

Although it might be zombies. She had it on for the sound more than anything. She was too tired to sleep, and she hated lying around in silence. It made new-moon nights so much worse.

They watched together until she couldn't eat any more. He finished his meal and then cleaned up and stored the leftovers in her refrigerator. She appreciated his making something she just had to heat up in the microwave.

He came back to the sofa to check on her, and his hand felt warm as he cupped his palm over her forehead. "You don't seem to have a fever."

"I'm cold," she confessed.

He moved to the far end of the couch and toed off his shoes. "Scoot over."

Her senses came alive as he wedged himself between her and the cushions. She felt him all along her back, radiating heat and comfort and sexiness. Especially when he wrapped his arm around her to keep her from teetering off the edge. It was a tight fit, but her muscles relaxed as he tucked her up against him. Safe, warm, and protected.

She settled her bare feet against his shins.

They watched the movie together that way, his arm tightening around her during those jump scares, laughing together when the hero's little dog scared the vampire off the porch.

"Can I ask you a question?" she whispered as they watched the hero creep through a darkened hallway with a wooden stake at the ready.

"Do I have to answer?"

"How do you fight sleep raiders in the dream realm?"

His hand went still on her stomach. At some point, it had not only slipped under the blanket, but under her T-shirt as well.

"Do you have weapons there?" she asked. "How do you vanquish them?"

"With a touch to their forehead."

Her air jumped into her throat. "Like you just touched me?"

"No," he said, the word slow. "I can't do it here, outside the dream realm."

"Are you sure about that?"

He shifted so she rolled onto her back, and he could look her in the face. "Yes, and it's all about intent. That's how I bestow dreams, too, by touching sleepers' foreheads and directing their brain waves."

"How do you know the difference, though? What if you screw up in the heat of the moment and do the wrong thing?"

"I won't. They're two very different actions."

She flinched when he pushed back a strand of her hair that had escaped her ponytail, and his lips flattened in an expression close to hurt. "I'm very good at what I do, Hunter, and I promise I won't hurt you."

She believed him, but it still made her nervous. Their families had been enemies for so long—what if it was reflex? Or what if one of his brothers tried? She'd felt more than strong enough to handle them under a full moon, but on a darkened night like this?

"I can't do it here in the waking world," he repeated, "and you can't enter the dream realm. We have a backup layer of protection."

True. She took an unsteady breath. "I didn't mean to offend you, but your brother was accidentally hurt because of my powers. I'm good at what I do, too, but when I'm charged up, things happen."

He nodded stiffly.

"We're so different, Tony."

He took the remote and flicked off the TV. "And we're so alike."

She let out a squeak when he climbed off the couch and lifted her in his arms.

"Get that light switch," he said as he stopped by the wall.

"Are you staying?" she said in surprise.

"Yes, either in your bed or on the sofa. It doesn't matter to me, but I'm not leaving you alone when you're like this. Let's get you back on the road to recovery and strong again."

* * *

Tony carried Hunter down the hallway, finding his way easily. She lived in a one-bedroom apartment that made it impossible to get lost. She felt light in his arms, even as she slumped into him, and his hold on her tightened. She was an amalgam of contrasts, bright as sunshine one day and sleepy as rain the next.

He was beginning to understand why. That was some rollercoaster of a life she was on, and it couldn't be fun— either the ups or the downs. Especially the downs. Did she have to plan her life around this?

She'd told him she'd be busy with a project for the next few days.

Some project.

He turned into her bedroom. Orange throw pillows added a pop of color against the white bedspread, and a yellow hula hoop leaned against the wall. At the same time, a window seat was softened with a gray cushion and a stack of paperback books. She'd made adjustments, no doubt.

It was going to take some adjusting to for him.

He set her down on the bed, and she tossed the orange throw pillows onto the floor. Working the covers down seemed to sap her strength, so he helped her with that. He knelt to help her get her sweatpants off, too. When she shivered, he swung her legs up onto the bed and tucked her in.

"Where do you want me?" he asked softly.

A smile pulled at her lips as she rested against her pillow. "That's a loaded question."

He smirked but waited.

She touched his arm. "You're warm. Get in here with me."

A knot in his chest unkinked. He would have stayed on the couch if that was what she wanted, but he'd rather bed down beside her. Trust hadn't come easily between them, and he didn't want to go backward.

"Let me get the light."

He checked that he'd left nothing on in the kitchen before stopping to look out the plate glass window in her living room. The inky blackness of the night had never bothered him before. It was his home, the welcoming arms of his heritage and his mother. He'd never thought much about the moon—other than dreading when it got full, and the Lunatics came out to play.

Menae...

But they weren't the only ones, were they? Animals were more active when the moon shone down upon the nocturnal world, and the tides of the oceans were stronger. This was nature—and *her* nature—and it wasn't something she could fix by working out or eating healthy.

He took off his shirt as he made his way into her bedroom, and he felt her gaze on him. She liked the way he looked, and the feeling was reciprocated.

Rounding the bed, he got rid of his shoes and shucked his gym pants. He kept his boxer briefs on as he slid under the covers beside her. When he turned to her, she slid right into his arms.

"Mm, you feel nice."

So did she, all soft hair and luscious curves. When he cupped the back of her head, he found her hair still gathered into a ponytail. That couldn't be comfortable for sleeping. Careful not to tug on the roots, he disentangled the rubber band from the long strands. Sinking his fingers into her hair, he massaged her scalp.

"Go to sleep. I'll be right here."

"It doesn't always hit me this hard," she said groggily.

"What's different?"

She shrugged. "I don't know. You?"

He frowned. "Are you saying that I'm sapping your strength?"

"No, but you made the high of the full moon really high."

And she needed to balance it out. He got that. Oh, how he got that. Dream Weavers were tasked with keeping things balanced in the dream realm, making sure nothing got out of kilter. It was a never-ending job.

She touched his face. "It's worth it."

His heart thumped.

She slid her finger along his lower lip and then leaned closer to kiss him. The effect was drugging. Hypnotic.

Pulling away, she settled against the pillow and watched as she traced the muscles on his chest and abdomen. He didn't know if she could see in the darkness as well as he could or if she was learning by touch. Either way, her explorations made his skin sensitized, and he was eager for where her fingers would roam next. Her touch was languorous, though, keeping his heart rate low, but pounding at double volume.

Her eyelids were at half-mast. Watching her closely, he skimmed his hand up the back of her thigh and under her T-shirt. She arched sinuously when he settled his hand at the small of her back.

He wanted to make sure he was reading her correctly.

"Are you sure you're up for this?"

His fingers tightened when she brushed kisses along his collarbone and then down his chest. When the tip of her tongue dragged over his nipple, he got the message she was sending.

"I'm logy, but I still have a pulse."

"Logy?"

She closed her hand around his biceps and gave a tug as she rolled onto her back. "Rock me to sleep."

Now that message was loud and clear, and so was his

body's response. He got hard fast, but the situation called for a different approach.

Rolling atop of her, in no particular hurry, Tony braced his elbows on the mattress on either side of her head. Catching her face in his hands, he kissed her deeply, lushly, yet just this side of hunger.

She wanted to be pampered.

He could do that.

Gently, he worked up her T-shirt. She wriggled to get it off, but he stopped her with his hands spanning her ribcage. She was naked except for her panties when he tossed the T-shirt aside. He'd known she wasn't wearing a bra when he'd held her on the couch, but that had been for comfort.

She was asking him to touch her now.

He swept his thumbs along the underside of her breasts, tracing the line of her curves as she'd touched him. She inhaled deeply, and he tucked his thumbs deeper, following the line where ribcage changed into soft curves.

She let out a hum of pleasure.

He kissed his way along her collarbone, and her breaths became choppier. Her fingers dug into his sides.

"Easy," he murmured.

This was all about the nice and slow.

Dipping his head, he ran his nose around one of her nipples. It stiffened, and he rubbed his cheek against her. He had enough five o'clock shadow by now to make the contact prickly. She arched slowly, like an ocean wave, when she felt the sensation.

"Tony," she groaned.

He opened his mouth on her and began to suckle. He swirled his tongue, and then suckled some more. Her nipple swelled and stiffened. Her hands moved up his sides, across his upper back, and her fingers dove into his hair.

He shifted at the press of her hips. He wasn't immune to what he was doing, but sometimes the journey was just as sweet as crossing the finish line.

"I'm not getting you worked up, am I?"

"No." She spread her legs to let him sink against her more deeply, "but I'd really like you to."

He ground against her, but there was still the matter of a few more clothes.

He skimmed his hands down her body, barely touching her, until he could hook his fingers in her panties. She lifted her hips as he tugged them down, and then she helped him get rid of his shorts. Flinging an arm out, she found the drawer to the nightstand by her bed.

Tony's eyes dilated as he looked down at her. The air in the room prickled with energy, all of it sexual. Her powers might be at low ebb, but she still had impact on him. He kissed her again, and the edge could not be contained.

She let out a hum and wrapped her arms around him, and then her legs.

His cock rubbed right against her softness, her wetness, her heat.

Rock her to sleep.

The words were like a mantra in his head. This was a marathon, not a race. Holding his cock in his hand, he rubbed the tip against her clit.

Her moan was low and long.

He slid a finger into her, and her body latched on, but with his weight atop her, she couldn't lift her hips to take it deeper.

"Don't tease," she said raggedly.

He was making her work too hard. He needed to ease her hunger. Give her what she needed.

He thrust into her slowly, drawing out the penetration until he was balls-deep. The moan she let out was full-throated this time, and he captured it with a kiss.

And then he began rocking.

In and out. Deep and then shallow. He stroked her in a rhythmic, sensual pace that had soft sounds coming from her throat. His toes curled against the sheets. It was fucking heaven the way their bodies joined. The way they stroked. The way they clung.

"Ah. Ah. *Ahhh.*" Hunter's eyelids fluttered as he settled in for the long haul.

Sweat beaded the small of Tony's back. His balls were drawn up tight, and, still, he rode her.

Her breaths hitched, and her body twitched. "Please," she begged.

"We're just getting started, baby."

Her eyes popped open. When she saw the strain on his face, she laughed.

The joyful tinkle of her laughter made Tony slip, and she cried out in victory when he gave three hard, fast thrusts.

He was daemon enough to slow back down again.

Her groan of frustration was real.

And he loved it. He kept things slow and deliberate, because he could feel the energy around them constricting and heating. The rising tide would not be held off.

When it came, it was like a great swell washing through them both, carrying them away. Hunter's fingernails bit into his back as her neck arched, and Tony rode the razor edge of the wave all the way to the shore.

When he rose back to the surface, he found her tucked underneath him. He lifted himself up to his elbows. Her eyes were dark and limpid as she looked at him, but then her eyelids drooped.

Mission accomplished. She was close to sleep.

He kissed her forehead and rolled until he was lying on his back beside her. He needed to hurry. She wasn't the only one eased by their lovemaking. His body was heavy, and all the ping-pong thoughts had settled down inside his head. It made crossing into the dream realm easy. One moment his body was sinking into the mattress, and the next, his spirit split from his corporeal form.

Once in the parallel plane, he waited.

Planting himself at the foot of the bed, he watched over her. She was fighting for sleep so hard, but she was hovering on the precipice. He looked at the two of them together, her curvy little body tucked up against his larger one. When he'd turned from predatory to protective toward her, he couldn't quite identify, but there it was. It had happened.

He tuned into her brain wave patterns. He knew her well enough to identify her rhythms, but these power swings… There was something familiar about the manic nature to them, although he couldn't quite place what it was.

Suddenly, a foreign energy pushed at his senses.

His attention widened. He braced himself, at the ready, when particles began to collect at her bedside. He watched as the being took form, and then he wasn't the only dream realm inhabitant in her bedroom.

"Sandman," he said, trying to keep the growl out of his voice.

The older man flinched, surprised to find anyone else who could see him. The shock quickly passed, though, as he evaluated Tony for what he was. "Dream Weaver."

How the hell was the guy looking down at him when he was half a foot taller? Sandmen were so snooty. They thought they were superior because they brought sleep rather than stole it, but too much sleep caused its own problems.

"You took your sweet time getting here."

A muscle twitched at the corner of the Sandman's eye. "And you're quite early." He looked at the bed. When he saw Tony's physical form there, beside Hunter, he let out a *harrumph.* "Then again, you had a head start."

Tony didn't want to hear it. "She needs sleep, the good kind. She's crying for it. Where have you been?"

The Sandman's chin lifted. "She's too tired to sleep."

"That's crap."

"It's true," the sleep bringer said. "When they get to this point, their summons are too low, too weighty to travel far. I didn't hear her until I was practically in the room."

"You know what she is." There was no way he couldn't; all night beings could sense one another. Although she didn't live in the dream realm, did she? Tony pushed right past the doubt. "You know what time of month it is. You should know you have to be here."

The Sandman's nostrils twitched. "*You* have the audacity

to tell *me* how to do *my* job?"

He looked to the bed and lifted an eyebrow in a meaningful arch.

Tony's hands fisted, and he took a step forward. "Just give her the sleep dust, pal."

The night creature slowly turned to face him, with his bare feet planted wide. He said nothing, but tilted his head in a way that was so dismissive and superior, Tony wanted to rip his shimmery robe off and throw it to the birds. Or bats. Whatever was awake out there.

One thing was clear, though—the Sandman was not intimidated. He knew he had the upper hand. Hunter needed what only he could give.

"A Dream Weaver and a Lunatic?" he said, his quiet tone full of menace.

And then there was *that.*

Tony's eyes threatened to go bloodshot as he forced himself not to react. Not to respond. The balance of power had shifted... or never been altered.

"Help her," he said. "Please."

The set of the man's shoulders changed. Apparently, that was the magic word after all.

"I am fond of her." Again, his gaze swept over Tony. "Although I do question her decisions from time to time."

"Sandy," Tony growled.

"Fine." The Sandman's robes flounced as he turned to the woman on the bed. He dipped his hands into the pockets of the voluminous robe and came up with two handfuls of dust. He sprinkled the air around her liberally.

Tony watched Hunter. She inhaled deeply, teetered, and then fell into alpha sleep. It was light sleep, but it was sleep. As long as she wasn't disturbed—and he'd make sure of that—she should get some relief now.

"It won't be enough, you know," the Sandman said as he brushed his hands clean. "Then again, maybe you wouldn't."

Tony was done with the guy's superiority complex. "Then give her more."

"What she needs is the moon to return," the Sandman said, "and something you're obviously not willing to give her."

"If you say one word about the two of us to anyone—"

The old man scoffed. "Like anyone I associate with would be interested in the sexual hijinks of your kind. That's all the Oneiroi seem to do these days anyway. It's no big news."

Tony couldn't argue with that. His brothers had been pairing up a lot recently, although he was the first to get involved with a goddess. That was gossip of the highest level, no matter what the Sandman thought. Although, in his myopic little world, maybe he didn't realize that.

The Sandman waved his hand as if the subject didn't matter. "There. She's asleep. *My* job is done."

"You can't give her more?"

"Not if you want her to awaken."

Tony reined in his concern. He was out of his area here. At least he'd answered the big question. She relied on Sandmen to sleep. "Be prompt if she needs you again tonight—and think about being early tomorrow."

The Sandman held his hands out at his sides, palms up, as he began to disperse. Like he couldn't do it with his finger stuck up his nose. "I have many sleepers."

"Don't we all," Tony snapped.

The Sandman began to fade.

"Hey," Tony said, a thought occurring to him. "Wait."

The sleep bringer kept going. He was see-through when Tony reached out and yanked him back. His particles snapped back together, and he swayed at the sudden change in direction. Tony lifted an eyebrow at him. The Oneiroi *were* the most powerful beings in the dream realm, lest the Sandman forgot that.

"*Eh,*" the sleep bringer grunted. He lifted a hand to his head. "Why did you do that?"

"Are the summons too low for humans that are getting too much screen time, too?"

The Sandman covered his discomfort by smoothing his

silver hair. There wasn't a strand out of place. "Whatever are you talking about?"

"Another Sandman told one of my brothers that you've been having trouble getting your sleep dust to work on people who spend too much time on computers."

"Well, yes, that is true… but not something we share widely."

"You just said that you can't hear Hunter's calls. Are you having trouble hearing theirs, too?"

"No, their calls are loud to the point of drowning out those with better sleep habits."

"Then what's the problem?"

"Their sleep won't hold. Their brain wave patterns aren't following the normal sequence."

That tracked. Just like their dreams. "Too much blue light."

"Their circadian rhythms are disturbed by it."

So, the Sandmen agreed with the Oneiroi. "That's what we've determined, too."

The older man straightened the cuffs of his robe. "It is… nice… to have confirmation."

"Yeah, maybe if you would respond when *we* called for you, we could have more conversations like this."

And there went the nose twitching again.

"The sleep raiders are winning," Tony said, his voice steely.

The Sandman's eyes flared. The nighttime world was out of balance, and it was only getting worse. "I'll pass on the message. Maybe regular conference between the Sandmen and the Oneiroi would be appropriate."

Tony didn't want to get too process-y. "Or maybe we could each identify a go-between."

"An attaché."

Whatever. "Yeah, one of those."

The Sandman nodded. "I will converse with the others. May I go now? I hear calls for my services."

Tony was hearing the calls of his charges, too. "Bring an

answer to me here tomorrow, when you bring *her* your fairy dust."

Vertical lines formed on the Sandman's forehead, and his mouth pursed. "We are not *fairies*."

Tony grinned, loving every minute of it. "See ya, Sandy."

The Sandman dispersed in a puff this time. It was good to know you could get past their superior attitudes if you poked at the right spot. Tony had no desire to be the frickin' attaché between their worlds, but he had plenty now to distract his brothers at next Sunday's IHOP gathering. They'd forget all about Hunter and her Lunatic ways once he handed the Sandmen to them on a silver platter.

Hunter.

He looked at her from her bedside. She'd moved from light sleep to deep in the time they'd been talking, and she was soaking up its recuperative benefits. His fingers itched. He wanted to touch her. He wanted to help. He felt the nearly desperate need to heal, but she wasn't a normal woman. Menae didn't dream.

"Fuck," he whispered into the night air. Not being allowed to help her just might push him into lunacy.

She moved closer to his form on the bed, seeking his warmth.

"Sleep well, baby," he said. "Tomorrow will be better."

And then he went off to find his charges, secretly hoping in the back of his mind that he'd run into a sleep raider. All he needed was one, because he was a grumpy Greek god with a Lunatic problem.

CHAPTER TWELVE

Hunter recovered faster than she thought she would, although the climb back up after the new moon was still more gradual than the free fall into it. Sleeping helped, and Tony made sure she was in bed on a regular schedule. Her sisters would be horrified if they knew an Oneiros was taking care of her during her power dip, but he'd been adamant that he wasn't leaving her on her own.

He was a protector, born and bred. He was used to watching over his sleepers during the night. She couldn't tell him that Dream Weavers were precisely what the Menae thought they needed protection from when they weren't at full strength.

She flicked her pen and looked around the apartment. It seemed quiet this evening without him here. She'd convinced him to go to a Solstice Satellites game with one of his brothers. Apparently, he'd worked with one of the players over the off-season. She couldn't remember which one…

"Focus," she muttered. She needed to get it together; she had a Zoom meeting with an important client herself—Pete Larimer.

She tapped her cheeks, trying to bring more color into them as the online meeting connected. She was on her sofa with her feet up and a pillow tucked behind her. She was using a fake background to mask her personal space, but she was getting back on track. If she got another good night of sleep, tomorrow, she might even feel good enough to leave her apartment.

But Pete was a night owl, and this time worked best for him, so here they were.

"Hi, Pete," she said when he connected.

"Hey, Hunter. Thanks for meeting so late."

"It's not a problem. How have things been going?"

He sighed and leaned back in his chair. It was black leather, and the Solstice skyline behind him was no design background. He was in Larimer Technologies' corporate offices on the fourteenth floor of the Mercury building downtown. "I went out with donor number three last night."

From the tone of his voice, it hadn't gone well. "No connection?"

"She took selfies and posted them on her LariLoop page."

Ouch. The woman had even used one of his technology platforms to do it. "Fangirl, huh?"

He rolled his eyes. "At least the other two were philanthropic."

Yet the winner had been old enough to be his grandmother. Bidder number two had been a nice guy, but gay. The two of them had at least had a nice sushi dinner together.

"You look tired," Hunter noted. As tired as she felt. "Are you still not sleeping well?"

He ran a hand through his hair. "No, but it's my own fault. I've been toying with a new idea. I don't get to do that much anymore."

"So you've been coding?"

"If you can call it that." He let out a self-deprecating laugh. "I'm rusty."

He reached for his keyboard to adjust some setting, and Hunter flinched when she felt a zing. "*Ooh*," she peeped.

"Don't act so surprised. I sit through more meetings than pair programming sessions these days."

"No, I..." Maybe it had been static electricity from

shifting on her sofa. It had been a dry month with little rain. "Okay, so the bachelor auction didn't produce the results we wanted."

"At this point, I don't know what will." Standing, Pete ventured over to look out the window. "Maybe I've moved myself into a category where there aren't potential matches for me."

She let out a frustrated growl, not caring if he heard her. She hated it when he used online dating terminology. "You've been looking at the pairing algorithms again, haven't you?"

He shrugged. "Logic is how I'm made."

"Logic has nothing to do with love. It's chemistry, and not the kind you find in a laboratory."

His lips quirked as he turned his back on the view. "Unfortunately, that's not my field."

"Your field is just one part of you."

A *bing* interrupted their conversation, and he picked up his phone. As he read whatever text had come through, Hunter's eyes rounded. She sat forward. *What was that?* She swore she could see a blue field, an aura of some sort, protruding from his phone.

He shook his head, set the phone down on his desk, and returned to his chair. Her gaze remained glued to his device. Only a corner of it was still within view of the camera, but the blue outline was gone.

"Hunter?"

She jumped. "What?"

"I asked what our next steps should be."

Next steps. To find him a girlfriend. Right.

"You're the whole package, Pete," she said automatically. Her brain was still on that blue haze. Had it been a trick of the lighting? It was evening, and the fluorescent lights above him were on. It was getting dark earlier and earlier these days.

She shook her head to get back on topic. "You ride dirt bikes, you're a foodie, and you're not a snob."

He chuckled. "Thanks."

"You just spend so much time working on those

computers." There, was that a blue haze around the overhead lights or was she staring too hard? "You're online constantly throughout the day with your computers and phone—and you said you like watching movies in bed when you can't sleep."

Which was often.

"I can't go out in public much, because I get recognized," he said. "Who's going to want to put up with that?"

"Lots of women."

"Who aren't fame or publicity seekers?"

Good point. It was tricky.

Hunter was struggling. She was still coming back from her monthly downward spiral, he had a tough situation, and her attention was split on what she thought she'd seen.

He reached for his keyboard again, and this time, she nearly fell off her sofa. There it was again, a blue sizzle of energy particles coming off the screen and heading for him. "Are you working on another screen?" she asked.

"Just responding to a few instant messages."

"Shut it down. Shut it down now."

The look he gave her was of a corporate CEO, but she didn't care. Begrudgingly, he turned off his second monitor and concentrated solely on her.

Hunter was nervous. What was she dealing with here? "Okay, we need to get serious. I'm going to give you an assignment. I want you to write down all the girlfriends you've had in the past, what qualities made you like them, and how you met."

"All right..." He seemed unsure, but he reached for his keyboard and started typing.

"On paper," she snapped. She swallowed hard and tried to calm down. "Do it tonight. No computers, no tablets, no television on in the background."

He lifted an eyebrow.

"Pete, you hired me to make life better for you, and I'm telling you that you need to get out of your office." Home wouldn't be any better. He'd just play a video game or watch television. "Go for an evening drive with the windows down. Head over to the Satellites game. I don't care what it is, as long as you're off technology and present in the moment. Clear your head and think about what you want to draw into your life."

He scrunched up his handsome face. "That sounds awfully *foofoo*."

"*I'm* foofoo. You've been putting yourself out there; maybe it's time to turn things around and consider how to attract what you want."

"You're talking about *manifesting*," he said, making quotation marks with his fingers.

Her feet hit the floor. Yes. Manifesting. Right now, only it was coming for *her*.

She could see the blue haze forming on her screen, billowing out across the keyboard. It jumped from key to key, and then pulled back. It ventured outward, following the edge of the laptop until it found the dongle that communicated with her mouse. It pulsed, and she barely yanked her hand back in time as it made the leap. "*Go back*."

Pete sat up straight in his chair as if he'd been poked.

The blue shimmers fell apart, but then tried to assemble again.

"Return to where you came from," she said, putting all her power into the words. She was far from full strength, but she was a Menae, a daughter of a Greek goddess. The blue twinkles puffed into a cloud before slinking back into the laptop screen.

Pete looked a little shell-shocked. "Is this a new technique or something?"

"Yes," she said, steadying her voice. She looked around his office to make sure the energy field hadn't merely jumped back to his side. "It's called going old school."

"Okay…"

"Slow down, stay away from your screens, and do some introspection," she said, thinking fast. "Write down your interests, too, and let's meet tomorrow to talk through what you've learned."

He automatically reached for his phone to pull up his calendar. "I don't know if tomorrow will work."

"Tomorrow, Pete." She scrambled for a reason why. "If you want to get a life, you need to go out and do that. What's more important at this point, another dollar or someone you connect with?"

His dimple appeared. "Another dollar?"

The poke of humor made her relax a little, but she was still scanning her screen and his office like a bounty hunter. "Okay, another hundred dollars."

He laughed.

"Hundred thousand?" She had no concept of what he made. It wasn't important to her.

"Let's call it five dollars, but you've made your point. A connection with someone is more important than all of it." He sat back in his expensive chair, and she could see the gears in his head turning almost as well as she'd seen that blue haze. He was beginning to like the idea—whatever it was she'd said. "How about lunch?"

"Perfect. Where?"

The blue thing, the blue light, seemed to be gone for now. The sooner she could meet with him, the better.

"My schedule is tight tomorrow. If you could come here, that would save me travel time."

"Not your office, Pete." There were so many computers there. She needed to wean him off those things, and fast.

"How about the sandwich shop again? The one on the first floor."

"There you go. I'll meet you there at noon—and what are your plans for tonight?"

He chuckled. "Have you ever thought about going into the software field? Somehow, I think that code would be written a lot faster with you around."

She gave a shudder. "Bite your tongue, and don't evade the question."

He sat forward and braced his elbows on his desk. "I'm

going to drive home with the windows down, grab some takeout, and write my list. On paper with ink."

"Atta boy." Hm, maybe she was onto a new technique. "And get a good night's sleep."

"Shutting down now, boss," he said with a smile. "Good night."

Hunter closed the Zoom meeting and then her computer. She pushed it away onto the coffee table. She'd seen it. She'd seen the blue light that was causing so many sleep problems.

But what the heck was she supposed to do about it?

* * *

Tony walked with Kimora and her coach from a parking garage in downtown Solstice toward the Mercury building. They were meeting with her business manager to plan out the next few months. With the tournament season ending in November, they had a couple of months to look at other objectives. He knew he was going to have to fight with her business manager if he was going to get in any off-season training with her. She'd had a fantastic season, but there was still room for improvement. She couldn't spend all her time doing endorsements and appearances if she wanted to stay at number nine in the rankings—or if she wanted to move any higher.

Still, they needed to celebrate her success. Hunter had taught him that.

"My brothers highly recommend this sandwich shop. Since your business manager is only a block away, I thought it might be a good place to meet."

"I'm fine not sitting in a stuffy office," her coach said with a smile.

Tony bent his head toward Kimora. "And I thought I might buy you a protein smoothie to go with it, one that's not green."

She looked at him suspiciously. "What for?"

Was he that much of a hard-ass? "For reaching your goal on your cross-court cuts. That might even rate something chocolate."

Her eyes rounded. "Really?"

"My treat."

Her face split in a smile that was blinding, and she executed something that could only be called a skip. Seriously? This woman had trophies, plaques, and medals—not to mention prize money. Who would have thought a chocolate smoothie would put a spring in her step?

Tony glanced at his phone. Maybe he should get one to go for Hunter.

Kimora gasped. "That's why. You called her!"

He did a double take at the intersection as they stopped for the crossing light. "What?"

"You called her, the woman you were talking about the other day. It's the only explanation for this."

Oh, gods. He wobbled his head on his neck. This was what happened when you let clients see into your personal life, especially female ones. "How in the hell did you arrive at that?"

"You've been in a good mood, you've checked your phone ten times since we left the car, and you haven't made me do mountain climbers for a week. I knew something was up."

"You need recovery time. Light days are important, too."

She waggled a finger at him. "Don't deny it. Just spill."

"Spill what?"

The light turned green, and she linked her arm through his and began to pull him across the street. "The latest. You've talked to her. Have you asked her out?"

"We went out." That seemed safe enough to share. She couldn't make much of an axe-throwing contest.

"You went out already? How did it go?"

"Okay."

"Ohmigod." She stopped in the middle of the intersection. "You slept with her, and it was good. Ah, Tony. That's fantastic."

"How... What?" Grabbing her arm, he got her going

again. Thankfully, her coach was already standing on the opposite street corner, out of hearing range. "How did you get all that out of *okay*?"

"It was the way you said it."

"It's two syllables—and I'm not saying you're right about any of it."

"Am I wrong?"

He gave her his most intimidating stare. "I'm about to retract my smoothie offer."

Smiling, the tennis pro finished crossing the street. She looked up at the glass and metal building that shimmered under the midday autumn sun. "So, are you texting regularly? Planning your next date? Give me the lowdown."

"There is no lowdown," Tony said as he shoved his phone in his pocket. "I'm just checking in on her. She's hasn't been feeling well."

Although she'd been feisty enough to make him go to the Satellites game last night with Bobby. She had more energy now that the moon was moving on to its crescent stage. He liked to think that the steady, dependable services of her Sandman had something to do with her recovery, too. He'd been making sure that happened.

He just hadn't seen her today to make sure everything was still on course. He'd checked on her from the dream realm last night, but he hadn't stayed over.

"Nothing serious, I hope." Kimora smiled at her coach when he held the door to the building open for her to enter. "Thank you, Johnny."

"She says it's not," Tony said quietly. He couldn't imagine cycling through an imbalance like that, over and over again. He worked with people to help them feel good and strong all the time.

"But you're concerned." Kimora sighed. "I wish I had someone who looked out for me like that."

"You've got me."

"Is that the place over there?" her coach asked. He, too, had a spring in his step. Who knew a simple sandwich shop could bring people so much pleasure?

"That's it," Tony said.

Kimora sidled up closer to him as her coach moved ahead to check things out.

"You're great. I've got a whole team of people around me. I'm talking about a special someone." This time, she was the one who dropped her voice so others couldn't listen in. "How did you meet her?"

That was not a story he could tell. "She's a friend of my brother's girlfriend."

"Aw. An organic meetup. I still dream of those, meeting someone out in the wild."

"The wild?"

"You know, no speed dating, no dating apps. Meeting the old-fashioned way."

"Yeah, it's tough." He caught the handle of the door to the sandwich shop and pulled it open. Her coach was already inside, drawn there by the promise of a pastrami on rye. "You'll find someone."

He had.

Tony stopped, dead center of the doorway. Because, speak of the devil, there Hunter was.

Sitting at a table with tech billionaire, and Oneiros family friend, Pete Larimer.

His thoughts went sluggish as he tried to process what he was seeing. Hunter and Pete? Together? How did they even know each other? Had Emily introduced them? The thoughts came faster and more furious, drilling right to the center of his brain.

The two of them were deep in conversation, with Hunter leaning forward as if to make a point. Pete lifted his hands and shrugged. She tapped on something in the notebook that sat on the table between them, and the answer hit Tony like a wrecking ball.

Pete Larimer was her big client. The bachelor.

"Tony?" Kimora said with concern.

He began drumming his fingers against his thigh, and he

felt the fidget spinner in his pocket. "Go ahead. I'll be right there. I see someone I know."

He was at a business meeting. They were in Pete's building.

Tony set his jaw and clapped a lid over his emotions. Locking eyes on their table, he made his way to it.

"Hunter."

She glanced up, and relief washed over her face. "Tony!"

Relief? What the hell? He'd just caught her, red-handed.

Her lunch companion glanced up.

"Oneiros." Pete smiled broadly, rose to his feet, and held out his hand. "I remember you. You're one of Zane's brothers, right?"

Tony nodded and shook the man's hand on autopilot.

Pete looked back and forth between him and Hunter, probably because Tony's gaze was locked on her. "You two know one another?"

When neither of them said anything, he had his answer.

He let out a soft snort. "I told Zane I couldn't compete with any of his brothers."

Tony had no idea what that meant, and he didn't really care. She was bold. He'd known that, but how many times had she been working with Larimer, right under his nose?

Hunter stared at him in confusion, but then her eyes narrowed. "This is my *client*, Pete."

"I know." That was the problem. "Can we talk for a moment? Alone?"

"Sure," she said, her voice just as clipped. She spun on her heel and led the way to the only empty spot in the restaurant, which happened to be the hallway to the bathroom. She whirled around to face him. "What is your problem? Are you territorial? Is that it? I'm not seeing him; I'm working with him."

Tony didn't suspect her of cheating on him. He trusted her that much.

Which was odd, because that particular arrow would strike closer to his heart.

And they'd never really defined their relationship…

"Pete Larimer is a friend of the Oneiroi." His jaw was so tight that only his lips moved. "He's under our protection."

"Your pro—" Her head reared back. "*That's* what this is about? The whole Oneiroi/Menae thing? Again?"

"That's how you choose your targets, isn't it? You take on life-coaching clients so you can manipulate them into doing the full-moon craziness bit."

"No."

"That's what happened with Emily."

Hunter threw up her hands. "I don't 'choose' anything. Do you choose your charges' dreams, Weaver?"

Tony took a step back. The shot was on target, but that was Zane's wrongdoing, not his. What chilled him more, though, was that she knew they were assigned to sleepers. Their charges. He'd told her things about the Oneiroi as they'd spent time together… things that he thought were harmless… or that they shared in common…

Had that been a mistake?

Had she influenced him more than he realized?

"Pete Larimer hired me," she hissed, "and it's none of your family's business."

"Bullshit. That guy has life figured out. What could he possibly want or need?"

Her eyes flared. "Again, you don't need to know, but *that* might clue you in."

She jabbed a rigid finger back at the tables.

Tony looked over his shoulder, but all he saw was Pete talking to Kimora. "I don't see any—"

The two were eye-locked and smiling at each other. Standing close.

Pete had made a play for Emily, too, until she'd made it clear she was interested in Zane. The guy hadn't been pushy or scummy about it. That fact that he was lovelorn had been pretty clear.

Oh, Tony thought dumbly. *Okay, so there might be that.*

"Do not play your games with him," he said as he folded

his arms over his chest. The reason for their working relationship didn't matter. It was just how she set the hook. Pete was not only a friend of the family, he was also a billionaire. A technology guru. Tony didn't even want to think about what the guy would come up with if a Lunatic unleashed him to explore his wildest impulses. On top of that, Larimer Technologies employed thousands of people. Pete was on the cover of magazines. This was one guy who couldn't go off the deep end, even for one night. Something like that would have far-reaching implications.

"I'm. Not." Hunter thrust her hands into her hair. "But it always comes back to that, doesn't it?"

"Apparently." She was a Lunatic, no matter what politically correct name was put on it. She wasn't going to stop just because she liked jumping in the sack with him. Screwing an Oneiros probably did it for her. The thrill of the danger, the draw of the forbidden.

All the while, he'd been drawn to *her*. The Lunatic thing was what he'd worried about.

With good reason.

"I'm done apologizing for what I am and what I do," she said, her entire body vibrating. "You want to talk about accountability? Let's talk about nightmares."

Tony's fingers dug into his arms. "People need those."

"Well, maybe they need some 'craziness' in their daytime world, too." Her eyes burned with wetness. "And to think I was going to ask you for help with him."

"Help? With Pete?"

It did look like he might have helped set him up. Kimora was smiling and twirling her hair around her finger.

"Never mind," Hunter said, pushing by him. She bumped up against him hard, not intimidated in the slightest. She was halfway into the lunch crowd rush when she pivoted and came right back. "He's the client I told you about, the one who's having problems sleeping because he spends so much time on computers."

Tony's gaze narrowed on Pete. Okay, maybe he needed to

talk to the Sandman about him, too.

"Last night, as I was on a Zoom meeting with him, I saw a Blue Lighter."

"A what?" His attention snapped back to Hunter so fast, his neck twinged.

"Figure it out, Oneiros," she tossed over her shoulder as she stomped away.

Tony went after her. What was she saying? She'd seen the actual blue light emitting from the screen? He supposed it was possible if the Menae could see different spectrums of light than humans. He didn't think the Oneiroi could see them, but he wasn't sure what he was looking for.

But that wasn't what she'd said. "Hunter. *A* Blue Lighter?" As in a thing? An entity?

She'd already joined the pair back at the table. "Hi. Kimora? I'm Hunter. Big fan."

"*Hunter,*" Kimora repeated, her eyes going wide. "You're the one."

"Might've been. Not so much anymore." Hunter swiped up the plate on the table with a big roast beef sandwich and chips. "Come on, Pete. Let's move this meeting up to your office."

"But I thought you didn't want to meet there."

Larimer's neck was getting a workout as he looked from her to Tony and back to Kimora. Mainly Kimora. It was clear that he didn't want to leave, but he could see what was going on. Fury was radiating off Hunter as if she were a contamination zone, and Tony was so worked up, he was ready to play fidget spinner with the ceiling fans.

"Um, okay. All right. Give me a minute."

Pete lunged for his phone and ignored Hunter when she let out something close to a growl. His thumbs moved fast as he typed, but then he held the device out to Kimora.

"Can I get your number?" he asked, his eyes moony.

Moony.

A muscle at Tony's temple clenched, but then he saw Kimora looking back at Pete the same way.

His toes dug into the floor as he came to a sudden halt. That dreamy smile on her face was not due to the promise of a chocolate protein smoothie.

"Sure." She took the phone and entered her digits. "I'll just text myself while I'm at it so I have yours, too."

Pete grinned, but Hunter was on the move. He grabbed the rest of their belongings and his lunch. He started to head for the door, but Hunter whipped around for one last word. Tony held his ground, but he felt it crumble beneath him when she hissed.

"And one more thing you might find interesting. It was *sentient.*"

CHAPTER THIRTEEN

Tony was at the gym, pounding the ever-loving hell out of a punching bag. His thoughts were swirling inside his head, pummeling his brain just as hard. A Blue Lighter. Was she serious? Or was she yanking his chain to get back at him?

He gave the bag the old one-two, before ducking and weaving.

He'd crossed a line, he knew. He should have had the discussion with her in private. Like real privacy. Not in front of their clients.

"*Hwuh*," he grunted, putting his fist practically through the bag with a left hook.

It hadn't crossed his mind once that she might be seeing Larimer romantically. It still didn't. Why did he have confidence in her about that?

Because that was about the two of them. The other was about their roles in the world. Their backgrounds, their upbringing.

Family.

He shuffled around the bag that was still quivering from the hook before moving in and letting loose with a barrage of punches.

He had to tell his brothers that she was mixed up with Pete, even if it was in a professional capacity, because they all knew what that would lead to eventually. He'd hid too much from them for too long. Family came first, and she was a Menae getting way too close to Zane and Wes's friend.

He kept pounding on the bag, giving it everything he had until his arms turned rubbery, his breaths raked at his throat, and sweat dripped from his brow onto the rubberized mat that covered the floors.

Breaking away, he took a walk by the windows to get his heart rate back down.

When the stars didn't stop blinking in his line of sight, he undid the Velcro on the gloves and tossed them to the floor. He wiped a towel over his face and took a swig of Gatorade.

His body was getting fatigued, but his thoughts were still going strong.

Sentient.

She'd had to leave him with a mic drop like that. Was she seriously telling him that whatever she'd seen had thought processes? Intent?

No, she'd known that if she threw something like that at him, she'd wind him up.

He looked at the bag. She was right about that.

He screwed the top back on the Gatorade so tight it might never open again. Hunter Mahina was a Lunatic and a master of manipulation. How had he ever forgotten that?

Because he'd been thinking with the head in his shorts, not the one atop his shoulders.

And maybe his heart.

Aw, hell. He didn't want to go there. He knew how to work out the harder emotions. If he thought about the tender ones, it would wreck him.

He reached for the gloves again.

A hand reached out and pushed them aside. "Enough."

Tony spun around. He'd been pounding on the stupid bag longer than he'd ever allow a client to, but the fight hadn't left him. Who was dumb enough to get in his way?

AJ stepped in front of him. "I said, that's enough."

Tony planted his wrapped hands on his hips, even though it made his arms quiver. "What do you think you're doing?"

"Stopping you from having a heart attack or a massive meltdown, one of the two." His brother peered at him. "What's going on?"

Tony hadn't even realized the ghost was here.

"Why have you been hanging around here so much?" he snarled. It wasn't a normal gym. They specialized in personal training for topnotch athletes, but their clients could come in to work out on their own when they wanted. He let his brothers do the same for a membership fee, because the place was quieter and less busy than the normal gyms. They could come and go with less of a fuss and fewer people eyeing the amount of weight they pushed around. Zane always went to the busiest gym in town, naturally, but he'd never seen AJ here as much as he'd seen him this week.

"Cael said to keep an eye on you."

"Are you serious?"

"I'm keeping an eye." AJ lifted an eyebrow at the punching bag.

Tony winced when he realized stuffing was coming out of one of the seams.

"I'm working out. How is that a surprise?" They knew what he did. They knew he hadn't gotten his strength by wishing for it. All the Oneiroi were ripped. He'd just pushed it to another level.

"You're not working out. You're trying to work out something."

Tony scowled. The quiet guy saw too much.

"What's wrong?" AJ asked, stepping closer.

Tony lasted all of five seconds before he tossed his towel to the floor. He'd been pounding on the bag, but he didn't want a fight. "I screwed up."

AJ waited. It was weird how effective an interrogation tactic that was.

"With the woman I'm seeing."

"Hunter."

Tony nearly fell over. "What?"

"Hunter Mahina, Emily's friend." AJ shook his head. "I

know it's not Kimora."

Tony was already feeling lightheaded as it was. "What am I, an open book? How the hell did you come up with that?"

He'd done everything in his power to hide it.

And that was what made her betrayal so bad… It had made him lie to his family.

AJ tossed something at him, and Tony automatically caught it. It was the fidget spinner, the one Hunter had given him. He immediately saw red. "You're going through my things now?"

AJ wasn't fazed, although he did transition his weight to the balls of his feet. He might be smaller, but he was faster. "I stopped by your office to find you. It was on your desk."

"Yeah?" Tony's thoughts spun off in another direction. "Well, it might be a kid's toy… but it helps."

Why was he covering? Hadn't he just told himself that he needed to spill the beans? AJ was just pushing up the timeline. Tony might not be ready, but the time had come.

He gave the spinner a twirl. "How did you know?" he asked, giving in.

AJ pointed at the whirling dervish. "It has her company logo on it, a crescent moon."

Tony closed his fingers over the gadget and looked at the center hub. Huh. He'd never noticed that before. He sighed, all his defensiveness leaving in a *whoosh*. "I'm sorry, man. I should have confessed a while ago."

"Whoa." AJ caught him by the arm. "You're wobbling."

His brother led him over to a weight bench. Tony sat down, and AJ cracked open his Gatorade for him.

It took two tries.

"Here," he said, shoving the electrolytes at him. He took a seat on the bench press machine three feet away.

They were the only two in the back room. Tony glanced at the clock on the wall. He hadn't realized it was so late. He'd been going at the bag for a while.

"What happened?" AJ asked.

Tony took a long drink. Where did he even start?

"I don't think she used her mind mojo on me, but she's so damn hot... and playful and funny and... You get the drift." He waved the cap around. They fit together in ways he'd never expected, and being with her just felt good. "I found myself going back for more and more. That's on me."

AJ held up a hand. "I don't care about that. It's your life. I'm asking what went wrong."

"Wasn't the whole damn thing wrong?"

"Tony, you've been happier and less stressed than I've ever seen you."

So the good part had shown.

"How did you know it wasn't Kimora?"

"You've been working with her for a while, but the changes only happened after the full moon."

The kiss. The one he was never going to live down, especially after the whole truth came out. All his brothers wouldn't be as accepting as AJ.

"That obvious, huh?"

"To me, it was."

Zane had been the one to start the Kimora rumor. AJ might resemble him in looks, but that was where the similarities ended.

"Am I really that high-strung?" He'd thought he played it off well. When it got to be too much, he blew off steam doing stuff like this.

Hunter had pegged him there. It was why she'd given him the fidget spinner in the first place.

AJ leaned forward and rested his elbows against his knees. "You internalize, and you put everything on your shoulders. Everyone thinks you're big enough to carry it all, but I have shoulders, too." He flexed, and it wasn't unimpressive. "Greek god shoulders."

"I betrayed the family," Tony said quietly.

"How?"

"By getting involved with her." He gave the fidget spinner a twirl. Why not? AJ knew what it was for.

"How does that hurt the family? I haven't seen you drop

the ball on your responsibilities. You've kept up with bringing dreams to your charges."

"I've been late some nights, though."

"We all do that. We all have lives. Why can't you?"

"She's a Menae."

"I'm talking about you. From what I've seen, you're not only feeling better, you've been rocking the Dream Weaver role. You started discussions for the first time in eons with the Sandmen, and you've been digging into this blue light thing."

Tony spread his feet wider on the floor. "About that... If you want to know what's wrong, what the tipping point was, I might have screwed that up, too—especially for you."

"For me?"

"Pete Larimer is being affected by it. He's your charge."

"I know. He's the one I was talking about at breakfast last week. He's not sleeping. The time he spends on screens is messing up his circadian rhythm."

"Hunter thinks it's more than that." Tony almost winced when he said her name aloud, but he couldn't stop now. "She saw something when she was on a Zoom meeting with him."

AJ went still. "Zoom meeting? Your Lunatic has been meeting with Pete?"

"As a life coach."

Tony saw the light dawn with his brother. It would only take a few more moments for AJ to catch up. Then he'd understand why his brother was such a snake in the grass.

"Pete Larimer is working with her as a life coach? Shit." AJ pushed himself to his feet and walked around in a tight circle. "Fool us once, shame on her. Fool us twice? Damn it. She might not be using her powers on you, but she has to be on him. What could a guy like that possibly want or need that he doesn't already have?"

"A girlfriend."

AJ's steps faltered. "That's true." He waited a beat before asking, "Is he hitting on *your* girlfriend now?"

"Nah." Tony jerked his thumb in the direction of the

punching bag. "I made the same leap you did. I accused Hunter of using her life-coaching job as a feeder system for her Menae night work. That's when everything went haywire."

"She didn't take it well."

"She's helping Pete find someone." Tony stared at the spinner as it went round and round. If all the moony looks and dreamy eyes meant anything, she might have just accomplished that goal.

"Okay. Back up. Your Lunatic thinks she saw something? What, exactly, did she see?"

"Menae," Tony said off-handedly. "I don't know. I didn't get a chance to ask."

Because she'd been walking away from him by that point. Stomping, actually.

"But she saw it in the waking world."

"She can't get to the dream realm."

AJ ran a hand through his hair, ruffling it. He was beginning to get the big picture. "You need to talk to her, Tony."

"I don't know if she'll even answer her phone."

"You call her, or I will."

Tony lifted an eyebrow.

"Pete's my charge. I need to know what she knows, unless... You don't think the Menae are behind this?"

"No." Tony flat-out knew they weren't. Hunter had been worried about her sleep-deprived client long before he found out who it was. And the fury in her eyes... No, she was as worried about it as they were.

"Then we need to work together. This blue light thing is bigger than any stupid feud."

"Blue Lighter," Tony said. She'd called it a Blue Lighter. "I'm afraid we might have a new sleep raider out there."

* * *

Hunter sat at a high table on the dark side of Night and Day. The quirky juice bar was quickly going from one of her favorite places to somewhere she dreaded. Tony had called and asked to meet. He'd been apologetic on the dozen or so messages he'd left, because she was screening his calls. He'd had gifts delivered, too, flowers and chocolates and even ribs from Kick Axe.

Those she'd accepted, because how better to feed her feelings than with ribs?

He'd hurt her. After all this time, he still didn't trust her. What did she have to do? Honestly, she was done trying, and that made her sad. She wasn't someone who gave up on things or people, but she couldn't change what she was at her core.

Apparently, neither could he.

Stupid Dream Weavers.

He was driving her to use one of her own fidget spinners. She pushed it into motion without even noticing. He'd asked her to meet him here. If she didn't want to hear his apologies, he at least wanted to hear about the Blue Lighter.

And she needed help with that.

She watched the spinner go round and round in a blur.

She'd reached out to the Menae network, but none of her sisters knew what to do about it. They'd all started keeping an eye out for the things, though, because they were encroaching on their territory. Light at night? Hello, the moon ruled there.

The problem was that her sisters didn't know how to deal with it when they did find it. They knew it responded to their powers, but they weren't used to fighting sleep raiders or vanquishing them. That was the Dream Weavers' specialty.

So, here she was, nervous and still angry, waiting for Tony.

She flicked the spinner. If she wasn't still worried for Pete, she wouldn't be here. At the very least, the Oneiros owed her.

Suddenly, the energy in the juice bar changed, and she looked to the front door. Tony walked in and, when his gaze connected with hers, a jolt went through her.

It had been that way between them from the very beginning.

Her gaze ate him up. He looked good, although he was

playing with the keys in his hand. He was nervous about this meeting, too. Instead of heading for the counter, he sucked it up and walked right toward her. Her foot began teeter-tottering on the rung of the chair where she'd rested it.

"You came," he said.

Oh, gods. His eyes were saying so much more.

"To talk," she managed to whisper.

"How are you feeling?"

He sounded concerned. She hooked her hair behind her ear. "I'm doing better. Feeling stronger."

"Good. I wasn't sure how long it took."

Longer when her heart was hurting, she'd found.

"Hunter," he said softly. "I'm sorry."

"You said that twelve times on the phone."

"So, you at least listened to the messages."

She sniffed.

He slid into the chair across from her, and, on a closer look, she saw creases on his brow and veins popping out along his biceps. He'd been hitting the gym hard.

"I wanted to tell you in person." He folded his hands atop the table, intertwining his fingers until they turned white. "I messed up. I saw you there with Pete, and I jumped to conclusions about your intent. I should have trusted you."

Her throat tightened. "I don't hurt people, Tony, or put them in danger. Not intentionally. I'm trying to help them in the only way I know how. So many people have forgotten how to have fun or cut loose, and the pressure just builds…"

"I know." He looked at the spinner in her hand.

They both felt the pressure.

"I've missed you."

She'd missed him, too.

"Don't do that," she said, her voice thick. "I agreed to come to talk about the Blue Lighter. Nothing more."

She didn't want to make another scene in this restaurant.

"Okay, you're right. Can you… Do you mind if my brother listens in?"

Hunter came off her seat when he gestured to another

man that she hadn't even noticed. Had he come in with him? All she knew was that she saw a blond. *Zane.* He'd brought freaking Zane, who despised her. Her gaze darted around, looking for more Oneiroi. Was this an ambush?

"No, it's not like that." Tony slid out of his seat and reached for her, but then pulled back. He rubbed the back of his neck. "Hunter, I'd like to introduce you to my brother, AJ."

She stopped. The guy looked like Zane at a glance, but he had an entirely different energy. He was calm like a lake in a forest, yet his vivid blue eyes were sharp.

"Hey," he said as he set two glasses of juice on the table.

"I remember you," she said. "You were there that night."

He'd been the one to run after the dirt bike on the half-pipe. She hadn't used her powers on him.

Hunter felt someone move up behind her and plant themselves at her side. Both Dream Weavers went still as they looked at the new arrival. They looked surprised, but she wasn't. She'd brought backup, too.

"Ganging up on my sister?" Berry said. "That's a low move, Dream Boy, no matter what she says about you."

"That one," Hunter whispered. She pointed at Tony, redirecting Berry's attention.

Her sister's eyebrows rose, and she hid her face behind her hand as she mouthed, *Wow.*

Tony's muscles bunched up. "Nobody's ganging up on anybody. Hunter, I'm introducing you to my family."

She blinked in surprise. They'd been running around behind everyone's backs, because they'd assumed that their families wouldn't accept the pairing.

Yet after their fight, she'd had to tell someone.

Had he really told one of his brothers about the two of them? Or was this all about the Blue Lighter?

Either way, her heart began to beat faster. This was a big step. Huge.

Tony shoved his hands into his pockets. "Pete is AJ's charge. He's the only other Oneiros here, I promise, and he's probably the coolest head in the bunch. We're here to listen. We want to learn about this thing."

"Okay…" Hunter gestured at her sidekick. "This is my sister, Strawberry."

Tony nodded. "Nice to meet you."

"You'll forgive me if I reserve opinion on you," Berry muttered.

Hunter smiled weakly. When she'd called Berry, she was in full meltdown mode. They might not look like sisters, but they were thick as thieves. While she was petite and dark, Berry was tall with red hair. She was normally as sweet as her name, but in her view, they'd been picking on her sister. The Menae and Oneiroi didn't get along to start with, but add that all up, and Berry was putting out some seriously pissed-off vibes.

In unspoken agreement, they all took seats at the table. It was way too small for the collection of power that had just assembled. Trust was tenuous, and they all sat on tenterhooks, ready for anything.

"Strawberry. That's June, right?" AJ finally asked. "Are you all named after your full moons?"

The tension had to be bad for him to break the quiet.

"No," Hunter answered, even if the question wasn't for her, "but it's tradition. Some of us follow it."

"Can you imagine a woman named Sturgeon?" Berry grumbled.

It eased the standoff a bit.

"So, the Blue Lighter," Tony said. "Can you tell us what you saw?"

Hunter folded her hands together, and they bumped into the fidget spinner on the table. For some reason, it embarrassed her. Tony tilted his head. Reaching out, he picked it up and began playing with it.

She let out a breath that was less anxious. "At first, I thought it was static electricity."

"You felt it, too?" he said quickly.

She pursed her lips. "I guess I did, but only for a second.

When I started paying attention, though, I could see it on Pete's side of the call. He was in his office, and it was evening, so it was dark outside. It made the blue fizzle easier to see."

"Where was it?" AJ asked. "Was the screen like a blue haze, or what?"

"No, it was moving. From his second screen to his phone to his keyboard."

"Like it lives in the electronics?" Tony asked.

She nodded. "Or at least, that's how it travels. I could see it billowing out, trying to reach him."

"This was in the waking realm?" AJ asked.

"But we know it's in the dream realm too," Tony said. "It's affecting sleep patterns and making sleep less restorative."

The brothers' heads were close as they tried to work through the situation, and Hunter watched them with interest. They didn't seem as hardcore and militant as she'd been raised to believe. It was what she'd been trying to tell Berry when she confessed that she'd been seeing an Oneiros.

"How do we fight it, then?" AJ asked. "We need to know where it's going to be. If it's traveling through electronics, it could be anywhere. How do we know where it will make an appearance?"

"More than that, if it can slide between realms, it's more mobile than we are," Tony said. "We can make the jump, too, but we don't have vanquishing powers on this side."

"We do," Hunter said.

"We do?" Berry said, swiveling her head around.

"Well, I don't know about vanquishing, but I was able to push it back when it came out through my computer."

"It came after you?" The fidget spinner in Tony's hand jerked to a stop.

Hunter shifted in her chair. "Maybe? It could have just been curious."

He leaned in. "What. Happened?"

"When Pete moved too far away from his computer, the

blue sparkles changed direction. I don't know… It must have followed the meeting connection? Anyway, it started spilling out of my screen onto my keyboard, and it freaked me out. I ordered it to go back." She shrugged. "It did."

"Wait. Was that the night I went to the football game?"

"Yes."

"Damn it. You were weak as a kitten on the sofa. I knew I shouldn't have left you."

Berry stiffened when she put together when on the calendar that might have been.

"It's all right," Hunter said, both to her sister and Tony. "I was able to handle it."

"I should have been there with you," he said.

Berry swung her head around, obviously disagreeing.

Hunter held up a hand to her sister as she spoke with Tony. "But you don't have powers in the waking world."

AJ looked to Berry, clearly unhappy that tidbit of info was being shared.

Hunter barreled on. "You would have been in more danger than I was."

"I don't care," Tony said.

"I do." Hunter caught herself leaning into him before she remembered why they were here. They weren't a couple. They were two people from warring families who snuck away for nooners. She folded her arms over her stomach when it gave a pang. "I'm the daughter of the moon goddess. Believe me when I say that we can contain Blue Lighters on this side."

"Um, I don't know if I can," Berry admitted. "I've never even seen one."

"Neither have we," AJ said, "on this side or in the dream realm."

"So that's where we start," Tony decided. "We need to find one."

Hunter pulled back when they all looked expectantly at her. "What? Right now?"

"Why not?"

"Look," Berry said, poking her in the side.

Hunter rolled her eyes. "Okaaay."

She looked around the juice bar. Karaoke was starting up, and excitement was bubbling. The day side of the establishment was bright, with white tables and chairs adorned with tropical greens and hot pinks. She ruled it out. They weren't going to see any night beings over there.

She turned to survey the night side of Night and Day. The lighting was dimmed, and the furniture was black. The pops of neon lighting didn't help her search, nor did the yapping of the emcee as he announced the first singer and song through the overhead speaker system.

Suddenly, she let out a gasp.

"What?" Tony asked. "Where?"

Berry stood up and tried to follow her line of sight. "I don't see it."

Hunter twirled her seat back around. "That's because one isn't going to come here. These people are out, having fun. They're not on their devices."

"There's a guy on his phone over there," AJ pointed out.

"We need to go to the quiet spots," she insisted. Did they not understand what this thing was and how it worked? "The libraries, people doomscrolling in their easy chairs, offices with computers on every desk, cafés in campus town."

"Sounds good to me," Tony said. "I'll partner with you."

She leveled a look on him.

"Anywhere you want to go."

"Tony."

"Is there blue light at a theater? We could catch a movie. Or I'll make you dinner as you get on your laptop. You can try another Zoom meeting with Pete."

"He has a date with Kimora."

"I'm trying to ask *you* on a date with *me*."

She blinked. He was asking her out right here in front of her sister and his brother?

"I don't care what we do," he said. "Hunter, we had a fight. Let's make up. Don't walk away from this."

Her breaths hitched, clogging up somewhere around her heart.

His hazel gaze bored into hers. "Just tell me what I have to do to make it up to you."

She felt pinned as a happy '80s song wafted through the air, sung by two women trying to do harmony. She wanted to give him a second chance—*them* a second chance—but relationships shouldn't be this hard.

Although… they'd been outed now. The secrecy part was gone. They both had siblings sitting right here, staring at them with mouths agape.

And Tony was acting like they *were* a couple, a couple who'd been so hot for one another they couldn't make it through a day without meeting to touch. A couple who cared how each other was feeling and doing.

"Serenade me."

"Excuse me?"

The words just came out, but she warmed to the idea. "Sing to me, up on that stage in front of everyone."

He stared at her like a deer in the headlights. Then he climbed off his chair. He hitched up his jeans and looked at the stage. With a nod, he headed in its direction.

"Holy shit," AJ whispered.

"He's actually going to do it," Berry said.

Hunter watched with wide eyes as Tony flipped through the song book and talked with the emcee. Her heart sped faster when she heard the announcement of the song selection: "Conditions Are Favorable," by her favorite band, Harbingers of Mayhem.

He took the microphone, and the joke was on her.

Tony could sing.

She nearly melted off her chair as he belted out the power ballad, putting his heart into it. The rasp in his voice made her squeeze her thighs together hard. All the while, he looked at her. Sang to her. Made it up to her.

As far as apologies went, it was a really good start.

CHAPTER FOURTEEN

Tony was ready when he finished the song, and Hunter rushed the stage and jumped into his arms. He kissed her soundly to the hoots and hollers of the crowd of juicers. With her arms wrapped around his neck and her legs around his waist, he carried her back to their table.

"*Hwuh*," he whispered into her ear.

Her smile was teary. "*Hi-yah*."

The knot in the middle of his chest finally released. He'd never sung in front of people before, but he was willing to make a fool of himself if it meant she'd forgive him. This was a better result than he'd hoped for.

He deposited her in her chair as a new singer hit the stage with another love song, hoping to have the same results. *Good luck with that, buddy.* Tony scooted his chair closer to hers.

Berry looked at AJ. "Do you sing like that?"

The color washed from his face. "No."

She cocked her head. "I bet you'd be really good at it. You should try."

"Strawberry," Hunter exclaimed. She swatted at her sister. "Stop trying to influence him. He's a god."

A smile finally lit up the redhead's face. "You can't blame me for trying."

AJ was the only one at the table who didn't think that was funny.

Tony felt Hunter's pinky hook around his. It made it hard to remember what they were supposed to be meeting about. "So," he said, "are we going out hunting?"

"It's the right time of night," AJ noted. "The sun set not long ago, and people are getting on their devices."

"But most of those places Hunter mentioned are in people's homes," Berry argued. "We can't go traipsing through living rooms looking for Blue Lighters."

"True." At least not in this form. Tony was so used to traveling the night in spirit form, he hadn't considered that. There was a reason why sleep raiders were supposed to live in the dream realm, damn it.

"What about the fraternity?" AJ said. "They're up at all hours."

"Same problem."

"I could go into the dream realm early and park myself there to see if this Blue Lighter shows up."

They were dealing with so many unknowns. Could Dream Weavers see the Blue Lighters in the waking world? Humans obviously couldn't. Would Dream Weaver powers work over here if they did encounter one?

"I don't like the thought of you taking one on alone, at least not until we know what we're dealing with," Tony replied.

"The university library may be our best bet," Hunter said.

"Do they let people who aren't students in there?"

"Don't look at me." Berry twirled a strand of red hair around her finger. "Libraries aren't really my speed, unless you're talking about those cute little ones on wheels. Bookmobiles? Yeah, those are fun."

Tony let out a grunt. They were spinning their wheels, all right.

"Maybe the commons area?" AJ took a drink of his juice as he thought about it. "We're going to draw attention wherever we go. We're too old. Wes would be able to pass."

"Bite your tongue," Berry said.

"Yeah, what she said," Hunter agreed.

Tony smiled and squeezed her pinky. It was good to see her lighter side again. It fit her so much better.

"Wes is a good idea, but it's too late to recruit him," he said. "This thing goes out early."

At least, if the Sandman had been telling the truth, it got there before he did.

Hunter's phone pinged, and she got a funny look on her face when she checked it. "It's Pete."

Tony sat back in his chair. There was still friction around that, no matter how many high notes he'd hit, yet he couldn't help his curiosity when she frowned. "What does he want? Is something wrong?"

"No." Her thumbs moved across her phone screen. "But this might be our answer right here."

She put the phone on the table for everyone to see. "He's hosting a professional gaming tournament in the Larimer offices next week."

"That's a thing?" Berry asked. "People watch other people play video games?"

"A big thing." AJ twisted his head to try to read the screen, but gave up and searched for the info on his own phone. His head began bobbing as he scrolled down. "You're right. This is it. Top gamers from around the country will be there. If this Blue Lighter is attracted to people who spend a lot of time looking at screens, it will definitely show up there."

"That's good, real good. We have a time and place." They'd just jumped to the head of the line on that, but Tony was still stuck on something else. "Why did Pete reach out to you for that?"

The moment he saw Hunter's face, he knew he'd stepped in it again. He lifted his hands. "Right, none of my business."

"Not totally." She went quiet as she read Pete's text message again. Squaring her shoulders, she sent a response. "You should probably know, though, that Kimora will be there, too."

"Kimora? Why the hell— Oh." Apparently, their

relationship had progressed to the point where they were willing to be photographed together in public. Tony had to give Pete credit; he was locking that down.

But their relationship was neither here nor there. "She can't go. She can't be infected by this thing."

Sleep was a key factor in performance, and she had one tournament left. A tennis tournament where people actually got off their duffs and showed some athletic skill.

"That's your concern." Hunter put her phone away and took a sip of her juice. "I have different priorities."

Number one being: get their clients together.

"Deal with it," she said.

"Oh, don't you worry about that, sweetheart."

Her eyes sparkled, and he grinned. Oh yeah, this was a much better way to deal with their conflicts.

"Should we head out to find a coffee shop in campus town?" he asked. "I still think a test run is a good idea."

This video game competition sounded like a big deal. It would be best if they started small before they went there.

"Sounds good to me."

"Wait," Berry said. "I want to sing a song first."

She was off her chair and heading to the stage before any of them could protest. Hunter gave a shrug and trotted off after her. Tony watched her unabashedly, soaking up the sight of her. She was so cute and sassy—and important to him.

He let out a breath that had all the tight muscles in his neck relaxing, and AJ gave him a slap on his shoulder.

"I like her—at least on a night like this. She's hell on wheels under a full moon."

Tony liked her, too. More than liked her. He'd fallen for her, big time. "You don't think I'll be cast out of the family?"

"There are some kinks that need to be worked out."

Yeah. Tony finished off his juice. "The King of Understatement."

They watched as the girls set up to do their song. With their looks and excitement level, they had the crowd on their side. Strawberry took the lead, and Hunter danced to the pop song with the emcee. When she lifted her microphone to join in on the chorus, though, the emcee jerked as if he'd just stepped on a live wire.

"Good gods," AJ said, pulling back.

Tony began laughing. Belly laughing. She was terrible. Off key and off the beat.

And she did not care.

Berry just sang louder, and the crowd jumped in to help.

Hunter didn't seem to notice the relief on everyone's faces when she went back to dancing.

"The Menae have more fun than we do," Tony said as he wiped his eyes. "I'll give them that."

"Yeah, well, you better plan on singing for your supper from here on out."

Tony busted up laughing again. "Otherwise, we'll starve."

The Menae were cheered/rushed off the stage when they finished their song, and he helped Hunter with her jacket. November had finally arrived with a chill in the air that made a person catch their breath. Without a doubt, the mosquitos at Comet Tail Lake were gone.

He took her hand as they headed to the door. "We can take my truck."

He was trying to devise a way to get her home with him, but he hadn't yet figured out the sister part of the calculation. He briefly considered dumping Berry on AJ, but the Menae would eat him alive.

They spilled into the parking lot, and the sign from the motel across the street caught his eye. She deserved so much better than that, but it had been fun, too.

Berry suddenly stopped walking. "Oh my gods. Is that what I think it is?"

Hunter stopped short to avoid running into her. "What?"

Berry pointed, and they all looked to the back of the building. A Night and Day worker stood outside the back door, taking a smoke break and looking at his phone. The area was well lit with an outdoor light, and puffs of smoke could clearly be seeing rising in the cold air.

Right along with a sparkling blue cloud that was pushing up from the phone screen.

"That's it!" Hunter said. "Can you see it?"

"I see it, all right." The hairs on Tony's arms rose.

AJ stood just as stiffly at his side.

Instinct kicked in, and Tony started moving. "Hey, buddy. Is that the game?" He shoved his fingers into the pockets of his jeans to try to make himself look less intimidating as he walked closer. He knew the vibes he put off. Sometimes they were helpful, others they were not. "What's the score?"

The scrawny kid looked up and then did a double take. He was wearing a Night and Day T-shirt that was black on the front and white on the back.

"Uh, yeah." He flicked ashes from his cigarette onto the asphalt. "Satellites are up by seven."

"Cool." Tony kept his eyes on the phone, both to keep the kid calm and to see how that blue sizzle reacted. "I've got twenty bucks riding on them."

The blue sparkles were focused on the kid until Tony got in actual eye range of the screen. Once he did, the blue cloud shifted in his direction as if sensing a bigger meal. He slid his hands out of his pockets, so he'd be ready if the thing struck. They were the best weapons they had against it, but he didn't know if they would work in the waking world. He might be as susceptible as a human.

The kid seemed uncertain, but he held out the phone so Tony could see. "It's still the first half."

The blue cloud shifted closer, but all at once, the sparkles stopped moving. Tony tensed, but then the cloud shifted away like a big gust of wind had come through. It swung toward the kid, decided it wasn't worth it, and began diving back into the screen.

"Tony," Hunter said sharply. Suddenly, she was at his side, breathing hard as if she'd just made a mad dash. "I told you to stop placing those bets."

She caught his arm and tugged him away from the kid—or, more precisely, his glowing phone. Which wasn't glowing anymore.

"Women," he said with a shrug.

The kid nodded knowingly, as if his sixteen-year-old girlfriend was the same drag.

Hunter stopped to look at him. "Don't those cigarettes taste nasty?"

Tony felt a wave of energy buffet him, and his lips twitched. He circled his arm around her waist. "Thanks, man. Have a good night."

He bent his head closer to hers. "Did you just use your mojo on him?"

"A little."

"Why didn't you just tell him to stop smoking?"

She rolled her eyes. "That doesn't work. You've got to plant the seed."

Tony looked over his shoulder and caught the kid smacking his lips and looking at the cigarette like it was bitter.

She was good.

He suddenly remembered the night of the full moon. All she'd said to Wes was something along the lines of "doesn't that half-pipe look like fun?" She hadn't told him to ride the dirt bike down it. He knew, because he'd been holding her in his arms when she said it.

"What did you learn?"

She did let people choose their own course.

"The Blue Lighter," AJ added when he didn't answer.

Tony shook his head to clear his thoughts. "It pulled back when it saw me. It knew what I am."

"Well, that answers that."

It answered a lot of things. "We can see it in the waking world, but it runs from us."

"So, it knows what we are and what we can do to it."

"*Might* be able to do to it," Hunter interjected. "You don't know for sure if your powers will work on it here."

"Ours will." Berry folded her arms over her chest and thrust out her hip.

"It pulled back into the dream realm," AJ said. "Where we

know *our* powers will work."

"We need to trap it," Hunter concluded.

Tony tightened his grip on hers. They'd gathered into a tight circle to talk and to fight off the chill. The wind wasn't the only reason for the shiver going down his spine, though. He couldn't stop thinking about her taking on that thing when she'd been weak and alone. "What do you mean, *we*?"

"I'll go to the video game event—"

"We'll go," Berry said. "I'm not leaving until we know how to handle this thing."

"*We'll* go to the video game event," Hunter said, "and when the Blue Lighter appears, we'll push it into the dream realm, where you two will be waiting for it. Um... if that's how it works. You said it's a parallel dimension, whatever that means."

"If the game is happening here, it's happening there," Tony said, working hard to avoid AJ's glare.

Typically, they avoided people who were awake when they were in the dream realm and only sought out the sleepers. Still...

"I don't like it," he said. "Next week, you won't be at full strength. The moon won't be full yet."

This time, it was Berry who grunted in frustration.

"We'll put Dream Weavers on both sides," he decided.

"What's to prevent it from running away through the electronics?" Berry said sweetly. Too sweetly. She was getting invested in this.

"She's right," Hunter said. "We can direct it. I wasn't at full strength when I dealt with it the first time, and everything turned out okay."

"And there will be two of us," Berry repeated.

Hunter jabbed her finger in the air. "And you don't have an invitation to the gaming event. I do."

Tony cocked his head. Seriously? She was going to block him from attending?

AJ scuffed his hand over his head. He wasn't one for drama, but he sat through plenty of it every Sunday at breakfast. "They're not going to reschedule the tournament based on the moon's phase, Tony."

Shit. They were right. Tony blew out a long breath. "I'm not doubting your capabilities, Hunter—I just don't want to be separated from you when this goes down. It would be best if we could combine our abilities."

The fierce set of her jaw eased. "I'd rather have you at my side, too, but we can't get into the dream realm. We can't partner that way."

Tony looked at AJ. "Don't even say it. I'm not leaving you alone over there."

Berry cleared her throat. "You don't know me, but I'm solid. I've got her back."

Two Menae and two Oneiroi. It was a strong plan, even if the niggling in his gut didn't agree. "Okay, I'm onboard if you all are."

One by one, they all nodded.

"We've got days to work out the details," AJ said.

"Okay." Tony gave his brother a look. "Give us a moment?

He pulled Hunter aside. "Are you good with this?"

"I am. Are you?"

"It's the best idea we have." He saw AJ heading for his SUV and Berry rubbing her arms as she waited by Hunter's car. He still hadn't figured out that part of the calculation.

He dropped his voice. "Want to come over tonight?"

"I don't think I should."

"Because I need to pay some more?"

"Maybe... but more because she just got to town. I can't leave her."

He was disappointed, but he understood. Crooking a finger beneath her chin, he lifted her face to him. Under the light of the moon, she looked like the goddess she was. He kissed her, deepening the contact when she fisted her hands in his shirt and pulled him closer.

He was breathing hard when he came up for air. "Here, take this."

He pulled out his keys and worked the one to his house off the key ring.

Her eyes widened when he put it in her hand, and he gave her a fast peck on the cheek. "Come over when you can."

*　*　*

The four of them worked out the details of their plan over the following days. They tried to flush out more Blue Lighters to learn about their ways, but for such an ever-present entity that was causing so many problems, they were elusive. Too soon, the time for planning had passed.

Hunter and Berry followed the directions to Larimer Gaming. Pete had his fingers in so many technological pies, it was hard to keep track. Hunter was beginning to see why his life was so complicated. She hoped she was helping with that.

They got off on the tenth floor of the Mercury building and were immediately hit with the magnitude of the event. Tables were set up with giveaways. Promotional posters hung on the walls. People crowded around, spewing trash talk and sharing high fives.

"Are we at the Geek Super Bowl?" Berry whispered.

"We just might be."

Not only were there gamers—there were teams supporting them. They wore T-shirts and matching jackets with names like Cyclone, WolverNinja, and JetTech on the backs. An electronic scoreboard hung on the wall, ready to keep track of standings.

"Hunter!"

She turned around to see a familiar face. "Kimora."

Her face warmed. Pete's fame didn't faze her for some reason, but she was more than a little in awe to be on a first-name basis with a tennis star. Especially this one. If she'd known Tony worked with her, it would have been hard for her not to pester him for details.

Kind of like he was with Pete…

She bit her lip. That might be the hardest part of their relationship if they worked through this Menae/Oneiroi mess.

"Hi," she said, giggling a little when she received a hug.

"Where's Tony? I was hoping he'd come with you."

"Oh, he's spending tonight with one of his brothers. They had a thing." Understatement of the year. How did she explain to a human that he was in the dream realm, ready to vanquish a sleep raider?

"Did the two of you make up?"

"We have. I'm sorry you had to see our fight."

Berry coughed. "Neanderthal."

"That's great. I'm glad you were able to patch things up. He's a really good guy."

It meant something that his client was standing up for him, but the last time Kimora had seen them, they'd been bickering in front of the lunch crowd at the sandwich shop just downstairs. Hunter winced. "It was a miscommunication. He overthought things."

"He does that."

Hunter's hair swung as she tilted her head. She liked this woman.

"I brought my sister, Strawberry, instead."

"Strawberry," Kimora repeated. "I love that."

Berry went bug-eyed when she got a hug, too.

For once, someone held back on making the comment that they didn't look like sisters.

Hunter tried to talk over the music that was playing. "How are things with Pete?" she asked.

It wouldn't hurt to get some feedback there. She wouldn't share it with him, but she might make some course corrections.

"Good," Kimora said, crossing her fingers. "It's so hard to find someone who's real, you know?"

Hunter nodded. The match was sounding better and better.

Kimora looked around before sharing, "Do you know that he invited me to play tonight, rather than just be his date?"

Hunter's smile froze. She'd forgotten about that. "Did he

now?" It was good to know that he listened to her advice, but that had been before they developed their plan. "You're both playing?"

She rounded her eyes at Berry. The goal for tonight was to free Pete from the Blue Lighter that was targeting him. She'd known there would be professional players, too, who might have attracted the menace, but she hadn't counted on having to protect someone as well known as Kimora Ikeda.

"Hunter," Pete called from across the room. He cut a swath through the crowd to make his way to them. He was wearing a Larimer Gaming T-shirt, the same as Kimora. Hunter appreciated that he looked like just another guy on the street when he did these types of things. Most CEOs couldn't let go of the pressed jeans and button-down shirts underneath. "Thanks for coming."

"Thanks for the invitation. We've never been to anything like this, have we, Berry?"

Berry held out her hand. "Hi. I'm Strawberry, Hunter's sister."

"Sisters?" And there it was. He looked back and forth between them. "You don't look alike at all."

"Show us around?" Hunter tried to tone down her impatience, but nerves were kicking in. "How does this all work?"

"Sure. Follow me." He swung an arm around Kimora's shoulders to help her cut through the crowd, and Hunter and Berry tucked in behind.

"This is the lounge area where people can take breaks, get some food, and talk strategy. Make sure to grab some T-shirts." There were more than just tables of food; servers were out and about, wearing Larimer T-shirts and jeans and shoes out of their own closets. They had to love being comfortable on the job for once. Berry plucked an hors d'oeuvre off a platter as they passed.

"The action happens in here."

Pete pushed open double doors that led into a gaming area that could only be described as nerd heaven. It was a small auditorium with seats for the crowd and overhead screens that would show each of the players' moves. Hunter looked over the setup with concern. Fortunately, the players were situated with their backs to the crowd. That would make seeing their screens and any Blue Lighters easier.

"Where are you and Kimora sitting?" she asked.

"Down here on the end. We probably won't play the whole night. It's more for fun."

"Talk for yourself—there's money on the line," Kimora teased. She went over to check out the setup and moved the controller to where she wanted it. "When I beat him, he's promised to make a generous donation to my charity of choice."

He chuckled. "It's my company's game, tennis pro. You're the one who will be paying up."

As a life coach, Hunter was happy to see attraction sparking, but as a Menae, her mind was on other things. "Can we sit here?" She had her eye on the two seats in the front row that were directly behind them. They were at least ten feet back, which worried her. Would their power project that far? Would they have to yell?

"You could, but those aren't the best seats. I saved two for you halfway up."

"Oh, but I want to see how you're working the controllers," Berry said with a feminine pout. She was checking out Kimora's gaming station. She lifted a pair of headphones on the sly and gave a quick thumbs-up.

Hunter blew out a breath. That would help. She didn't want to disturb the two of them from their gameplay.

She wrung her hands. There were more spectators here than she'd expected, and even journalists. They couldn't see Blue Lighters; they wouldn't know what was happening if she and Berry started yelling random comments. She didn't want to make another scene in front of Pete, but she feared that the two of them were about to earn the Lunatic nickname they'd been given.

Berry took one look at her and jumped in to start asking

questions. "What video game are you playing? What's the top prize? Where are all the players from?"

Hunter looked around the elaborate setup. It was bigger than she expected. More players and certainly more screens. She tried to sense Tony. Was he here? Were he and AJ in the dream realm watching what was going on? Was he hearing any of this?

She touched the fidget spinner in her pocket. She was getting way too worked up. She needed to be ready. She needed to be strategic.

Finally, Berry caught her hand and dragged her to their chosen seats. Apparently, she'd won the negotiation on that.

"Pull yourself together. It's game time."

They sat, rigid with anticipation, as a host talked through the rules and introduced the players. They clapped at the right time, and Berry hooted when Pete and Kimora were announced.

Hunter was still on the lookout for signs of Tony.

Then the clock was ticking down, and gameplay exploded in flashes of color and explosions of sound. She nearly came right out of her chair until the audio crew got the volume corrected. Still, it was a swirl of movement and action that she hadn't prepared herself for.

Berry let out a hoot. "Go, Kimora!"

She got no reaction, as Kimora was immersed in the gameplay with headphones covering her ears.

Berry gave a thumbs-up. Nobody else in the crowd mattered.

Hunter sat forward in her seat. Her gaze jumped from one screen to the next. She assumed the players' personal screens were the ones to watch. They were the ones who'd put in hours behind them.

Her breath caught. "There."

That hadn't taken long.

It was the player on the opposite end from them, but she caught the distinctive blue haze just entering the corner of his screen. That wasn't part of the game graphics. It was starting already.

"Crap," Berry said. They watched as the blue powder puff grew in size. "Go home, Blue Lighter."

"I don't think it knows we call it that," Hunter said, raising her voice to be heard.

Yet the blue cloud shrank in size.

"It knows I'm talking to it. Just direct your intent," Berry said.

Hunter nodded, but she flinched when she saw the blue miasma on the screen of the player next to Pete. "Go back to the dream realm," she said forcefully.

It pulsed.

"*Now.*"

It pulled back, but another one popped up, this time at Kimora's station. "Get away from her," Hunter ordered it.

"This isn't your playground," Berry said, right on top of her.

The puffs popped, sending sparkles outward.

"No," Hunter said sharply. "Into the dream realm with you. All of you."

The particles skittered like spiders back to the screen and into it.

The last of them weren't gone, though, before a new smear of blue appeared elsewhere… and then on another player's screen… and one on the viewing screen above…

Berry caught Hunter's shoulder. "There's too much, too many."

"Keep pushing back." What they were doing was working; they just needed to talk faster. Push back harder. "Go into the dream realm. Stay away from here. You're not wanted."

Berry rose from her seat to go to the other side of the room. "Whoo! Great move. Get your ass away from him, Bluey."

If people were confused, they didn't complain. They were too immersed in the action. Coaches, junior players, and marketing agents had their own roles to play here. None of them even saw the blue light that was affecting their health and their sleep every night.

Hunter worked harder. Talked faster. Got more specific. Who knew there was so much of this stuff? Was this one being or multiple?

Tony. Tony and AJ. They weren't prepared for this. Vanquishing the night raider had to take more time and more effort than what they were doing.

"They're everywhere," Hunter cried.

Berry changed her approach. "Try to vanquish them! You, yes, you, Cyclone. Woohoo! Implode, you blue slime. Go *kablooey*."

Hunter tried. "Freeze, Blue Lighter."

The blue sludge stopped. It had taken her suggestion literally. It looked like a thick blue ice pack. She just couldn't utter the words to take it further.

Berry could. "Die, you freaky blue thing. Splinter."

Her look turned panicked when it turned and started crawling toward her instead.

Hunter sprang from her seat. Their power couldn't make people do things totally against their will. "Stop if you know what's good for you," she ordered it.

The thing paused.

It was sentient. It knew what it was doing. It was searching for power. Feeding itself.

"There's lunch at home. There's lots of energy in the dream realm."

The tentacle that had reached out to Berry hesitated and then curled back on itself.

"Hunter, keep going." Berry waved her on, even as she looked around the room. A guy in the audience watched her strangely, and she grabbed a pom-pom off the wall. "Go, Larimer Gaming!"

Hunter's power was waning. She'd already expended a lot, and it was too early. She had to stay strong. If this thing got past her, it would affect everyone in the room, including Kimora and Pete.

What would it do to her and Berry?

She thought fast. They needed help. Tony and AJ needed backup.

She whipped her phone out and did the unthinkable. She called Emily. "Em, I don't have time to chat. I need to talk to Zane."

"Zane?" Emily said in surprise.

"Tony needs help."

"Hold on, I'll get him. Is everything okay?"

"No!" Maybe that would put a spring in her friend's step.

"Lunatic?" Zane said when he came on the line. "What do *you* want?"

"Zip it, Oneiros. Tony and AJ need you. They're fighting a Blue Lighter... multiple Blue Lighters... They're in the dream realm at the Mercury building. Tenth... Berry, are we on the tenth floor? Yes. Tenth floor, in the Larimer Gaming room."

"Wait. What's a Blue Lighter?"

"The blue light coming from electronic screens. It's combined into a... a monster."

"Are you screwing with me? How do you know this?"

"Because I'm fighting them too. Send help. Send all the Oneiroi that you can."

Berry ran to the back of the room where nobody was looking. She twisted the rod on the blinds over the windows so they opened. The moon sat dead center of the glass pane, just rising from the horizon.

"Yes!" Hunter cried.

The moon wasn't full, but it was plump. Waxing gibbous, in the terms of the astrophysicists. It gave her the boost she needed.

As one, she and Berry refocused on the swarming blue blob that was overtaking the room. Putting the power of the moon behind them, they pushed back.

"Go home, Blue Lighters. You're not wanted here. Get out!"

CHAPTER FIFTEEN

Tony dodged out of the way of a blue tentacle and leapt on another one. They weren't prepared for this. They were battling a freaking kraken. The Blue Lighter was turning out to be bigger than they thought, with arms stretching out in every direction. It fed on electronics, and it had grown to gigantic proportions. Just when they got one tentacle subdued, another would appear.

"AJ, duck!"

The Menae were successfully pushing the Blue Lighters through, but they kept coming. It was impossible to tell where one stopped and the next began.

Or where the head of it all was.

A touch to the forehead was all it took to vanquish other sleep raiders, but they didn't know if that would work with this one. Lopping off tendrils didn't. Another would only sprout.

AJ narrowly avoided a swinging blue arm, but he got caught by one on its way up. It knocked the wind out of him, and Tony pounced to get him out of the sleep raiders' clutches.

They were outgunned here, but retreating wasn't an option. The thing had them surrounded.

"Stick with me," he yelled. Touching the being was all they had to do to injure it. They just needed to follow all these leads back to their center.

AJ held out his hand, getting between him and a limb that was whipping toward Tony's head. It sliced off clean, saving him from getting his bell rung.

"There, I think I see it," Tony yelled. "Pin it down there."

AJ didn't ask questions. He just threw himself on a sparkling blue limb that was feeling along the ground. Tony followed the path his brother had opened up, punched another whirling tendril, and dove for its core. There was no identifiable face. No eyes, no mouth.

The thing was a new creation, spawned out of the time and energy people were putting into their devices. Their tablets, TVs, computers, and phones. He thrust his hands into the middle of all the flailing arms and spread his fingers wide as he touched the head of it. The heart of it... whatever it was. He hoped that by covering more surface area, he'd get to the source of it.

The Blue Lighter heaved, trying to buck him off, but he held tight, wrapping his legs around the thickest tentacle coming out of the center.

AJ swore and threw his weight on top of that one, too. Arms flailed above them, and the sparkling blue light dimmed, flared, and then dimmed again. The Blue Lighter bucked once more, trying to shake them off, but then shuddered. It went dark and still. When the light extinguished, so did the being. Its particles drifted apart like a spent dandelion caught in the wind.

"Yes!" Tony yelled. They could vanquish this thing.

"Watch out," AJ said as he grabbed him and rolled. "There's more."

Tony's heart was pounding, and his muscles burned. There wasn't just more; there were too many.

Hunter. Was she being overrun on her side, too? Dear gods, what had they done?

"Fight," he said. It was all they could do. They had to fight to get out of here. He'd work to get AJ out of here, at the very least.

A massive blue arm came at them. AJ dove to the floor and got out of its way, but Tony had nowhere to go. The thing caught him around the middle and lifted him into the air. It began squeezing just as he felt a change in the crazy, kinetic energy all around them. He recognized the power, and the being that formed to his left.

"Cael," he wheezed. "Use your hands on it."

His big brother brought his hand down like a knife, slicing through the sparkling blue arm that was cutting off Tony's air.

He dropped to the floor and watched as more Oneiroi appeared around them. Derek manifested next to AJ and gave him a hand up. Then Mac and Bobby were there, backing them up too.

Hope roared to life inside him. "The core. Use your hands at their core to vanquish them."

More Dream Weavers evened up the battle. Pairing up in twos, he and his brothers took on the sleep raiders. It had been a long time since they'd had to fight as an army, but the future of the dream realm was at stake. This thing had grown right under their noses, and the balance was so far out of whack, it might not even be salvageable.

But they had to try.

"Derek, stay with AJ," Cael ordered his brother as he squared up at Tony's side. "How much do you have left in you? Do you need to waken?"

"Hunter… and Berry. They're all alone on the other side."

"No, they're not. Zane and Wes are with them."

Tony nearly went lightheaded with relief. They might not be able to vanquish the Blue Lighter on the waking side, but it would run from them.

And come here.

His hands curled into fists. He had to stay. They needed all the Oneiroi in the dream realm they could get.

Off to his left, he saw Mac wrestle his way to the core of another of the damn octopus-like creatures. Bobby protected his back, slicing and dicing any sparkles of blue that came his way.

Derek and AJ were using an inline approach to get them both closer to the core of another one.

"Cael, watch out," Tony barked. Another limb was swinging their way, only the Blue Lighter was adapting. Instead of waving its arms about, it had begun jabbing them. He jumped at the arm that was punching toward his brother and sliced it off with a karate chop.

He never saw the one coming for him.

* * *

Hunter had never been so happy to see someone who didn't like her in her life. She and Berry had nearly pushed all the Blue Lighters out of the gaming facility when Zane and Wes talked their way into the event.

She hurried toward them when they entered the gaming room. A roar went up as WolverNinja made a move to overtake Cyclone. None of the humans had an ounce of awareness of the war going on around them.

"Can you see over there?" she asked, putting on the brakes just before she crashed into them. "Into the dark realm? Can you see Tony at all?"

Zane caught her, but his eyes rounded when he saw the blue sparkles of light emitting from the large screen overhead. Wes stepped between them and the Blue Lighter, and the moment it sensed him, it skittered away.

"Tony and AJ," she said, grabbing Zane's shoulders. "They're over there, trying to vanquish what we're sending, but it's not just one. There are too many. Can you see if they're all right?"

"I can't see from here." He moved her away from the screens and all the gameplay. "I'd have to astral-project."

"Astral what?"

Wes cut her off. "Cael sent us here to help you on this side. He and the others have gone to back up Tony."

Hunter saw the familiar sparkles lighting up the phone of a spectator sitting in the aisle seat. Leaning down, she hissed.

"Get out of here, you evil blue demon. Back to the dream realm. Now!"

Zane's eyes rounded when the blue fizzled and pulled back sharply. He looked around the room. "You've got it contained."

Only because she'd had help from her sister and the moon.

"We just stopped it from coming over here. It's mainly in the dream realm now, but I don't know what's happening there. If he gets hurt... They get hurt..." She turned to Wes. "Go over there. Add one more to the mix."

"Sorry," he said. "It's not going to work this time. I have orders."

Work? "I'm not trying to coerce you; I'm trying to help him."

"Why?" Zane demanded. "How did this even happen? Did one of your games spiral out of control again?"

"No!" She wrenched herself away from him. "Both of you, go. Astral-project... Do whatever you need to do. Just go help him. It can come back this way. I don't care."

Zane's eyes narrowed in confusion. "Why? Why do you care so much?"

"Because I love him, you idiot."

Zane rocked back on his heels, and Wes spun around so fast, he lost his balance. "Love him?"

Berry was suddenly at her side. "Get your hands off her, Dream Weaver."

Zane gestured in frustration. "Who the hell is this now?"

"One pissed-off Menae."

His jaw clenched as he glared at Hunter. "So it's not Tomora, but Tonter?"

"No, Huney," Wes said with a grin.

Hunter pulled at her hair. She didn't know what they were talking about. "You're taking too much time."

Zane planted his hands on his hips and looked Berry over. "Can you fight?"

"Can I fight?" She surveyed the room. A blue fizzle flared

on the screen of the player closest to them, and she stamped her foot. *"Git!"*

The fizz ducked its head and disappeared.

"Good enough for me," Zane said. He moved out of Hunter's way. "Go to him."

"I can't get to the dream realm."

"Go to wherever he's sleeping on this side," he growled, lowering his voice so Berry couldn't hear.

Hunter's chin snapped up. She twisted toward the doorway but stopped. "Berry."

She couldn't leave her sister alone with two Dream Weavers she didn't know, much less trust. More Blue Lighters could show up at any time.

Her sister waved her off. "I'm good. This is wild. I'll hang with your celebrity friends once it's over."

Hunter clapped her hands to her head. She'd forgotten all about Pete and Kimora. "Are you sure?"

"Go to him. You're of no use here anymore anyway."

She wasn't. She truly wasn't.

She ran out of the room, past the tables full of swag and degrading cheese puffs. She punched the elevator button ten times before it arrived, and security went on alert when she ran past them.

Too bad they couldn't help with the bad guys this time.

"My boyfriend has been in an accident," she made up on the fly as she pushed past the uniformed man.

Gods, she hoped it wasn't true.

At full speed, she ran to the parking garage and then to her car. With adrenaline pumping and uncertainty making her sick, it took everything in her power to drive safely.

What was happening in the dream realm, that place she imagined as so dark, dangerous, and scary? Had she caused more harm than good? Could Dream Weavers even vanquish the thing? It had been so strong and unending.

What had humans done?

Was this the price of technology? Their sleep, their health, their sanity?

She tapped into the power of the moon again. It was earlier than she'd realized, still in the middle of prime time. She gasped. Even she was doing it, judging time by what was on television.

She felt herself start to unravel, but she pulled herself together. She needed to be strong for him. She didn't know what she was going to find, but she couldn't fall apart. He needed her.

"*Agg.*"

Hunter was frantic when she pulled into the driveway at Tony's house. His truck sat big and quiet. She slammed her car door shut and ran to the front door.

The key.

Her eyes flooded with tears. He'd given her the key to his home. She hadn't wanted to use it for a situation like this, but she flipped through the keys on her key chain to find the one she needed. Her hands shook so hard, she almost couldn't get it into the keyhole, but then the door opened.

She ran through the living room, down the hallway, to his bedroom.

"Tony."

He lay still on the bed. She scrambled onto it with him and put her hand on his chest. His breaths were light, so light, and he was so still.

He slept this way. She'd thought she'd gotten used to it.

She'd just never imagined what might be going on when he was on the other side.

"Tony, I'm here with you. Nobody will get to you here." She stroked his chest, wishing she could do more. If he could hear any of this over there, she didn't want to distract him. "You're strong and smart. You can outwit them and out-wrestle them." She wasn't sure about that. The dang things had so many arms. "I have faith in you."

He'd be fighting to protect AJ more than himself. He took the responsibility of being a protector too seriously, to the point where he put himself in jeopardy. She'd seen it.

Suddenly, his body jolted, and she let out a cry.

He went back to being still, which scared her even more.

What had that been? Had he been hit? Was he hurt? She tried to feel for a pulse, but she couldn't hear his over the thumping of her own in her ears.

He'd told her once—without words—that if something happened to him over there, he wouldn't wake up here.

"Oh, gods. Selene." She needed the moon goddess. Flopping off the bed, she ran to the window and opened the curtains so she could see the moon. It was up in the very corner, about to move out of sight.

Good enough. It slanted across the bed, bathing Tony in its light.

She slid back into bed with him. The moon wasn't full, but she summoned all the power she could. "Come back to me, Tony. Come back to me now."

She got no response. Not even a tremble.

She kissed his cheek. "I'm waiting for you, here, in your bed. Our families are working together. There's no reason to hide anymore. I love you, Tony Oneiros. I'm a Lunatic who's crazy about you. Come back. I love you, and I need you here."

He suddenly sucked in a heaving breath and pulled his knees upward.

"Tony. Oh, my gods. Tony, are you all right?" With a groan, he rolled onto his side, toward her. She cupped his face. She needed to see his eyes, those beautiful hazel eyes. "What can I do? Where are you hurt?"

A coughing fit consumed him, and she rubbed his back until he got it under control. Still, he pressed a hand to his chest. "The son-of-a-bitch punched me."

"A Blue Lighter?" She pushed up his T-shirt so she could see. There was no puncture wound, but a bruise was already starting to form, all red and blotchy. It looked bad. Really bad. "You need to go to the hospital. Can you walk?"

"No hospital. I just need... *Ah*, fuck that hurts."

"Ice." He needed ice.

"No, wait."

She was already halfway to the kitchen. She dumped a trayful of ice cubes into a kitchen towel, gathered it up, and ran back to apply it.

"Careful, that's cold," he hissed, but then he eased back against the pillows. She held the ice pack over the bruise and looked him over to see if there were any more. Reaching up, he caught a strand of her hair as it dangled near him. "I'm okay."

"You're not okay. You're curled up in the fetal position, and you took your sweet time getting back here."

"I didn't want to leave before I knew all my brothers were safe."

See? Wasn't that what she'd thought?

"Are they? Did everyone get out?"

He coughed again, following it quickly with a groan. "No casualties."

"Oh, thank the gods. You got them, the Blue Lighters? I don't care if you didn't. I was just afraid we sent too many your way. We didn't know. We were trying to protect the people in the room." The people in the room who were slowly being worn down by the blue light, not being bashed in the chest by them. "We should have stopped. They're more dangerous to you. We should have waited until we figure out how to better fight them."

"Hunter, slow down. Stop." He tugged at her until she was lying down beside him again. "Are you okay? I was worried they were flooding back over to the waking world toward you."

She shook her head. "The moon. We used the power of the moon to push them back."

"You're okay? Berry's okay?"

She nodded. "AJ?"

"He's good. Banged up, but good." He brushed a hand through her hair. "You sent backup just in time."

She pushed his T-shirt up higher until he took it off, and she looked him over for any more damage. The bruise on his chest was the worst. "Are you sure you don't have broken ribs?"

"I'm sure."

"We should run you to the emergency room, just in case."

"Hunter, baby. Nothing's broken, and if it is, I'll heal. I'm a god." He cupped her face. "You did so good. The people of Solstice should sleep better tonight."

"But there are more Blue Lighters out there." She was sure of it.

"You're right, but now that we know about them, we can fight them. Together."

She took a shuddering breath. "Are you really okay?"

"Do you really love me?"

"You heard me?" she squeaked.

"I heard you, and I felt you pulling me out of there." He ran his hand down her arm to her biceps. "You're strong for such a little thing."

"Well, you convulsed on the bed. I knew something bad had happened, and I had to try."

He folded her in his arms and pulled her closer until only the ice pack sat between them. "Shh, it's over. Everyone is fine."

"I'm not good at vanquishing," she blubbered.

"That's okay. I love you anyway."

She lifted her head. "You love me too?"

"I love you with everything I have."

"Tony." She kissed him softly, taking care of his bruised chest.

He carefully rolled onto his back, and she adjusted the ice pack. "Just give me a little while, and I'll show you how much."

Hunter felt all the weight of her worry and fear ease. It was still there, lurking on the edges, but she went limp beside him. They weren't leaving this bed for hours. She wouldn't let him. He needed to recuperate.

Her breath caught when she thought of something. "You don't have to go back, do you?"

He went into the dream realm every night. He had

sleepers who needed dreams, but the thought of sending him back terrified her.

"The others are covering for me." He caught her hand and settled it back on his chest, next to the ice pack and over his heart. "Tonight, I'm all yours, and you, my fierce Hunter, are all mine."

CHAPTER SIXTEEN

Hunter awoke to the sensation of Tony nuzzling at her neck, his big body pressed up against her side. His arm lay heavy against her stomach, and his legs were tangled with hers. She snuggled closer to his warmth, but stretched away from the tickle. Sleep was heavy upon her, and she wasn't ready to wake up.

She didn't care what the sun had to say about it. It glared in her eyes, coming through the uncovered window to pester her.

The nuzzle returned, this time against her ear, and she turned her head away. When he kissed her temple, she pulled up the sheet and rolled over. In the process, her elbow bumped against him.

Her eyes popped open.

Oh, no. Last night. The battle. His injury. Had she just hurt him?

She sat bolt upright and twisted toward him. "Ohmigosh. I'm sorry. Did I get you?"

"Not yet."

His voice was morning rumbly, and she couldn't tell if he was in pain or not. When he sat up beside her, she pulled the sheet down to look him over. She knew he didn't want to go to the hospital, but if that bruise looked any worse, he was going. She didn't care if she had to put him in a wheelbarrow and push him there.

"Oh." She shifted to let the light land on him and spread her hand wide over his ribcage. It hadn't been an optical illusion. The discoloration was nearly gone. "You heal so fast."

"God's blood."

"If it's that good, those damn mosquitos will have survived the cold snap, and they're still out there waiting to get us." The relief she felt made joking easier. She suddenly felt like a balloon, ready to lift off, after spending the whole night under a heavy weight that threatened to make her pop.

His warm hand settled on her hip. "I'm better, but the back end of a truck doesn't sound that comfortable. Let's just stay in bed all day."

She lifted an eyebrow. Her ear was sensitive to suggestions, and she could tell he was serious. "You don't have any clients today?"

"I'll cancel them if you do."

"Done." She'd never made a deal so fast in her life.

He pushed back the mess of her hair. "You're a night owl, I can tell."

Going from sleep to panic left her brain feeling dazed. "It takes me a while to get going."

"Maybe I can help with that."

He kissed her. Hunter loved how strong he was, but how tender he could be at the same time. He was a Greek god of dreams, but he was vulnerable, too.

She could have lost him last night.

She wound her arms around his neck and straddled him so he didn't have to crane his neck. He rewarded her by skimming his hands up the back of her thighs. A shiver went through her. She hadn't planned on spending the night here, so she'd slept in her Larimer Gaming T-shirt and panties. It wasn't the sexiest combo, but he seemed to like it.

She let her head fall back when he kissed her neck again and touched his tongue to her pulse. "Ooh," she said on a shuddering breath.

"You were amazing last night."

"I was petrified."

"You held your ground—and you called in backup when I really needed it."

She put her hand over his mouth. "Don't tell me that."

He kissed her palm. "Okay. Maybe I should just show you my thanks?"

"That would be great."

He chuckled. "I'll see what I can do."

He pushed his hand under her panties to cup her bottom. When he squeezed, her toes curled. "Tony," she whispered.

He shocked her by opening his mouth on her breast, T-shirt and all. When he poked at her nipple with his tongue, she reflexively rose to her haunches. She caught at his shoulders to hold him right where he was.

He used the opportunity to pull her panties straight down. Catching her bottom in both hands, he turned and soon had her flat on her back.

Her panties came off and her shirt went up. She was pulling it over her head when his mouth returned to her breast, taking her nipple in deep. Need coiled between her legs as he licked and tugged at the sensitive tip.

She squeezed her thighs together, but he wanted them open. He worked a knee between hers to make a spot for himself, and his weight pinned her to the bed. With her thighs spread wide, he ground against her, and she nearly came.

But he eased off.

She groaned in frustration when his mouth left her breast as well. Moving downward, he pressed soft kisses along her breastbone and her stomach. It was rising and falling as her air came shorter and faster. She clenched the sheet as he kept on his trek, moving down her abdomen and, finally, to her core.

"Ahh," she cried as his mouth touched her intimately.

He kissed her there and then gave a long, slow lick. Hunter nearly slapped him on the back of the head, she reached for him so fast. "Oh, oh… *Ooh.*"

She couldn't breathe without moaning. Her hips rocked and rolled, but he stayed with her. He loved her with his mouth until her muscles couldn't tighten any more and anticipation was razor sharp. When he swirled his tongue around her clit, she came with her heels pushing into the mattress and her fingers digging into his scalp.

She'd just collapsed against the pillow when she heard him distinctively say, "*Hwuh.*"

Laughter bubbled up inside her and spilled out. It made her even happier that she could laugh with him when they were getting hot and heavy.

Tony was visibly focused on the latter. His eyes were locked in, and his jaw was set. Sliding off the end of the bed, he pushed down his briefs. He climbed right back on, and before Hunter knew what was happening, he'd flipped her on her stomach. He pulled her hips up and entered her in one hard thrust.

As hot and slick as she was, the feel of him was even better. "*Hi-yah.*"

A sound somewhere between a snort and a groan left him, and then he was thrusting hard, fast, and deep.

The world tilted again as he pulled her up so that she was sitting in his lap, straddling him again. With his legs thick as tree trunks, her knees couldn't touch the mattress, but he had her. His arms came around her, one going to her breast and the other going back between her legs. Hunter gasped and held on as he fucked her. Reaching up, she caught the back of his neck as he panted against her ear. Reaching down, she sank her fingers into what she could reach of his hip.

He shuddered when her nails scratched.

It was too hot to last long, too intense. When he jerked and buried himself deep, she came again.

And then they were both useless.

They sprawled out on the bed, limbs tangling and breaths coming hard. When she reached for her pillow, she discovered it had been knocked to the floor. She didn't have the ambition to pick it up.

She frowned. "What's that gurgling sound?"

"Coffeemaker."

"Ooh, coffee."

"Want it before or after we shower?"

She opened one eye to peek at him. "I'll probably need it before."

It was a good call.

Round two happened in the shower, this time with her returning the favor by going down on him.

It was midmorning when they finally lay facing each other on the bed, with the pillows put back in place and tucked under their heads. It had taken that long. It had taken that much touching and loving to get over the scare from the night before.

"You're not immortal," she whispered. Last night, that had been painfully clear. "I'm not either."

His hair had dried wet from the shower, and it was rumpled and sexy as he looked at her. "I didn't think so, but it's good to know I won't be accused of being a dirty old man as we age."

He thought about them growing old together? It did funny things to her heart. "I'm not actually the daughter of the moon goddess," she confessed. "I'm the daughter of a daughter of a daughter... all the way back to Selene. The role of Menae is handed down from generation to generation."

"Because you're half human, and you age."

"The percentage is indeterminable now, but yeah. Selene and Endymion had fifty daughters. He was said to be so handsome, Zeus put him in a never-ending sleep so he wouldn't compete with the gods."

Tony plumped his pillow. "I don't have a father."

"You don't?"

"Nyx reproduces at will, so she's continually replenishing the army of Oneiroi."

"So you don't know all your brothers." He couldn't. It just wasn't possible. He had to have family all over the world.

Even with fifty, it was a challenge for her to remember all her sisters' names.

He shook his head. "It's all right, though. We formed little family units, and if we ever want to move, there's always new family around."

"Have you been with your Solstice brothers long?"

"Cael's moved around with his job, but Derek and I have been together a while. AJ, Zane, and Wes came a little later."

"I can't even imagine."

"As kids, we learned how to weave dreams by practicing on animals. Dogs, horses, birds… they all dream."

She was fascinated. "What do they dream about?"

"Oh, you know. Chasing rabbits, being a wild mustang. I once had a dog dream that I was its owner, but then I realized I'd accidentally gone on a dream ride, and I was the one who wanted a dog."

She smiled. "One of my first full moons, I spent with a friend reading under the covers with a flashlight. It seemed rebellious at the time."

"We all start somewhere."

She shifted, and her knee rubbed against his. "Will your charges suffer aftereffects if you missed them last night?"

He brushed his toes against hers and kicked the covers down further. "My brothers were supposed to cover for me, but one night of missed dreams won't hurt sleepers. Any more than that, though, and they can get manic—"

He stopped abruptly, mid-sentence.

Hunter reached for him. "What? What is it? Is it your chest again? Are you in pain?"

Oh, gods. And they'd just had a workout like that?

"Tony?"

"Manic…" He sat up. "You're mortal, half human."

Hunter held the sheet to her chest as she got to her knees. She didn't understand, and he was making her nervous.

He caught her by the shoulders. "Hunter, I know what will help you with your energy swings. *You need to dream.*"

CHAPTER SEVENTEEN

Everything clicked in Tony's head. The familiarity of Hunter's symptoms... the frenetic highs of her full moons... the desperate moodiness of her lows... The same thing happened to Cael's charges when he'd started seeing Devon and his regular schedule fell to the wayside.

Hunter was the descendant of a mortal human. She needed to dream. It made perfect sense.

"Menae don't dream," she argued. "None of us do. We never have."

"I'd lay odds that isn't true." Tony clapped a hand to his forehead. The Sandman had even told him so. She needed what *only he, Tony, a Dream Weaver, could give her.*

She shook her head sadly, obviously trying not to hurt his feelings. "I just need the moon."

"I'm not saying it will fix your situation entirely, but it should make the highs and lows less extreme. That would make life more livable for you."

She shrugged her shoulders out of his hold. "That's okay. I don't need to dream."

Everyone needed to dream, even if they were only daydreams, but that was another matter.

"Hunter." He had to play this right. He was ready to jump in and start now, but she needed to warm up to the idea. "If I thought there was any chance of your being hurt by this, I wouldn't recommend it."

She'd been told her whole life that she couldn't dream and that the Oneiroi were the enemy. He'd react the same way if a beautiful woman with a wild glint in her eye told him he needed to ride a dirt bike on a closed course under the moon. But they'd moved past that.

"I hated seeing you like that, so wiped out."

She was like a bright flame that had been dimmed to a flicker. He couldn't let her suffer like that if there was anything he could do about it.

She looked at his hands.

Hands that had just been used to vanquish a sleep raider.

The light bulb dawned. Oh, hell. Where was his head? She didn't need to just get used to the idea. She was scared. Terrified.

He wrapped his arms around her and settled back against the headboard. "You've asked me to trust you; now it's time to trust me. I would never hurt you. I truly believe this is what you need."

"I know you do."

"You're worried I'll make a mistake."

She gave a nervous hum. "It's not just that. I'm worried that because I'm half human, I'll respond differently than a full-blooded one. What if I react like a sleep raider?"

"You're not a sleep raider. You're a goddess. I don't know how the Menae were ever mixed in with that bunch."

"Because we thrive at night. We stop people from sleeping."

"But you live in the waking world. Sleep raiders live in the dream realm."

She went quiet as he rubbed her back. He'd made inroads with that argument, he could tell. The more he thought about it, the surer he was that the feud was the source of the problems.

She turned her face into his neck. "I'm not ready."

"It's okay. We won't do anything until you are."

"And if that's never?"

He wouldn't act without her approval. It was her call. "Then I'll keep making spicy stir-fry and watching old movies with you."

She went quiet for a long while. Tony racked his brain, trying to think of another argument to make, but this wasn't about him. Just because he was excited didn't mean she ever would be.

"What would I even dream about?" she whispered.

"Who knows? That you're flying or late for a test?"

"And I'd think it's real?"

"Most people do."

"I have no concept of what it would even be like. What if my first dream is scary?"

"I don't think it will be." And it wouldn't, because he'd make sure of it. Even if she needed a nightmare to work something out, it could wait. He wouldn't allow her to be scarred by a nightmare as a first dream. "But I could ride along with you, if you like."

"You can do that?"

"Zane does it all the time." And his brother took flack for that. Tony was beginning to see the merits of breaking that particular rule. Hunter had never experienced the wild, unpredictable nature of a dream. Why would he toss her into that kind of a situation all on her own? "I promise to stay with you through it all until you wake."

She picked at a wrinkle in the sheet. "What if I don't like it?"

"What if it makes you feel better?"

Her sigh was heavy. "I need to think about it."

Hunter was scared. What if something went wrong? She knew Tony wouldn't hurt her on purpose, but why would they even try this? *Menae did not dream.*

There had to be a reason for that.

Unless it was all because of the stupid Menae/Oneiroi feud...

The wrinkle in the sheet twisted as she picked at that thread. When had the feud started? And why? She needed to learn more about it.

Maybe Berry knew.

Berry, who'd dropped everything at a moment's notice to come defend her. Berry, who'd knowingly walked into the lion's den of the Oneiroi. Berry, who'd battled Blue Lighters at her side.

Hunter's sinuses clogged.

What if he was right? What if she could bring a cure to her sisters who suffered as much as she did with every new moon? She was in a perfect position to try what he was suggesting. She had an Oneiros lover. None of her sisters would let one get within spitting distance.

And then there was Tony.

He took care of his charges every night. He worried about them and looked over them. He'd just taken on an army of Blue Lighters for Pete Larimer, who wasn't even on his list. He had the biggest savior complex she'd ever seen, along with the... *ahem*... equipment to back it up, but what if her brain was different? What if she reacted the opposite of humans to dreams? Or what if the energy swings got even worse?

That would have been a good reason for the Oneiroi to stop bestowing dreams on the Menae. If they'd ever dreamt at all.

Oh, it was going to drive her insane.

"Will you stop if things don't go right?"

"Yes, but nothing's going to go wrong." He cocked his head. "AJ could act as a backup, if that would make you feel better."

"No," she said automatically. If they were going to do this, she only wanted Tony. "Okay."

"Okay?"

"Let's do it."

"Just like that?"

Just like that? She'd wound herself up like a clock. She couldn't keep going round and round. "Tonight. Tonight, when I fall asleep, do it."

"Are you sure?"

"Yes, get it over with." She was a born risk-taker. If she couldn't take a risk for the Menae, she didn't deserve her goddess status.

He hugged her and kissed her temple.

"Your trust means a lot," he said softly. "I won't do anything to lose it."

* * *

Hunter was worked up, thinking about the impending night. Tony did everything he could think of to settle her down, because the Sandman wasn't going to get anywhere near her at this rate. He made her chamomile tea and gave her a neck rub. It was a rainy November day: gloomy, cold, and overcast. They stayed off screens, and she tried to read a book. He found a can of lavender air freshener under the bathroom sink, and he went from room to room spraying it. Lavender was supposed to be calming.

Finally, he did something he knew would calm her.

He took her against a wall, holding her close and looking deep into her eyes. Then, satiated and limp, they lay together on the sofa. He pulled his Satellites blanket over them, making sure to cover her feet, as they watched the rain come down. Once she stopped thinking so hard, the warmth, the comfort, and the quiet did their trick.

Soon, she was napping.

It was now or never. If he didn't give her a dream, she'd get worked up even worse and never sleep tonight.

He closed his eyes and drifted off. Once his physical body was asleep, he astral-projected into the dream realm. Crouching down in front of the sofa, he gently placed his hand on her forehead. Curious, he analyzed what was there before he did anything.

Her brain waves were unique. He'd been able to identify that from a distance, but at the base of it all, he detected theta waves.

The same as human sleep.

And yet he waited to see if she'd cycle through the phases like her ancestor, Endymion, would have. Legend said that the man had been an excellent sleeper.

She moved into deeper sleep, through the spindles and K complexes, until delta waves were coming at regular intervals. He let her body soak up its healing properties for her muscles and immune system.

And then it was time.

He caught the next delta wave that passed. Making sure his hold was gentle, but firm, he led her up. Her heart began to beat faster, and her blood pressure rose. When her muscles locked down, ensuring she wouldn't act out, he knew he was right. She needed to dream. This was natural to her. Her system was hungry for it. Voracious.

He opened the door to the dream realm and stepped inside with her.

"We're here," he said, taking her hand. "Where do you want to go?"

The environment changed. Color flushed out. A dusty wasteland appeared before them with a bluish-gray cast. Overhead, a blue marble floated in a black sky dotted with twinkling stars. He heard the tune to "Conditions Are Favorable," and, when he looked at Hunter, he found her buck naked and grooving to the song.

He bit his lip. So close. She was dancing naked on the moon under the Earth.

A breeze swept through, and he stopped laughing when he felt it in places he shouldn't.

"Gods damn it." How did he always end up naked in the dream realm?

"Come on," she said as she caught his hand. "Loosen up."

She wanted him to dance with her. He stepped awkwardly from side to side, but not even in a dream could he move the way she did.

She gasped, and her hold on his hand changed to a tug. "Hurry. Over here."

A dune buggy suddenly sat beside them. She hopped in

behind the wheel, so he climbed in the passenger side. She hit the gas so hard, the back end skidded sideways. Moondust kicked up behind them, and then they were plowing forward, shooting up over drifts and hugging the edges of craters.

He held on to the roll bar. They couldn't get hurt. They were in a dream. Heck, they were breathing on the moon, where there wasn't any oxygen. That didn't mean that his stomach didn't react like he was on a rollercoaster.

She was driving like a bat out of hell.

"Where are we going?" he asked.

"The Meneiroi can't catch us together."

Meneiroi?

"They'll make us go to jail."

The buggy jumped over the lip of another moon hill, and the environment blipped. The gray-blue ground switched to vibrant hues. Green trees. Yellow fire hydrants. Brown gorillas. They were back on Earth, and she slammed on the brakes as they pulled up to a wooden building.

Jail? he wondered.

She hurried to the door, but he caught the handle before she did. "Nice dress, babe."

She was suddenly swathed in a Grecian-style gown with one shoulder bare. Her choice, not his.

He'd just wanted to make sure she didn't find herself naked in public. That was a common dream, and not a particularly fun one. He conjured up some jeans for himself.

He recognized the place when they stepped inside. It was Kick Axe, or something inspired by it. He looked around. He didn't see any of this newfangled Meneiroi her mind had come up with. Her sisters and his brothers, he assumed.

Unless that had been the gorillas.

They walked down a long wooden hallway that morphed into a throwing lane. His jaw set when he saw the target. Instead of the standard bull's-eye, there was a shape that looked ominously familiar with a circular center and arms radiating outward. It might have been a sun, if not for the blue color.

A nightmare was looming.

He'd known she needed an outlet. Her brain waves had told him so. He just needed to be careful what she was exposed to. If the experience was bad, she'd never let him bring her to the dream realm again.

She yanked an axe out of the holder. Grabbing it in both hands like he'd taught her, she waved it once... twice...

The target on the wall began moving. The arms on the octopus began to grow outward, hitting the ceiling and crawling back along it toward her. She held the axe overhead, her eyes wide with fear and even her hair trembling.

"*Uuuuhh*." Her mouth was open, but the sound came from her throat.

Tony snapped to. She'd hit the dream sludge, that state where she wanted to throw something or run, but her appendages weighed a thousand pounds. She was trying to scream, but very little sound was coming out.

He grabbed another axe and whipped it down the lane. It lodged in the target, dead center.

The arms shrank back, and then collapsed to hang loosely. He snapped his fingers, and the target was replaced by a standard, run-of-the-mill bull's-eye. "*Hi-yah*," he said.

Fun. They were having fun.

With her emotions high, she was on the verge of slipping out of the dream and waking up. The dream state was closest to waking, and if she made that jump, it was likely she would remember at least parts of the dream.

Especially the way it made her feel.

He gently removed the axe from her hands. At his touch, her rigor broke.

The dream flashed again, and they were back to the nighttime world. Their world. The world of the night and the moon. His balance shifted, and he realized they were on his blow-up mattress, the one he'd had in the back of his truck.

"Whoa," he said, dropping to his knees before he fell off.

They were floating out in the middle of Comet Tail Lake. As if lit from below, its color was electric blue.

"Stir, Tony. Put some of those muscles into it."

He felt the weight of an oar take shape in his hands. *Stir.* What did she want him to stir? The lake?

She had an industrial-sized bottle of yellow food coloring that she was pouring into the water, drip by drip by drip.

Stir. Okay.

He began paddling.

"It's working!" she said. With each drop of yellow, the blue turned less blue. "It's changing to green."

He paddled along, helping her get rid of the blue light.

"Hunter's green," she hooted in victory.

A fish jumped, startling her. An electric-blue one.

He didn't have time to step in to change the dream. She'd already jumped out of it entirely.

She'd woken.

* * *

Hunter woke up mumbling, "Stir, stir."

Groggily, she rubbed her eyes. Realizing she was lying right on the edge of the sofa, she grabbed it to make sure she didn't fall off into the... water...

She looked around the living room, disoriented. Had a pipe broken?

Obviously not. She heard rain hitting the roof. Water must have gotten in, but where had it gone?

"What happened?" she asked.

She was so confused.

Tony was watching her closely. "You had a dream, baby. Your first dream."

"We were on the lake."

Comet Tail Lake. She remembered the sandbar that stuck out from the shore. That really existed. Dreams couldn't be that detailed, could they?

"You were adding yellow food coloring to make it Hunter's green."

"What?" That felt familiar, but she couldn't quite pull the memory back. It was flitting away like a tissue pulling apart in the wind. "That makes no sense."

"It kind of does."

She gasped. It was midday, but she distinctly remembered a dark sky full of stars. "Were we on the moon?"

He nodded.

She went still. It was a sign. She'd dreamt, and Selene had brought her home. Tears pricked at her eyes, and she had to clear her throat.

"Do you remember the dune buggy?" he asked.

"Dune what?"

He chuckled and pulled her into a hug. His big, strong arms made her feel protected. Safe, when she was suddenly questioning the thoughts that were in her very head.

"How do you feel?" he asked.

She wasn't quite sure. "That was bizarre. That's what dreaming is like?"

"Yes, although I'd hoped you wouldn't wake from one your first time. They're more easily remembered if you do."

She swung her feet to the floor and sat up. "You didn't want me to remember?"

"I didn't want you to be scared."

"But that was a trip! Why don't people remember all their dreams?"

"So, you liked it?"

"I..." She pressed her hand to her pounding heart. The feelings had been intense when she woke, but they were washing away, too. "That's supposed to help people's mental state?"

"It cleans out the clutter—and you had a lot of cleaning up to do." He glanced at the clock on the wall. "You spent nearly all of your nap in REM sleep."

"Ooh, rapid eye movement! Did my eyes do that twitching thing, too?"

He lounged back against the arm of the sofa. "I don't know. I took a dream ride. I was in the dream with you, not watching you from outside it."

"Is that too much time to spend there?"

"For you?"

She nodded. She didn't want to get stuck... which was a horrible thought. She hadn't considered that when she gave him the go-ahead.

"I think you just needed to dream so badly—or maybe you don't have sleep cycles like humans? I'll have to figure that out."

"We're doing it again?" she squeaked.

"You don't want to?"

Her hands fluttered. She was hard to keep up with, she knew. "I don't know."

"It's just new... although probably really, really old for your kind." He tugged on a strand of her hair. "Dreaming comes naturally for you."

Their gazes connected. She'd just never had someone to take her there. None of the Menae had.

"Let's try it for a while and see how it affects you."

"Will you stay with me the next time? Do the dream ride thing again?" She got the feeling it wasn't normal for Dream Weavers to do that.

"Absolutely. It doesn't feel like we did anything wrong, does it? Your head doesn't hurt?"

She did feel clearer in her head; that never happened after a nap for her. "I'm actually a little lightheaded. Was it hard to get me into the dream realm?"

"You were exactly like all my human sleepers."

"Not the dogs or the horses?" she teased.

She sprang off the sofa and gave a twirl. "Tony, I'm excited."

He grinned. "I'm excited, too. Want to go on this adventure with me?"

"Are you kidding? I'm Menae. I was born for adventure."

CHAPTER EIGHTEEN

When Tony entered IHOP with Hunter, they were both on edge. He was bringing a Lunatic to the weekly meeting of the Solstice Oneiroi. What could possibly go wrong with that?

He knew he should have invited everyone over to his house and served tea and crumpets, but this was already on the calendar. Everyone would be here. No doubt, they were all waiting for an explanation about what had gone down the other night anyway. He and Hunter might as well make their relationship official while they were at it.

He let out a harsh breath. Adrenaline was pumping inside him like a broken water main. He knew a fight was coming, but he was usually the one who stepped in and stopped tempers from flaring. Who was going to play peacemaker this time?

He didn't want to go against any of his brothers, but he would.

It was time to set the record straight. On everything.

"I don't know if this is a good idea," Hunter said. She was flitting around like a nervous butterfly.

He squeezed her hand. "It will be fine."

He'd make sure of it.

He tensed, though, when they walked into the back room. As he'd expected, there was a full contingent of Oneiroi here today. That was what happened when you fought an epic battle with a new sleep raider that looked like a sparkly blue kraken. Even Mac and the two new guys, Nick and Jalen, were here. They covered Dream Weaver duties during the day, so third-shift workers were going without dreams right now.

Which only increased the pressure.

"Where's Emily?" Hunter whispered. She was cutting off the circulation to his hand, she was holding on so tightly. "You said there was a girls' table at these things."

Shit. He'd hoped Emily would be here to smooth out things. Hunter needed her support. "I don't know. Maybe they stayed home so we could talk about the Blue Lighter situation?"

Anxiety was coming off her in waves, so he stopped to dig into his pocket for his keys. It wasn't fair to bring her here, outnumbered like this. "Take my truck and go. I'll talk with them on my own."

The cat was out of the bag anyway. His brothers knew they'd been seeing each other. Hell, Hunter had reached out to Zane to get help, and nobody was going to shut that blabbermouth down. Tony was surprised that no one had shown up at his door already, demanding answers.

"No," she said. "We agreed we were going to present a united front."

"They're my family. I can handle them…"

Conversation at the table drifted off when his brothers began catching sight of them. Instinctively, Tony pulled her closer to his side… and maybe a bit behind his hip. He wanted to get between her and anything hurtful that might be directed her way.

He cleared his throat. "Morning, everyone. This is my girlfriend, Hunter."

He added a glare, daring any of them to say anything. He could still put any one of them on their backs.

"Hi," she said softly, giving an uncertain wave.

"Hey, Hunter," AJ said.

It was a lone voice in the wilderness.

She shifted, sensing hostility, and pulled back. "You're right. This wasn't a good idea. I'll go."

Tony's keys dug into his palm. His brain was cramping, and his rage was spiking. This wasn't right. She'd fought at their side the other night. He appreciated the hell out of AJ even saying hello, but couldn't just one of the others—

Cael stood. "Glad you could make it."

Tony looked at him sharply. Where Cael led, the others usually followed.

"Please, sit," his big brother said. "We've been wanting to hear about this."

Tony glanced at Hunter. It was now or never. She nodded, and he pulled out the empty chair next to Cael for her.

"Never thought I'd see the day that a Lunatic was invited to the Oneiroi breakfast table," Bobby muttered.

Tony whipped around. "Hey, show a little respect."

"Respect?" Planting both hands on the table, Bobby pushed himself to his feet. "You're the one disrespecting us, bringing her here like this. We've been fighting against Lunatics and cleaning up after their stunts for centuries. You can't expect us to forget all that just because you let one get into your head—and, obviously, your pants."

Tony exploded into action, only to slam directly into Zane, who hopped up in front of him as he tried to get around the table.

Bobby only worked up more steam. "You despised Lunatics more than any of us. You can't tell me she isn't messing with your head."

Ice washed through Tony's veins, even as his temper went white hot. He looked back to Hunter. "I didn't know what I was talking about then. I do now."

Bobby shoved away Mac, who was trying to get him to sit down. "Are we forgetting what she did to Emily?"

Wes jumped up at that, joining Zane in holding Tony back.

"What the hell, Wes?" Bobby said. "She hurt you, too."

The new guys got in the mix, jumping between them to

keep them apart.

They wouldn't let him around the table? Tony would go over it.

"Tony," Hunter cried. "Stop."

Zane and Wes were losing ground.

"Enough," Cael snapped. "Both of you, cut it out. We're in a public restaurant."

"No," Tony said, straining against the hands that were holding him back. "This whole problem is *because* we stopped."

"What are you talking about?" Derek said.

"The whole Menae/Oneiroi feud... that dirt bike thing... It's all partly our fault."

"Yeah, yeah. Turf wars." Bobby stepped back from the table and shook everyone off. "I'm sick of hearing about it."

"I'm not talking about the turf war." Tony worked one arm free and banged his fist on the table so sharply, silverware clattered. "The crazy highs that the Lunatics experience? That's on us."

"What the fuck are you talking about?"

Tony looked around the room. He'd sufficiently gotten their attention. Even Sally, their usual waitress, was looking at him wide-eyed. The restaurant manager was probably on the way.

He planted his hands on his hips and tried to get his thoughts in a row. The controversy over his relationship status was one thing, but above all, they needed to understand this. "The Oneiroi abandoned the Menae. At some point, we stopped bringing them dreams."

A hush settled over the back room. Hunter was pale as a sheet. Tony backed away from the table, and Zane and Wes let him go so he could stand at her side.

He lowered his voice. He didn't need to yell anymore, and he could tell that the patrons in the next room were worried about what was happening. He took Hunter's hand again. When his thumb started drumming a beat, he didn't try to stop it.

"I don't know what caused the breakdown, but the Menae are hyperactive during the full moon because they need dreams. It's like what happened with Cael's charges." Tony winced when his big brother rocked back on his heels, but there was no getting around that sensitive piece of their history. Without it, he never would have figured out what was going on with Hunter. "They haven't had the mental clearing process of dreams for centuries. Without it, they've just gotten wilder and wilder."

"Hey," Hunter protested.

Tony tilted his head. "Well, it's true."

"Do you seriously think we'll buy that?" Zane asked. "They get pumped up by the moon. Everyone knows that."

Hunter stepped forward. Zane was one Oneiros she wasn't afraid of. She'd taken him on before and won. She'd taken on four of them.

"We still follow the stages of the moon, and yes, we'll still encourage spontaneity in humans. That's *what we do*, but since Tony has been giving me dreams, my energy and thought processes seem to be stabilizing. I'd never dreamt before... You want to talk about *wild*."

Nine Oneiroi stared at them, stunned. The idea of bestowing dreams on a Lunatic was akin to kissing a rattlesnake. It just wasn't done.

Or it hadn't been... and that was the problem.

"Endymion," Derek said, catching on. As always, he was ten steps ahead of everyone else. "The Menae are descendants of a human."

"How did we miss this?" Cael asked.

"I don't know," Tony said. "Something must have gone down, way back when."

"The Menae have no recollection of ever dreaming," Hunter said, "so we don't blame you. For *that*."

"Come on, Cael," Bobby said. "This changes nothing. Lunatics still put our charges at risk. They trick them into doing dangerous things."

Hunter's lips thinned. "It's Menae, and our intent is to free their minds, to get them away from their worries and fears. People are so stressed and depressed. We're trying to help them—at least, I am."

"Hold on," Zane said. "Are you telling me that Emily was stressed and depressed?"

"Well, you kept putting her in the friend zone, blondie."

AJ covered his mouth with his hand.

Derek turned to Cael. "Is it just me, or does that mission sound familiar?"

Cael wrapped his hands around the back of his chair. It was a lot to take in, Tony knew. "Could it be? Two sides of the same coin?"

Derek shrugged. "The Menae covering the day shift and the Oneiroi on duty at night?"

Hunter bounced up on her toes. "You think the things we do are crazy, but they don't come close to the bizarre things I've run into in my dreams."

Derek stared at her. Hard, in that intimidating way that he had. "We need to do some digging into our history."

Hunter reined her excitement back in, and it pissed Tony off. She shouldn't have to hide her light—he loved her personality of fun—but she was still facing off against a roomful of Greek gods who'd been brought up not to trust her.

She fumbled her hands together. "We're Greek goddesses, but, at some point, we got lumped in with sleep raiders."

"I have some thoughts on *that*."

Oh, hell no. Tony swung around. "Don't even think about it."

Zane held up his hands. "I have questions. I think I have the right to ask them."

Tony remained an impassable mountain until Hunter squeezed around him. She put a hand on his chest as she eyed Zane warily. The status of protector had shifted. "Say what you have to say. I can take it."

Tony tensed, but Hunter just lifted her chin and shook back her hair.

"Why Emily?" Zane asked.

"We met at the adventure park, and she hired me. She chose me, not the other way around."

"Why Tony?"

"Have you looked at him?"

AJ let out a snort, and Tony felt the tips of his ears grow hot.

Zane pressed on. "How long have you two been seeing one another?"

"Since the full moon."

"So that kiss…"

"Was the first of many. He's a good kisser."

Mac coughed, and the new guys grinned.

"Ugh." Zane scrubbed his eyes. "Too much damn information. Okay, straight up—are you working your mojo on him?"

"No, and you should have more faith in him."

Tony stood a little prouder. He wasn't used to being protected. It felt nice.

"That octopus thing the other night." Zane waved his arms to simulate, as if they all hadn't been there to see it. "Was that something you started that got out of control?"

"No. The Menae have no relation to Blue Lighters."

Tony leaned in. "Although she was the first to catch one trying to enter the waking world."

"So, the other night… You guys were, what? Partnering?"

"Yes," AJ said. "It was a Menae/Oneiroi joint operation."

Eyes turned on him, relieving the pressure momentarily.

"We'll get into that later." Zane turned his interrogation back on Hunter. "I still don't like what you got Emily into."

"I know."

"But you reached out to me when these two got in over their heads." He waggled his index finger at Tony and then AJ. "You didn't hesitate."

"Why would I?"

Zane cocked his head. "Do you really love him?"

Tony blinked, not expecting that.

"Yes," Hunter replied, "but I'm pissed as hell that you made me tell you that before I could tell him."

Zane's eyes sparkled, and then his lips twitched. Like recognized like. "All right. I figure that makes us even."

Hunter's face went slack.

He stuck out his hand. "Truce?"

She closed her mouth. She hadn't expected this kind of reaction, because honestly, Tony hadn't either. He watched as she clasped Zane's hand, and they shared one brief, but meaningful, shake.

Holy. Hell. Zane was playing peacemaker?

"And you," Hunter said, waving at another brother. "Wes, is it?"

"Yeah."

"I'm sorry you got hurt on my full-moon night. It wasn't my intent."

He shrugged. "I've got a date with the nurse who patched me up, so…" The grin he gave her was sly. "I'm going to say we're even, too."

"Hunter! Tony!"

Everyone turned when they heard a familiar, excited voice. Emily rushed their way.

"You two came clean? Finally?" She squeezed between the two of them and gave them both side hugs, happy to see them here. Her pretty face was lit up.

"Wait," Zane said, his eyebrows lifting. "You knew? And you didn't tell me?"

"Of course I knew."

"How?"

"I listened. You should try it sometime."

"I'll go old and gray before I can listen to all these knuckleheads. You need to help me out with these things."

"Old and gray… You'll still be irresistible." Emily brushed her lips against his cheek. She looked at the empty chairs around the table. "Why is everyone standing? Sit, I'm hungry."

"Yes," Cael agreed. "Let's sit."

Tony looked to Hunter to make sure she was okay. She looked as shell-shocked as he felt. He helped her back to her seat and hoped things would stay calm for a little while.

"So," Zane said. "What kinds of pie did you order?"

Emily ticked them off on her fingers. "Pumpkin, chocolate, and apple. Wait, are you two coming to Thanksgiving dinner?"

When it became clear she was asking them, Tony glanced to Hunter. She squeezed his pinky finger under the table. "Sure. Thanks for the invitation."

Zane was concerned about other things. "No pecan?"

"Isn't three kinds of pie enough?"

"Pecan is my favorite."

The moment he used his puppy-dog eyes on her, Emily gave in. She folded her napkin and set it on the table. "Fine, I'll go back and add it to the order."

The moment she left the room, Cael took control of the meeting. "Are your sisters willing to come to the table to discuss things?"

Hunter flinched as she tried to keep up with the ping-ponging conversation. "Some of us are, some will never be."

"If we start bestowing dreams on them, would that help?" Wes asked.

"Not without permission. I've only talked to a few who are interested in exploring that. The others will drop you where you stand if you even try."

"Okay," Cael said. "We'll pursue discussions about that, but we need to talk about the Blue Lighters before Emily gets back. How the hell did that happen, and how did it spiral so far out of control?"

Tony saw the questioning look on Hunter's face. "Emily knows the story of the Oneiroi, but she thinks it's mythology. She doesn't understand that it carries on today."

"You're not telling her?"

"Got any advice on how to break it to her?"

Point made. Hunter's brow furrowed when she came up against the same brick wall they all had on that topic.

"Focus," Cael demanded. "How did we end up with a five-alarm emergency at that video game event, and how do we ensure it never happens again?"

Tony didn't know about the others, but his balls tightened up when the leader of the Solstice Oneiroi used that tone of voice.

"I first saw one hunting Pete when I was on a Zoom call with him," Hunter shared.

"Larimer?"

"Yeah," Tony said.

"Why didn't you tell me?" Zane asked. "He's my friend."

"Or me?" Wes said, piling on. "I work with him, too."

"We looped in AJ. Pete's his charge."

Derek and Cael both nodded in approval. They'd followed protocol on that.

"This sleep raider is different, because it can cross realms," AJ said. "We can see it in the waking world when it encroaches, but we can't vanquish it."

"We don't know that for certain," Tony interjected. "It senses what we are when we get close, and it runs. It travels through electronics. If AJ is right and we can't vanquish it on this side, we could have bigger problems coming."

"Dang," Wes muttered.

"*Our* powers do work on it." Hunter squared her shoulders. She was the only one here to represent the Menae. "Our plan the other night was for us to push it from the video game event back into the dream realm."

"Who's us?" Cael asked.

"The redheaded whirlwind was her sister," Tony said. "AJ and I were waiting in the dream realm to take on the Blue Lighter. We thought there was only one. The plan was solid."

AJ agreed. "Two Menae and two Oneiroi."

"But you ran into a platoon of the things." Cael had been there. He'd seen how many flopping arms and blue sparkles there were.

AJ grimaced. "We had no idea they could get that big—or were that strong. Or that there were so many of them."

"In retrospect, the gaming event was the wrong choice," Tony said. "We knew they'd be there. We knew Pete had one targeting him. We just didn't know that video games would attract so many Blue Lighters."

"Like deep-fried Twinkies at the state fair," Hunter murmured.

Cael's lips twitched, and he rubbed his nose. "I think you were on the right track with your plan, but you should have run it by us here before you went off and nearly got yourselves killed."

Tony shifted in his seat. That would have required that he tell them about him and Hunter. He didn't know how that would have gone. Ironic how the Blue Lighters had made it easier. The enemy of an Oneiroi enemy was a friend?

Cael nodded at Hunter. "We need to work with the Menae."

"As long as you don't try to trespass in the waking world, I've received approval to coordinate with you."

The Menae couldn't battle them alone, either. Just the thought made Tony shudder. Hunter had managed to push back one at her weakest when it had come through her laptop, but he'd seen how she froze in her dream. Vanquishing wasn't part of her repertoire.

Nor should it be.

Like the Oneiroi, each of the Menae were different. The more he learned about Hunter, though, the more he understood she was about joy and light. Moonlight, to be specific. She just got carried away sometimes.

He was curious to see how that might change now that she was dreaming regularly.

"We need to develop better fighting techniques," he said. "We know it's like an octopus, and the head is vulnerable to our touch, just like any other sleep raider. With all those arms whipping around, though, it's hard to get to it."

Hunter's eyes went wide. "*That's* what was happening on your side?"

Tony absently rubbed his ribs. The thing had been

learning to punch, too. "I've got some ideas on how to combat it."

"I can help with that," Jalen offered. "I have a background in martial arts."

"Great." It would be good to establish relationships with his new brothers in town.

Cael sat back in his chair. "Tony, you've shown real diplomatic skills these past few weeks, first with the Sandmen and now the Menae."

Tony went still. He'd just been doing the same thing as always. "Just trying to protect everyone."

"Yes, but Derek and I should be consulting more with you for ideas and strategy."

Derek nodded in agreement and followed Cael in offering his hand.

Tony's chest puffed up so much, it made it hard to breathe. He'd never been acknowledged for his brains. It had always been his brawn that was considered the most useful. He shook his big brothers' hands, but he could only manage a tight nod in response.

"What the hell," Zane said. "I'll buy you some peach crepes, big guy. You've earned them."

"Crepes?" Emily said as she returned to the table. "That sounds good." A big smile was on her face when she placed a hand on Hunter's shoulder. "Want to join me at the girls' table?"

"Oh gods, please," Hunter said. She gathered up her purse and pushed back her chair.

Emily blew a kiss to Zane. "Finally, it's my turn to invite someone."

Tony frowned at Hunter. "Hey, where's *my* kiss?"

She rolled her eyes. "First, you don't want them to see us kissing. Now, you do. How am I supposed to keep up?"

"When in doubt, kiss."

"But leave his pants on this time, would you?" Zane said with a laugh. "At least until you get behind closed doors."

"I'll close your door." Tony waved a fist in the smart

aleck's face.

Hunter stopped all the nonsense by catching his chin and turning him back her way. The kiss she planted on him made him see stars when the sun was bright on the horizon.

And it made all the hassle with his family worth it. They had just one more hurdle to get over.

Hers.

CHAPTER NINETEEN

November, Beaver Moon

"Hurry up, Tony. It's time." Hunter stood by the back door, waiting impatiently.

"It's too damn cold out for this," he complained.

She halfway agreed, but she couldn't control the weather. The day had been beautiful, with the sun shining and the sky so blue, she'd wanted to swim in it. The air had been crisp, but when she and a client had taken a hike and kicked up the fallen leaves, it seemed nice. Now that the sun had set, though, the crispness had more bite to it.

"Mind over matter, big guy. Come on."

"This big guy is going to have some tiny balls if you make me go out there like this."

She adjusted the blanket around her shoulders. "We won't be out there long. Just one dance. You can do it."

"But the neighbors…"

"We're not going to turn on any lights. They won't even know we're out there." She'd waited long enough. Whipping open the door, she darted down the steps into his backyard.

And it was bliss.

The sky was cloudless, and the full moon was bright. She lifted her face to it and basked in its rays. Her power was surging, but it didn't feel risky or erratic like it might have on full-moon nights in the past. All she felt was power. Clean, sweet power that she could control. Her mind was crystal clear.

Dreams. The dream world that Tony had opened up to her had done this.

She watched as he braced himself in the doorway. He was clad the same as her, but he was much less enthusiastic about her plan than she was.

"Beverly has got to be loving tonight." It was a super moon, which meant it was closest to the Earth along its elliptical orbit. It looked huge on the horizon, almost as if she could reach out and touch it. She couldn't wait to hear how her sister had spent her special night.

Tony stepped onto the back stoop but pulled his foot back sharply from the cold concrete. "Ah, foot cramp."

Hunter dropped her blanket and gave a suggestive wiggle. His bitching and awkward hopping stopped. She crooked a finger at him, and, as she expected, he bounded down the steps without complaint and trotted across the grass to meet her.

"Darn it," she said. "I forgot the music."

He looped an arm around her waist when she started to run back to the house. "We're not turning on that, either. This is a family neighborhood."

She narrowed her eyes at him. That wasn't part of her vision for tonight, but a new, better plan formed in her head. "Then you can sing."

"What?"

"Sing to me—or I'll go find Harbingers of Mayhem on Spotify."

He began crooning the opening line of "Conditions Are Favorable," and she melted. Yes, this was so much better.

Letting her head drop back, she lifted her arms and began to swirl around his backyard. The soft bluish moonlight illuminated every inch of her. Crickets chirped along with Tony's singing, and the scent of the night air made her want to remember this moment forever.

The tune drifted off as he watched her. "You're so beautiful."

"And you're cheating." She pranced his way, fully aware she had his attention. The heat in his gaze was enough to make her forget the nip in the air. She fisted her hand in his blanket. "Drop it."

He grimaced, but sucked it up and let go.

Hunter tossed the blanket aside and backed up to take a look at him. In the moonlight, he looked like one of those marble statues of Greek gods from ancient past.

Even if the temperature was having the effect he'd predicted.

"It's the cold," he said, shielding his groin with his hands.

She smiled. "I'll warm you up."

She stepped up to him, wrapped her arms around his neck, and was soon snug in his embrace.

"Mm," she said. As much as he complained, he felt warm to her.

"Okay, you're cold, too," he said, tucking her up close. "Your nipples are like daggers against my chest."

"Dance, Oneiros."

He began to sway stiffly from side to side.

"How do you feel?" he asked.

He wasn't talking about the cold anymore. "Incredible."

"The upswing hasn't been as high?"

"It's high, but it's not as sharp. Like, the rollercoaster isn't shuddering as it reaches the top of the first hill, you know?"

He rubbed his hands against her sides. "I know."

"I can feel my power, but my thoughts aren't all over the place. The dreams are helping."

"I'm glad." He tried a step back and seemed surprised when she followed. They ended up doing a full turn, and he nodded, proud of himself. "Hopefully, the lows won't deplete you as much, either."

She rubbed her cheek against his chest. "I'm so glad you figured it out."

"I knew I recognized something in your brain wave

pattern. I'm no Derek, but I can be street smart when I need to be." He rested a hand against her upper back and swooped her into a dramatic dip.

Hunter yelped and hung on.

He smiled as he looked down at her. "You haven't even noticed how I kept you away from Pete tonight."

"Pete?" she squealed as he lifted her back upright.

"No racing scooters in front of the TV station, no streaking down the Satellites' sidelines, no climbing trees on Kimora's property…"

"Oh, you silly boy—although those are some good suggestions. I'll have to write them down in my notebook." She laid her hand on his chest. "I never wanted to spend my full-moon night with Pete Larimer. You were always my objective." She let out a tinkling laugh. "I've got an Oneiros dancing naked with me under a full moon—*and* serenading me while we do it. I'll go down in Menae history as a legend."

"You already are legendary, baby."

"Both of us are. A Menae and her dream lover." She winked at him. "*Hi-yah.*"

He grinned. "*Hwuh.*"

ABOUT THE AUTHOR

Kimberly Dean is an author of contemporary and fantasy romance. When taking the Myers-Briggs personality test in high school, Kimberly was rated as an INFJ (Introverted-Intuitive-Feeling-Judging). This result sent her into a panic, because there were no career paths recommended for the type. Fortunately, it turned out to be well-suited to a writing career. Since receiving that dismal outlook, Kimberly has become an award-winning romance novelist. She has written for seven publishing houses and was the recipient of an EPPIE award for independently-published authors. Her book, *Haunted Hearts*, was a finalist in the Romance Writers of America's RITA contest.

Learn more about Kimberly's books and sign up for her newsletter at https://kimberlydean.com.